Praise for What She Had To Do

The author's clever prose—a cross between British and American style that perfectly reflects Penelope's inner conflict—provides sharp dialogue and a group of charming, eccentric characters straight out of a BBC television series An enthralling, well-written family novel.
—KIRKUS REVIEWS

A touching and suspenseful novel, a brilliant portrait of a difficult, dying woman and her complicated daughter, and the ambivalence of love.
—DIANE JOHNSON,
author of the forthcoming *Flyover Lives*

Here's a novel that reads like a movie. In scene after scene, Mary-Rose Hayes takes on the complex bonds between a mother and daughter, moving the story skillfully towards its surprising finale. It is an excellent and satisfying read.
—LYNN FREED,
author of *The Servants' Quarters*

Mary-Rose Hayes thoughtfully examines territory many a family will recognize, and also provides compelling mysteries. An intriguing read from an accomplished storyteller.
—SANDS HALL,
author of *Catching Heaven*

Sensitive and gracefully written. Mary-Rose Hayes captures the ups and downs of maternal romance with accuracy and insight.
—MOLLY GILES,
author of *Iron Shoes*

Also by Mary-Rose Hayes

Novels:

The Neighbors
The Caller
The Yacht People
The Winter Women
Amethyst
Paper Star

With Senator Barbara Boxer:
A Time to Run
Blind Trust

Poetry:

From the Garden of the House in Bali

*Sue —
with much love
always!*

What She Had To Do

A Novel

Mary-Rose Hayes

Mary-Rose Hayes
11-14-2013

WHAT SHE HAD TO DO

This is a work of fiction. The characters and events in this book are fictitious. Any similarity to real persons, living or dead, is coincidental and not intended by the author.

Copyright © 2013 by Mary-Rose Hayes

Originally published by:
Cavendish Hill Press
2520 Octavia Street, Suite 120
San Francisco, Ca. 94123
www.cavendishhillpress.com

All Rights Reserved. No part of this book may be reproduced or transmitted in any form or by any means, graphic, electronic, or mechanical, including photocopying, recording, taping, or by any information storage or retrieval system, without the written permission of the Cavendish Hill Press.

ISBN 978-0-9898145-0-8
LCN 1-977334671
Printed in the USA

For Patrick

PART ONE

1.

    The call comes very early in the morning.
    I'm in bed with my husband Liam in San Francisco, and this is what I'm dreaming:
    I'm a child again, it's summer, and Mother and I are staying in a small hotel at the beach. Mother says it's no better than a boarding house and yearns for the fancy place on the cliff with the turrets, emerald lawn and the pretty umbrellas on the terrace which even at six years old I know we can't afford, but I've never been away from home before and everything is new and thrilling.
    I love that our hotel has a name, like a real person. It's called "Vie en Rose." Our own house is just called Number 12.
    I love the stained glass fanlight over the front door which throws a red, blue and green peacock-tail across the hall floor whenever the sun comes out.
    I especially love our room. The carpet has a rose pattern on it; there are more roses on the wallpaper, enormous overblown red ones; and our pink-quilted beds are so close we can reach out and touch. The room smells of the sea and very faintly of the rose-painted potty in the cupboard between our beds which Mother complains the maid doesn't wash properly—a unique blend of salt and old pee which for the rest of my life I'll associate with total happiness.
    And we're here for two whole weeks!
    On sunny mornings Mother and I go to the beach to build sandcastles and poke in the tide pools, me in my new red bathing suit with blue balloons on it, she in the red sundress with the blue flowers. We could be twins, she says. When it rains we put on rubber boots, walk along the cliffs and watch the waves smash up

on the rocks below. After lunch we explore the town, go to the cinema, or out to tea. I'm too young for the hotel dining room at night so Mother brings me supper in bed, bread and butter and a boiled egg from the kitchen, and sits with me while I eat it.

Each day the tall, dim rooms at No. 12 drift further away, as does the silent man whose eyes follow me everywhere when he thinks I'm not looking, and whose return from work each evening prompts a hectic, welcoming gaiety from Mother and my banishment to my bath and then bed. Here, at Vie en Rose, I have her all to myself, beautiful Mother with her slanting, green-gold eyes, her red smiling mouth and the thick black hair which she pins into snail coils at night to make it curl. "Like a regular film star, your mum," says Mrs. Babbacombe the landlady, and I agree that everything about Mother is beautiful, even her name: *Imogene Amanda Sayle.* Surely nobody else is called Imogene Amanda!

The best times are the early mornings when she lets me climb into her bed.

She looks so young without her powder and bright lipstick. She smells of sleep, of last night's perfume, and a sharp sweetness which I don't yet know is gin. She wraps her arms round me, buries her face in my neck then demands, eyes wide with pretend surprise, "Penny darling, you naughty thing, what *are* you doing in Mummy's bed?"

"I want to always sleep with you!"

"Only on holidays. Mummy sleeps with Daddy at home."

"But *I* want to be with you, for always and always!"

"Me too, darling—but someday, you know, you'll get married and leave me!"

It's just a game we play, but each time I'm shocked she should even think such a thing let alone say it. "I don't *want* to get married! Promise you'll never leave *me!*"

She smiles and tickles me under the chin with a lock of her hair. "Of course I promise!"
Suspiciously, "What about when you die?"
"Don't be a silly goose, darling, Mummy will never die. ." which is when someone screams, loud and shrill, once, twice, three times; Mother's beautiful topaz eyes, the bright window and the rosy wallpaper swirl together and fade into darkness; I wake disoriented, the phone is ringing, the glaring green numerals on the clock radio say 3:00 and an English-accented stranger is telling me how Mother has been found unconscious on the kitchen floor and I must come home at once. *Surely you know Imogene's dying,* he says—though the part of me in violent denial and clinging to sleep wonders how can that can possibly be when, seconds earlier, Mother was young and beautiful and tickling me with her hair.

2.

Twenty four hours later.

I'm in England, and the car Liam hired to bring me here from the airport is pulling up outside No. 12, Regent Crescent.

The Crescent is historic and architecturally significant, a two-hundred-year-old semi-circle of tall Georgian town-houses flanked by an apron of emerald lawn smooth as a billiard table. It overlooks the lushness of the Victoria Park, the city spread out below, and the hills beyond. People are impressed when I say I used to live here, and ask how could I bear to leave.

Mrs. Ship, who will have been watching and waiting, throws the door open before I even ring the bell. She has been the building's caretaker for as long as I remember, a specter of a woman who seems always to have been sixty years old, to have worn the same flapping floral housedress, and whose proverbial cup is always half empty. She greets me as if I've been gone merely days, not the ten years since my father's funeral. "There you are, Penelope! Glad you could come so quick; your Mum's waiting. I took the post and paper up to her earlier. Isn't this heat something awful and it's that close and stuffy makes it hard to breathe. Difficult for the kiddies and old people; lady died of heat consumption over Bristol way."

I ask after Mrs. Ship's health; receive the standard answer: "Been better but can't complain." However, despite her gaunt frame and chronic smoker's cough she's strong as an ox and insists on carrying my heavy bag up three flights of stone stairs.

Mother's apartment door stands open; from her bedroom down the hall her voice rings strong as ever: "Penelope! *Darling! At last!"*

I close the front door, drop my bags and wipe my suddenly damp hands on my pants' leg. I haven't seen Mother for over a year, not since her last visit to San Francisco, over eighty but vigorous as ever after a flight through eight time zones, her hair its usual age-defying ebony, her powdered and rouged public face carefully reapplied in the lavatory where she will have spent far too long before landing.

Mother's beauty is legendary and painstakingly nurtured—but now I imagine her yellowed and gaunt and hope I can control my face when I first walk into that room.

Why didn't she tell me she was so ill? Why for god's sake didn't anybody *else* tell me—though I suppose it's my fault, I should have guessed because this year, for the first time ever, Mother postponed her annual summer trip to San Francisco. She was feeling a bit under the weather, she said, and would come for the Christmas holidays instead and I didn't press for details because Mother is old and old people are often under the weather. And of course I was so grateful for the reprieve. . . .

"*Penelope! What are you doing, hanging about? Come in here!*"

I draw a deep breath, march resolutely down the hall, go in—and thank god it's all right after all, in fact it's fine, Mother actually looks better than she has in years and strangely youthful, reclining against a pile of bright pillows, wearing her yellow velvet bedjacket which, though crushed and stained with a button missing remains, like Mother herself, defiantly glamorous in old age. Her ancient quilt is laid across her knees, worn and torn and leaking feathers. She has patched the worst places, using slivers of a gold brocade vest, a black and lime-green striped miniskirt and the purple satin number I wore to a party with Johnathon back in the 'seventies. Her stitching is impatient and careless. Mother has always enjoyed fine embroidery but everyday sewing is for maids.

"Oh Penny!" She holds out her arms. "I was so happy I could have *cried* when dear Simon said you were coming!" Why does she look so young? Then I realize she has given up coloring her hair which is now a gentle greyish-brown; the thin, surprised eyebrows so fashionable in her youth are no longer pencilled in halfway up her forehead; nor is she wearing her signature firehouse-red lipstick. I blurt, "You look fantastic!"

"That's what they all say," Mother agrees complacently, "Isn't it *absurd!*"—and I'm overwhelmed both with relief and admiration that instead of a haggard invalid I find a gypsy queen lounging on bright pillows as if for a lover.

I lean down for her embrace. Mother drags me onto her chest with surprising strength, squeezes too tightly, and to my further relief smells just as I remember of face-cream and powder.

Nor is there the faintest odor of disease in the elegant though threadbare bedroom, dominated as always by Mother's portrait as an eighteen-year-old-debutante in white satin evening gown, elbow-length kid gloves and pearl tiara. Morning sunlight gleams from the many gilt-framed mirrors on the walls and the facets of the crystal pitcher beside her, filled with her favorite apricot-colored roses. I'm sure a man brought them for her. Mother has always been a woman to whom men bring flowers.

I sit on the bed and take her hand. It's light as a leaf, the skin sliding silkily over delicate bones. "You should have told me you were ill."

"I didn't want to bother you in case it turned out to be nothing."

Before leaving San Francisco I have managed to talk both with Mother's general practitioner and her oncologist. I have learned about the grapefruit-sized tumor which has invaded her abdominal wall and the organs beyond; that in no sense can her condition be described as 'nothing.' I ask, "And what's this about you falling in the kitchen?"

"Wasn't that silly of me! I was boiling the kettle for tea, I remember feeling a bit dizzy and watching the floor come up at me, and the next thing I knew I was lying half under the table and couldn't move. Luckily Mrs. Ship came soon after that with the newspaper, and she rang Simon. Simon Morley—you talked to him, he's the one who phoned you. Poor thing, I *did* give him a scare!" Mother chuckles at the memory. "He's such a dear man; a brilliant architect. He brought me these lovely roses. Of course there's nothing *physical* between us," she assures me serenely, "He's actually a raging queer—but just the kindest man on earth and such fun! You'll meet him tonight, he's coming for a drink, him and some other people. Do you know, he used to be married and has a son about Caitlin's age. Isn't that peculiar? He must have decided he was queer afterwards. Though we're supposed to say gay now, aren't we. I wonder why?"

I refuse to be sidetracked. "Why didn't Mrs. Ship call an ambulance?"

Mother's mouth tightens. "She knows better than that."

"Then Simon Morley should have."

"Certainly not! They both know how I feel about hospitals. Those places are infested with germs, you go in there and you don't come out again."

"What did the doctor say?"

"Just a little fainting spell. I expect I'd forgotten to eat breakfast."

And as for the rest of it, the reason she'd been unable to come to San Francisco, she's determinedly opaque. "Just tummy trouble. Don't make such a fuss, Penelope! It's not as if I had Big C or anything horrid. That specialist, Dr. Savage, said it was only a tumor—"

"But Mother—"

"—so there was no point taking the damn thing out! Such a relief! I was terrified in case I had to have an operation. They botched my appendix, I've showed you, haven't I? A scar from here to *here!*" Mother holds her hands wide apart like an angler bragging about his catch. "Anyway I feel *much* better now, just supposed to rest in bed for a bit. And dear Dr. Alice, she's my G.P., has given me some new pills which work *wonders!*"

The bottle is on her nightstand, half hidden behind a silver-framed photograph of my father who stares sternly into the camera wearing full dress navy uniform of 1936 complete with gold epaulettes, with his ceremonial sword holstered at his hip.

I reach for the bottle; read: *Morphine sulphate, 30 mg. 4 X daily.*

"Put that back!" Mother orders. "I refuse to talk about boring medical things, not now you're here! Stand up and let me see you properly!" She takes me by the wrists and holds me at arms length. "My goodness, don't you look American!"

I'm wearing jeans, cotton turtleneck, black leather jacket and sneakers. I don't think I look especially American, just stiflingly overdressed because England has surprised me with a September heatwave, but Mother always sees what she expects to see.

She pats the quilt beside her for me to sit down again. "Tell me all about your flight! Was it horribly crowded?" Her thin fingers worry at one of the patches on the quilt and she drags a feather from a gap between her slapdash stitches. "Such a long way, eleven hours, and all those dreadful films, sitting in the dark. Goodness, I've done it so often; once a year since Caitlin was born! Nearly twenty times! Do you remember when you picked me up that first time when she was only a month old . . . ." It's one of Mother's favorite stories, she has told it so often and in such relentless detail I can recite it word for word, with identical pauses and inflections. " . . . . And would you believe, the conveyor thing was broken down and we had to wait hours for our luggage! In America where everything's supposed to be so efficient! Honestly! I told that Customs woman or whoever she thought she was how it was iniquitous making us wait so long when we're tired, and she was so rude. Women officials are always the worst, give them some authority and they behave like little Hitlers!"

I'm in no mood to revisit Mother's first arrival on American soil but, clearly, she is disinclined to discuss anything relevant and potentially dire, at least not yet, so I wait it out, glad the re-telling gives her pleasure and she has the energy for it.

Mother asks, "And how *is* my Caitlin? How much I miss her! Is she having a wonderful time? Does she go to parties and have masses of boyfriends? Is she in love? Tell me e*verything!"*

Caitlin, with her slender body, topaz eyes and dark hair springing from a deep widow's peak, is an almost eerie reincarnation of Mother when she was young and provides her with the perfect vehicle through which to re-live her glory days. When I inform her that Caitlin's summer job volunteering at the marine mammal sanctuary precludes an active social life, Mother sighs in disapproval. "What a shame! This is the time of life when she should kick up her heels and go out dancing every night, the way I did when I was her age!"

"It's also the time she should be thinking of her future." I explain how the sanctuary is a perfect fit, that it's a dream summer job and Caitlin is lucky.

Mother is unimpressed. "She's too pretty to be a boring old scientist. She'll get married right away, you'll see, and all this college business will be wasted."

Through everything, Mother has clung to her ideal of romance and how a woman is not merely incomplete but a downright failure if she has not snared a man before the age of twenty-five. I was barely seventeen when she had a potential husband picked out for me, Johnathon Price, a handsome young law student with expectations – *he's got his eye on you, Penny, I can tell!*

Now, "This college Caitlin goes to," Mother wonders— "Remind me?"

"The University of California, Santa Barbara."

"You're sure it's the right place for her?"

"It has a fine marine biology program. That's why she chose it."

"But does she meet the right *kind* of young man at a state school? If you know what I mean."

Mother was raised with certain indelible attitudes. It's unfortunate but unavoidable. I know exactly what she means though I pretend I don't; just tell her that out of roughly twenty thousand eligible males one or two might make the grade.

Mother sighs. Then she asks for pictures. "I hope you've brought the latest. Run and get them for me!" She reaches up to smooth the hair away from my hot forehead, tells me not to frown because I'll get wrinkles and while I'm fetching the photos to pour myself a drink, I look as though I need one. "There's a new bottle of gin in the booze cupboard, I sent Mrs. Ship to Sainsbury's to stock up. Give yourself a big one."

I point out that it's only mid-morning.

"Well, so what? Celebrate! You're on holiday!" and as usual I marvel how, despite all those years with my father, Mother still manages to equate alcohol with frivolity and fun.

3.

I head for the kitchen, longing not for Mother's off-brand supermarket gin but a strong cup of coffee, knowing, of course, there'll only be instant. Mother endures domesticity as a necessary evil and for as long as I remember the most sophisticated item in her kitchen has been a can opener.

Today, though indeed I only find a jar of Nescafe, there are herbal teas in pretty floral packages and the refrigerator, usually a depository for dessicated dabs of leftovers, is sparkly clean and stocked with fresh goodies. Somebody has been helping out. Mrs. Ship? Simon Morley? Whoever it is, I'm sincerely grateful.

I boil the kettle and find my purse. In the rush to get away I never thought to bring photographs and the only one I have is in my wallet: Caitlin and Liam leaning against his new, bright blue Ford pickup.

I find some scissors and cut Liam's image away.

"Is this all you've got?" Mother's cup rattles in its saucer and she places it safely on the night stand, using both hands. She doesn't care for the picture. "What ugly clothes Caitlin's wearing. Those heavy black boots and raggedy jeans." She peers closer. "And her bra strap's showing."

"It's how kids dress these days."

"But she's not a kid; she's a beautiful young girl. She should have some pretty things. And why can't you have a portrait taken by a real photographer, the way *we* used to, with her hair done nicely? Something I can be proud of."

I glance at the picture of me which stands to my father's left. I'm sixteen, in three-quarter profile, wearing the pink tulle evening gown I despised but which Mother thought sweetly romantic and bought without asking me first. She genuinely doesn't find my expression sullen but touchingly contemplative, that of a young girl poised on the brink of womanhood. "Yes," she nods, "Just like that. Caitlin mustn't let herself go, although," eyeing me critically, "You're not exactly a good example, Penelope. You need to look after yourself better. You girls spend too much time in the sun, you're getting dried out and leathery and you're still so beautiful, or you could be." With a fingertip, she traces the lines bracketing my mouth. "There's no need for those."

"Mother, I'm forty seven."

"If you say so. But at least you've had the sense to get rid of that nasty grey hair that was coming in"—and I don't tell her that the white badger stripes at my temples, which I thought rather distinguished, were actually sacrificed for Sirvas and Segal, Advertising, where the average age of my co-workers is approximately half of mine.

Mother returns to the photo and runs her finger down the sheared-off edge. "You've cut somebody out. Who didn't you want me to see?"

"I trimmed it to fit my wallet."

"It's a man, I can see a hand and part of his arm. I suppose it's that husband of yours." Mother seldom refers to Liam by name as if, by so doing, she can persuade herself he's not really a working class, Catholic Irish-American and I actually married a high-toned, protestant doctor, lawyer or wealthy landowner like the daughters of her friends.

She adds, "At least she doesn't look like him," and I have a flashed image of myself in my hospital bed; my new daughter all red and wrinkled, tucked under my arm in a pink blanket; a roomful of Foleys gazing critically from me to the baby to Liam and Granny Foley, a tiny slat of a woman with quick, black sparrow eyes and greying hair wrenched into an agonized topknot, complaining how Caitlin was the spitting image of me—"with not one drop of himself in the child!"

"Here." Mother thrusts the photo back into my hand.

The only picture of Liam in this apartment was taken at our wedding. I am beaming in a hippyish floral gown, Liam stands stiffly erect in his rented tux, the wind is gusty and damp and my veil is blowing half way across his face which must be why Mother tolerates it. She has never forgiven me for letting her and the family down so badly. Of course Liam was quite good-looking in a rough sort of way, yes, she could see that, "But why on earth," she has sighed more than once, which quite shocked me the first time, "Couldn't you have just had an affair with him and got him out of your system?"

Of course I've never admitted to Mother that the first time I saw Liam, on the construction site just down the block from my office, my immediate thought had absolutely been all about sex and how soon I could get him into bed.

How huge and dusty he was, what a hunk, his black hair curling beneath the rim of his yellow hard hat, his smile a white slash in his dirty face.

The next day he was waiting for me, he said hi, where was I from, what sort of accent was that, Brit or Australian, and what did I do in that building? The third day, Friday, he asked me out for a beer after work, I thought about him for the rest of the day, what would happen later, and how disappointing, having fan2tasized about a violent sweaty thrash among plaster dust and scrap lumber, to find him showered and brushed and changed into a clean shirt and ironed jeans. Even more disappointing when he caught me by the wrists in his powerful, work-roughened hands and held me firmly away from him, so clearly wanting me but saying this might be for real and we weren't about to screw it up till we found out.

So we waited and he was right and we've been married twenty four years now.

I fix soup, scrambled eggs and toast for lunch though Mother only sips at her soup and crumbles the toast on her plate.
Afterwards I leave her drowsing among her tattered pillows and seek the refuge of my old room, which is virtually unchanged since my childhood.
Here are the same twin beds with the red-and-white-striped rayon covers; the glass-topped vanity where my grandmother's silver-backed hairbrushes are still laid out; the cedar storage chest (for fur coats, Mother has said although she has never owned a fur coat) where I stored all the detritus of my childhood and girlhood including notes and cards from Johnathon when Mother's hopes were still high; and the mahogany bureau upon which, when Mother began to sleep here after I fled all those years ago, her crucifix used to stand (a beautiful piece, Florentine, she said)—only it's gone now, replaced by another photograph of my father which I at once bury face down in the bottom drawer.

The room is hot and breathless and the turmoil of the past twenty four hours is catching up with me. I fling the window open, collapse on the bed in my underwear, pull the cover up to my waist, feel it weigh too heavy on my legs and kick it off again.
I long for sleep, my eyelids droop as if there are physical weights attached to them, but the cells of my brain and body still crawl with inner motion from the endless, anxious journey, the vibration of jet engines, the long car ride, and the burbling echo of Mother's voice.
Eventually, however, I sink into a half-way state: asleep enough to dream, awake enough to know I'm dreaming.

It's another hot afternoon many years ago and Mother and I are walking along an empty street lined with high stone walls. Doors are set into the walls at regular intervals, she pauses now and then to check the house numbers and it's all so immediate, so *real* I can taste the dust, feel the sweat on my forehead, and the heat striking up from the road through the soles of my sandals.

Where are we going? Who are we looking for?

How old am I?

I must be quite young because I have to reach up to tuck my hand in the crook of Mother's arm.

I'm compulsively trailing the fingertips of my other hand along the rough wall beside me. They're wearing smooth and beginning to smart and every few minutes I check for blood.

"Don't do that!" Mother says.

One door stands open; as we pass I feel a wave of delicious coolness, and glimpse a narrow, unruly garden where a naked stone boy perches on a rock in the middle of a pool. He's holding up a shell from which water gently trickles. I long to go in, sit at his feet, take my shoes off and dabble my toes in the water.

I suck on my fingers. Ask, "Would Daddy have loved me if I'd been a boy?"

"Silly girl! What a question! He loves you just as you are."

"No he doesn't."

"You're quite wrong, Penelope. He just doesn't know how to show it. He's never understood children."

"Why not? He was a little boy once—" though I can't imagine my father ever being young.

We walk on, turn a corner, our shadows stretch out darkly in front of us while the still potent late afternoon sun burns the back of my neck. "His parents were quite old when he was born and he didn't have any brothers and sisters," Mother explains.

"He never wanted any children of his own. He even asked me to sign a paper promising I'd never have a baby. Of course I didn't sign, but it was very hard. I had to fight for you tooth and nail for years. Oh, what I had to do to get you, Penny!"

I'm thrilled that she'd fight for me tooth and nail; I tell myself I don't need a father anyway when I have her.

"Daddy was so afraid of me having a baby that he'd wear two French letters, one on top of the other when we made love," Mother says (my present-day partly-aware self wonders would she *really* have said that to a small child?) and, then, I have a fleeting image of my father kissing Mother with foreign-stamped envelopes stuck to his back—but by now I'm more interested in my fingertips, tissue thin with the red flesh pulsing beneath, and I examine them as we walk on and on, our footsteps muffled in the heat.

Fifty nine . . . Seventy three . . . we're pausing again and, "I think this is it," Mother says with a glance over her shoulder as if she's scared someone might see us. We're crunching up a gravel path toward a black front door with an inset panel of frosted glass, she reaches for the bell, the old fashioned kind you pull, it peals over and over—and I'm flung back into my childhood bedroom, hot and dizzy and feeling a bit sick, Mother leaning over me, shaking my shoulder, looking shockingly aged with my father's ancient, brown-flannel bathrobe—how well I remember that robe, how I hate and despise it—clutched across her chest. She cries, "Tell them to go away!"

I rub at my grainy eyes. "Who? Where?"

The bell rings again.

"*Don't let them in!*"

I haul myself off the bed, run across the passage into the dining room and lean out the front window. A young blonde girl stands in the street below. She sees me and waves. She holds a large, brown-paper-wrapped bundle in her arms; calls up, "*Laundry!*"

I buzz her into the building, the front door slams, feet clatter on the stairs and moments later in she bursts, plump and panting—"Hi, I'm Sue"—returning Mother's clean sheets and towels and collecting the used ones, which I learn is a free weekly service provided by the local Council for ailing seniors.

"Sorry to go on and on ringing, Mrs. Sayle, but I didn't think you'd heard me."

Mother is at once herself again, panic forgotten. "Dorothy! How nice!" And politely, as I stand there in my bra and panties, "you must meet my daughter Penelope! She's come all the way from America to take care of me!"

"That'll make you feel lots better won't it, Mrs. Sayle!"

Mother sinks into an armchair by the window while Sue and I strip the bed and fold sheets.

"Dorothy has a boyfriend," Mother tells me brightly. "With the gas company, isn't he, dear? And you're getting married!"

"Next June, Mrs. Sayle."

"You'll invite me to the wedding, won't you!"

"Wouldn't hardly be the same without you!"

"Such a long time to wait, though. Can't you hurry it up?"

Sue flushes and giggles. "You know how it is, so much to do, these things take time!"

"Then they shouldn't!" Mother is stern. "Not when two young people are in love. Once we'd made up our minds, Frank and I were married in three weeks flat."

"I'll bet you were a beautiful bride, Mrs. Sayle. Must have looked a picture all in white."

"I'll show you one of these days," Mother says, who had indeed yearned for a white wedding with all the trimmings but to save expense had to be content with a neat little black suit and the registry office. "It was so long ago but sometimes it seems it was just yesterday."

"He was a lovely man, the Commander!"

"The handsomest man in the navy." Mother gazes dewily at his picture. "Everyone said so."

Sue departs with her new bundle. I help Mother back into bed between clean sheets and ask, "Why do you call her Dorothy?"

"What else should I call her? Dear Dorothy! She's always taken such care of me. She used to do all the cooking!"

"Was she the one who stocked the refrigerator?"

Mother looks confused. "Dorothy's been in the fridge?"

I don't pursue it. "What were you afraid of? Who did you think was at the door?"

"Those other people." Mother picks at her quilt again. They come around poking their noses in. So *nosy!*"

"What people?"

"The social workers. Senior services. The church women. I see nothing but women. I hate women. Except for that last little girl. She's sweet; takes such good care of me. Such pretty hair and good skin. She's getting married soon. Her boyfriend works for the gas board."

I shoot a measuring glance at Mother, in whose head, I'm realizing, the gears have begun to slip.

"She's not like those others. They say I shouldn't be here alone, that it's dangerous and there could be an accident, like a fire. They want to put me away and I won't go. Why should I have to live in some horrid, poky little room? I hate little rooms, they give me claustrophobia. They'll have to carry me out of here feet first." She repeats with emphasis, *"Feet first!"*

Then she reaches out, grips me tightly around the wrist and drags me forward until I'm half sprawled across the bed.

"But I don't have to go anywhere now, do I," she smiles in triumph, "Not now *you're* here!"

4.

Six o'clock. I've unpacked, taken a cold bath in Mother's antique catafalque of a tub and dressed in a black tank top and the floral cotton skirt, sadly crumpled, which I'd luckily thrown in at the last minute. Who could have expected such weather?

Mother has changed back into her yellow velvet and finds my outfit disappointingly dowdy—"At least put on some lipstick!"—otherwise she's in good spirits. She has always loved company and guests are imminent: not only Simon Morley the gay architect but Colonel and Mrs. Augustus McBryde, and a woman called Bethany Loveless, a retired librarian who has launched a second career as a psychic.

"They can't wait to see you!" Mother says, as if these people are my friends too, although apart from Simon Morley the names mean nothing to me. Has Mother mentioned them on the phone, or in the letters she still occasionally writes? I'm ashamed how little I actually know of her life in England as if, between her annual visits to me in San Francisco, I stash her away like a seldom-used article of clothing in a drawer.

Simon Morley, first to arrive, has brought Mother a copy of Architectural Digest, containing pictures of an Elizabethan barn restoration he's recently completed, which he presents with a flourish and a smacking kiss before turning to me with a politely outstretched hand. "Glad you were able to get here so quickly, Penelope," says Simon. He's in his early fifties with a sturdy waistline and a brown/grey beard. He wears chocolate-colored corduroy pants, an open-necked blue-and-white checked shirt and nothing about him 'rages' but Mother tends to qualify anyone outside her immediate understanding or experience with superlatives. Gays of either sex are 'raging,' the rich are 'stinking', Roman Catholics, according to their social status are either 'ardent' or 'rabid' as in, *Penelope married a rabid Catholic though of course* (as if I'm a glass of milk which refuses to sour) *she never **turned!***

    Colonel and Mrs. Augustus McBryde are next. I've envisioned a bluff old codger in tweeds, his spouse in cardigan twinset and stout brogues. In fact the Colonel cuts rather a dashing figure in an ancient but well-cut ivory linen suit as if he's about to stroll a coastal promenade in the South of France while blonde pony-tailed Felicity (a second wife?) wears a scarlet blouse over a short navy skirt and looks younger than me. She hands me a paper bag containing a ripe avocado and a lemon. "I thought Imogene could have half for supper tonight with a squeeze of juice, and the rest for lunch tomorrow. She does adore them and I can always get her to eat some. You have to tempt her appetite, she picks like a bird!"

    "Pet," orders the Colonel in the strident voice of the hearing impaired, "don't be so bossy!"

    Mother strokes Felicity's arm. "You dear thing, always so thoughtful, just like a *real* daughter," while Felicity sips sparingly at her glass of Mother's cooking sherry and promises to bring over a container of home-made soup which she has made from scratch using fresh vegetables from the garden. "Gus and I are frightfully keen gardeners," she tells me with ingenuous pride. "You must come and see it! Have you got a garden in San Francisco?"

    I say not really, just a brick patio with plants in pots, and Felicity says how much she envies me all that California sun, and when she thinks of San Francisco all she imagines are hippies and car chases although she's sure it's not like that really. "Nothing's ever the way you expect it to be, is it. Like you, for instance." Her blue gaze takes in my tired face and wrinkled skirt. "I thought you'd look sophisticated!" blurts Felicity, then flushes to her hairline. "Not that you're *not!* I mean, it's just that you never really—"

Simon smoothly interjects that you can't help but create a picture of someone in your head though it might be quite wrong when you meet them, just as the psychic strides through the door. Mother has gushed, "Such a sensitive person, so *empathic*" and I've pictured a gypsyish wraith in veils and hoop earrings; Bethany, however, is large and booming, wears knee-length brown twill shorts, an emerald sports shirt a size too small, and carries an obese Aberdeen terrier which she pitches unceremoniously onto Mother's bed.

"Bethany, dear! How lovely! And darling Scottie come to see me too!" Mother leans over to tousle his ears, Scottie unleashes a silent but deadly fart and attacks his nether regions in a flurry of grunts and growls from which everyone tactfully averts their eyes.

Bethany offers me a workmanlike hand, "The prodigal daughter I presume," accepts a glass of whisky and chugs it down like a sailor.

Mother, always a pushover for the occult, tells me how I absolutely *must* have Bethany read my Tarot cards while I'm here: "She's quite extraordinary! She told me I'd soon be having a visitor from abroad, and here you are!" Then she grabs my wrist and demands of the room at large, "Will you tell me the point of having children when they run away from you and live the other side of the world?"

"So sad for you," agrees Felicity, clearly challenged in the tact department; "Just like poor Gus's son in Australia. He hardly ever comes home, not even for Christmas, does he, dear," and the Colonel, reminded, looks mournful.

"There was this young solicitor, so handsome, desperately in love with her, but no, she must needs rush off to California, as far away as she could get!" With a tinkle of laughter like breaking glass, "Dear Penelope!" Mother sighs, "Always so independent!"

There's a brief, digestive pause, broken simultaneously by Simon who apologizes for calling me at such an ungodly hour but he was so worried about Mother he'd forgotten the time difference; by Felicity who says at least I got here, everybody had been wondering whether I'd come at all; by the Colonel who rumbles "Now then, Pet" when she bites her lip and blushes again; by Bethany who wonders whether I'm a working girl back in San Francisco, or a lady of leisure.

I explain that I'm a copywriter with an advertising agency.

Mother, of a class and a generation whose women only took jobs upon failure in the marriage stakes, insists it's not real *work,* that I just make up slogans for the papers.

Simon argues that copywriting surely counts as real work, and Mother shrugs dismissive shoulders. "She doesn't *need* to work at all, her husband's stinking rich!" Making the defiant best of it, "He's a builder you know; and they all are, aren't they, *stinking!*—but she still insists on going to that office, day after day." Mother chuckles and swipes at my arm again. "Claims they can't do without her!"

Just yesterday—was it really only yesterday?—"How long do you think you'll be away?" wondered my boss Andy Sirvas, creative director of the agency. "Two weeks? Three?"

Andy is a lot younger than me, with the Napoleonic complex of many short men. His crisply fragile hair is remorselessly thinning back and front and he takes out his terror of baldness on his subordinates, many of whom hold him in dread, which I know he relishes. He does not do sensitivity well and regretted Mother's timing, if not selfishness, in choosing to die with the Enraptor campaign about to take off.

I reminded him it was 1997, that I was taking my laptop and cell phone, we could email, fax and talk every day and that I'd stay for as long as it took—eventually walking away with two weeks full pay (accumulated vacation and overtime) with up to three months' unpaid leave of absence.

Now, I'm wondering whether three months will be enough. Could the doctors be wrong and Mother is in spontaneous remission?

Although grateful I am not, after all, attending a harrowing deathbed there seems something almost anticlimactic in my rush to Mother's side and I think, with a groundswell of resentment how, if I was a man, I would never be expected to drop everything, put my life on hold, fly six thousand miles and move in 'for as long as it took.'

Then I think of the morphine, the pain she won't discuss, the disease she will not name, and admit the significance of her undyed hair and unlipsticked mouth: that she's no longer striving to look youthful because she's too damn tired to bother.

5.

When the door has closed on her visitors and their chatter faded down the stairs Mother's face instantly wipes clean of its bright social smile. She sets down the drink she has barely touched with a hand which trembles worse than before. "Take this away, Penelope, or drink it yourself. I know I said I wanted it and I like to hold it and smell it and, you know, look as if I'm having a good time, but I can't swallow any, it makes me feel sick."

Mother's guests, who at first so energized her, have exhausted her. Patches of feverish color flare on her cheekbones. "I've got this silly pain again and I was so *sure* I was getting better."

She gropes behind my father's picture, finds the bottle and fumbles with the cap. I pour water, put the glass in her hand, guide it to her mouth and hold it as it rattles against her teeth. I suggest, "There were too many people at once. It was too much for you."

"No," Mother says faintly; "I like to have them all together, it makes it like a party," and I remember how much she enjoyed parties, how she was seldom able to attend one let alone give one and that of course, when she finally threw that one and only triumphant celebration, I was the one who ruined it for her.

She leans into her pillows and appears to fall into a light doze. I tiptoe around the room gathering up glasses, straightening chairs and, turning, find her regarding me with puzzled eyes. She says, "I can't *imagine* why Johnathon hasn't rung. I'd have thought he'd be on the phone first thing."

I remind her that I haven't seen Johnathon for ten years; that he's over fifty, long married, with two grown sons.

"He's still a boy to me," Mother says. "So handsome. I'll always remember how you two looked together. You were made for each other. That night, that awful last night . . . watching you both . . . . ." she peels off the yellow bedjacket to reveal a man's undershirt, once white, now dingy and stained, which I have a horrible feeling also belonged to my father, along with the bathrobe. It's downright creepy and I vow that tomorrow, first thing, I'll buy her something nice to wear in bed.

She heads for the door and clings with lowered head to the door handle. I try to support her but she swats me away and wends her shaky way to the bathroom alone. When I follow, she closes the door firmly in my face and insists, "I'm all *right,* Penelope!"

I tidy the bed and fluff her pillows.

She returns. Back in bed now, the quilt tucked across her lap.

The phone rings in the living room and her face lights up. "There you are!" she cries, "That'll be him now! I just *knew* he'd ring! *Quickly,* Penelope! *Answer it!"*

6.

"So I guess you arrived safely," Liam says, his warm, drawling American voice a welcome balm after a day of clipped British accents. "How was the flight? Get any sleep?"

"On and off. Dozed a bit."

"How's Imogene?"

I think of Mother in the next room just feet away, Mother, whose acute ears can hear the dust settle inside walls, who *just knows* this is Johnathon and won't want to miss a syllable. I say, "I can't really talk right now."

Liam understands at once. "Okay, I'll ask the questions, you just keep it general. Have you seen the doctor?"

"Tomorrow morning."

"So you don't know anything more?"

"Not really."

"And how are things between you and her? Can you say?"

"Fine so far. A little sniping, but basically white noise."

"Poor Imogene." I can sense his rueful smile across six thousand miles. I've told Liam many times I don't know how he puts up with Mother. She'd consider it woefully ill-bred to be downright rude, but she accomplishes a lot with the occasional brittle laugh or chilling silence. Liam, however, is a genuinely kind man. He has a deep respect for family and a tolerance for difficult old ladies. He never complains and unfailingly turns the other cheek which I know infuriates her.

He has never allowed Mother to get to him during those endless summer visits, unlike me, however hard I try. After the brief, jetlagged honeymoon period she'd recover her energy and veer once more onto the attack, the verbal knife-thrusts launched without warning. She'd accuse me of being cold, hard, and a bad daughter, sounding so angry and bitter I'd realize she must hate me. I'd feel sick to my stomach, gulp down Tums and count off the remaining days, wondering exactly when Mother's promise to live forever became a threat.

But, I remind myself, that was then. Now, after all, Mother has turned out to be mortal. She's ill, in pain, and she needs me. She's hardly likely to rage at me now and, even if she does, how can I be angry with someone who's sick and dying?

Liam's saying, "Go easy and take it one day at a time, and if you want me to come over, just holler."

He would too, no matter how busy, even though he's an unenthusiastic traveller. To my certain knowledge, apart from a spell in Vietnam in the service, he has left the United States twice, once to Hawaii for a family beach vacation which hardly counted, and once to Mexico for a deep-sea fishing trip. He has never been to Europe.

I tell him I'll do that. That I'll holler. Then we fall silent, neither of us sure what to say next, we've never been apart longer than a week and we're not used to intimacy at long distance. Eventually he says, sounding slightly awkward, "I miss you, Pen. Last night was lonely."

I say, "I haven't even been to bed yet," and think of us together just yesterday—was it really only yesterday? So close, our bodies touching all the way down at shoulders, hips, thighs and feet; moving into each other, his hands on my shoulders, my breasts, his hard, calloused fingers so gentle and knowing.

I'll be sleeping alone in my narrow childhood bed tonight—and for how many nights after that?

"I miss you too," I say, "I'm lonely too." I feel my throat tightening and ask hurriedly, "What are you and Caitlin doing tonight?"

"We'll probably pick up some Chinese."

"I'll be thinking of you."

"Try dreaming instead. It'll be three, four in the morning where you are."

"You can't control what you dream. Being awake's better."

"Well then, if you're awake, call us!"

And as if I'd set an alarm clock I wake at 3.00 a.m., tired to the bone but knowing I'll never fall back to sleep, thinking how it's early evening in San Francisco and Caitlin and Liam might even now be climbing from his big blue truck loaded with plastic bags from the Five Happiness Kitchen.

I watch them in my mind's eye, mounting the steps of our Potrero Hill cottage with the magnolia tree outside the living room window and the high view across to the East Bay hills. We bought the house sixteen years ago as a near ruin and Liam has been fixing it up and adding to it ever since.

Now they're in the kitchen unpacking: fried rice with prawns, Mongolian beef, spicy chicken and noodles. Our usual order. I see them seated on stools at the counter, their backs to me as they watch the lights glitter across the Bay and the ships heading in or out of the Port of Oakland, Liam dark and hulking, Caitlin small and delicate-boned, her glossy braid reaching below her shoulder blades. They're spooning the food into bowls. Passing soy and plum sauce. Caitlin deftly uses chopsticks; not Liam. It takes too long, he complains, and what are forks for, anyway?

They finish eating and their heads lean together companionably as they crack open their fortune cookies.

"*'You'll soon be making a journey,'* Caitlin reads. "Think that means Santa Barbara or England?"

"Either—or both," Liam says. He's sitting on his customary stool beside the wall, the phone on his immediate right which is forest green to match the granite counter tops. I think about creeping into Mother's living room—*call us!*—but the whirring of her rotary phone will seem excessively loud in the silence and even a whispered conversation will wake her: *Penelope, who on **earth** are you talking to at this time of night?*

I don't want Mother to be ill. I don't want her to need me. I don't want to be here. I want to go home.

Once I was glad to be an only child so I wouldn't have to share her with anyone.

I wish I wasn't an only child now.

7.

In the relative cool of early morning I've walked downtown, located an internet café, visited Milton Street where all the better shops are located and bought Mother a sunshine-yellow terrycloth bathrobe and three nightgowns: peach silk, white cotton lawn, black satin with lace trim.

Mother wonders, "What's all this for?"

"They're a present from me to you. You can't sleep in my father's old undershirts."

"Why not?"

"Because they're old and full of holes. They're a disgrace."

"So what? They make me feel closer to Frank. Anyway, nobody sees me."

"I see you."

"For god's sake, Penelope! I'm your *mother*. What does it matter?"

"It matters to me."

"Rubbish! I've never worn a nightdress in my life and I'm not starting now."

I'm momentarily diverted, I hadn't known Mother slept in the nude. I ask, "Won't you at least try them on?"

But she's resolutely stuffing them into the shiny pink bag they came in. "I said I don't want them. Stop badgering me. Keep them for yourself, or return them and get your money back."

"At least the dressing gown—"

"What do I need a dressing gown for? I've got Daddy's."

"I'll put it in your closet for later on. In case you change your mind."

"Oh all *right* then! But mind you close the door."

I hide the sunny bathrobe away and shut the door with barely controlled violence.

"There!" Mother says. "And while you're at it, Penelope" — critically regarding my sleeveless navy-knit top with the white piping around the neck—"Next time you go to the shops be sure and buy yourself a new blouse. That thing makes you look like a priest."

The day lurches on, the morning alternating between specious argument and sweaty trips back and forth downtown; the afternoon with the parade of women Mother has deplored: *how I hate women!*

Not even Mother, however, can object to the first caller, Dr. Alice Cameron, who is young, soft spoken and clearly pregnant, who brings out all Mother's maternal instincts.

"Do you know, Penelope, this dear person is expecting in January!" And, clearly regarding the doctor's visit to be social rather than professional, beckons and pats the bedside. "Come and sit down, my dear, you need to get off your feet or they'll swell up. Mine did. I remember it so well, all those years ago but it could have been yesterday. Do you know how I first knew Penelope was on the way? I got this absolute *thing* about soap. I couldn't stand washing, couldn't bear the smell, so horridly sweet. I had to use that harsh, rough stuff you wash clothes with which wasn't scented but even that nearly made me sick. My mother got quite cross with me and said the baby would be born dirty but when Penelope arrived she was absolutely perfect!" She reaches out, grabs me by the chin and tilts my face up to the light. "And you could tell she was her father's daughter the minute she appeared! See that forehead? And that chin?"

Dr. Cameron, who has cleverly managed to check Mother's vital signs and whose hands are now splayed across her abdomen, hurriedly glances from me to my father's photograph and agrees I'm the spitting image.

In full flood of reminiscence, Mother describes how I was born in the middle of a thunderstorm, how she hid under the bedclothes and put her fingers in her ears, and was in labor for twenty four agonizing hours. "People didn't usually go to the hospital in those days to have babies, but we lived in a small flat in London and dear Theo—that was my brother—took me down to our aunt's house in the country. My Aunt May—my mother's sister, she was a Waterstone—married a London banker. Stinking rich; he died though. Such a beautiful house, with a grove of silver-birch trees in the garden. I stood by the window and looked at them across the lawn and counted them—there were nine—and they looked so beautiful gleaming against the black clouds. It had started to rain, the lawn was bright, bright green, there were birds on the grass fluffing their feathers and it took my mind off the pain for just a moment before it started again. There's that moment every mother knows when you realize it's just going to go on and on and won't stop till it's all over. The midwife was a darling but she wasn't allowed to give me anything and the doctor didn't even get there until after Penelope had arrived. I'd no idea you could suffer like that, nobody told me, and I thought Penelope would be born dead!"

The story of my birth is another of Mother's favorites but although I hear of my grandmother soaking Mother's forehead with cologne and Uncle Theo drinking gin in the living room to steady his nerves, my father seems conspicuously absent.

Once I asked where he was at the time but Mother was vague: "He was still in the navy then; he would have been at sea"—but he wasn't at sea, he had a staff appointment with the Admiralty in London.

"Even if he didn't want a baby," I said, "Wouldn't he have wanted to be with you?"

With genuine astonishment, "He couldn't possibly have taken the time off! He was *very* senior. And good heavens, you know Daddy! Can you imagine him hanging around for that sort of thing? Having babies was a woman's job."

I pointed out, "Uncle Theo was there."

"Uncle Theo was different," which seems to have been indisputable. As an adult he would have been described as a confirmed bachelor; at high school he was nicknamed Rapunzell on account of his hair which he insisted on wearing just too long. "They called him a sissy, too, because he liked artistic things better than sports," Mother said, "But of course he never cared what anybody thought, he just laughed at them."

Unlike my father, Theo certainly had no hang-ups about childbirth and upon hearing of my arrival came roaring down to Aunt May's house in his Jaguar, carving a gravel trench right outside the front door, so excited he kissed Mother, Granny Waterstone and even the midwife, then swept me into his arms and pranced around the house singing his own adaptation from Aida, "That famous aria, you know the one," and Mother warbled: " '*Prin*cipessa Bam*bi*naaaaa!' . . . He had a lovely voice, Theo; a beautiful tenor, he should have been an opera star, but he decided to be a writer instead."

That was why he went to Tangier when I was still very young, to be a writer, though he never seems to have written anything, at least nothing that was published. My father would sometimes hint at something disreputable about Uncle Theo and his circle of friends, "And God only knows how he makes a living!" But Uncle Theo never forgot my birthday and always sent deliciously unsuitable presents: a belly dancer's jingly coin belt, finger-cymbals, liqueur chocolates, and once a check for a hundred pounds which bounced. Mother thought my father should make up the money to me, but he never did.

Uncle Theo died soon after that though nobody told me about it for weeks and if there was a funeral out there in Tangier Mother didn't go.

It was sad, but I hadn't seen him for so long I didn't cry. Mother didn't cry either but I remember her white face and an uncharacteristic silence which lasted all day.

Dr. Cameron is asking now, "Any discomfort here? And what if I do this?"

"Can't feel a thing!" chirps Mother.

The slender fingers probe some more. "There?"

"Nothing. I feel tons better! Do you know, I haven't had a single twinge since Penelope got here!"

Afterwards I walk the doctor to the door. We step out onto the landing, I pull the door closed behind me and tell her, "That's not true. She was in pain last night."

Dr. Cameron suggests Mother might have overdone things yesterday in the excitement of my arrival; that it could be gas pains or an acid stomach. She tells me the morphine dosage was adjusted upward only last week and the pain relief should be constant provided Mother follows instructions; "Just don't let her take more than the prescribed dose," and impresses upon me how easily that could happen: "She could forget she'd already taken a pill and pop in another one; or if she had some breakthrough pain, she might think the morphine wasn't working properly, take another to make sure, and because the drug works on a time-release system it could all clock in together and she'd go a little haywire."

I ask Dr. Cameron what she means by haywire; learn that Mother could become disoriented and even hallucinate, when I recall a memorably awful night in San Francisco back in the 'seventies trying to persuade a tripped-out friend that blood was *truly* not oozing from the walls.

"Ideally," the doctor says, "You should keep track of the pills and dole them out yourself," when I think with dismay about coming between Mother and her medication. Mother loves pills. In the past she would hoard stashes of valium around the house and the threat of the pill bottle, at certain stressful moments, was her ultimate weapon against which not even my father could prevail.

I ask what I should do if Mother does start to hallucinate; am told I just have to use my judgment and walk her through it, "And in an emergency dial 999."

Dr. Cameron glances at her watch. She has already allotted us a generous amount of time and will have other patients waiting. I ask exactly how I should 'walk her through it', Dr. Cameron says there should be no problem provided Mother stays with the program, and now we're back where we started, she's shaking my hand, hitching her battered leather satchel over one shoulder and trotting away down the stairs, leaving me more worried than before she came.

8.

Next to appear is Nurse Follis, a strapping blonde with a fog-horn voice and thickly muscled forearms. She strips away Mother's sheet and tells her to roll on her side, loudly explaining how one must regularly checks Mum's bottom and hips for bed sores because they could blow up with no warning, and now that Mum's lost so much weight I should lay a sheepskin pad under the sheet to spread the pressure.

Mother declares how she won't have me or anybody else look at her bottom, she hasn't lost an ounce, and she neither wants nor needs a sheepskin.

"Of course you do, dear."

"And don't call me 'dear!'" Follis whips out a notebook, writes down the name of a medical supply house, tears out the sheet and hands it to me. "It's in that little shopping center by the railway station. You'll find everything you need there."

Mother says, "I told you I don't want a sheepskin. I'll be much too hot."

I say, "I'm not getting her one if she doesn't want it."

Mother snaps at us both, "Don't talk about me as if I'm not even *here!*"

"No need to get hot under the collar, dear." And Follis suddenly declares, with narrowed eyes, "How did *this* happen then?"

I gaze in dismay at a purple-black swelling the size of a saucer on Mother's upper thigh. "I've no idea. Perhaps when she fell in the kitchen?"

Follis looks from Mother to me. "Nobody said anything about a fall."

Mother jerks the sheet up to her waist and holds it rigidly in place. "It's no business of yours!"

Follis doesn't reply. She's writing in her book.

"Don't you dare put that in a report," Mother says.

"It's not a question of dare, it's procedure," Follis says.

An explosion is brewing, luckily stalled by bathtime to which Mother has been looking forward.

I'm invited to join them and perhaps I should in case there are more bruises and contusions but if this is so then Follis is sure to tell me, Mother will hate me to see her naked, and in any case it's an opportunity to count pills.

Mother leaves on the nurse's arm, looking both martyred and furious. I hear water running, Follis's parade-ground voice and Mother's deafening silence. There are twenty-three morphine pills in the bottle which I hurriedly replace behind my father's picture because they're returning already, Mother tight lipped and swathed in a towel, the nurse gripping her by both elbows. I know it's for support but the image created is of a guard with a prisoner.

Follis departs on her next call with a hearty "Cheerio!" and long before she's out of earshot Mother roars, "I can't stand that woman! She's bossy and rough and common as dirt. Dyes her hair, too. It'll be dried-out straw by the time she's much older. And she doesn't let me have any time to enjoy the water, just rushes me in and out." She regards me with an unfathomable expression. "That's what it would be like in one of those *places*. People I don't like bossing me about. Unfriendly, rough hands touching me. People who don't care."

"Surely they can send us somebody else."

"I've got to have her. It's the National Health."

"But if you don't like her . . . ."

"They'd only send someone worse."

"You don't know that."

"She'll tell them about the bruise."

The doorbell peals.

"Oh *god!*" cries Mother.

I lean out the window; yet another woman waits expectantly below. She's wearing a navy blouse with white trim just like mine, only hers really is a clerical collar.

Mother is peering over my shoulder. "It's that priest creature from St. Stephens. Mildred something or other. Can you imagine being called Mildred? I don't want to see her. Don't let her in!" But it's too late, Mildred has seen my face at the window and given a cheerful wave.

I buzz her into the building; listen to plodding footsteps ascending the stairs.

"Keep her away from me!" orders Mother.

"What do you want me to tell her?"

"Whatever you like. Tell her I'm in the bath. Tell her I'm asleep. Tell her I'm *dead!*"

"You must be Penelope!" Mildred takes my hand in hers and presses it between large, moist palms.

I make excuses for Mother. "I'm afraid you're stuck with me, it's too bad you had to climb all these stairs for nothing," but Mildred, unlike the doctor and Follis, seems to have all the time in the world.

She sits at the dining room table, thick legs sturdily planted. She has a long face, unusually wide-set brown eyes and large teeth, and reminds me of a friendly horse. I offer tea which is gratefully accepted, along with a ginger cookie which she dips in her cup.

"You poor thing, you must have been so worried but I want you to know we've been doing all we can!" She eats with her mouth slightly open, the cookie is brown mush on those equine teeth and I look away. "We're all so glad you've come home. You're very much *needed,* you know. We'd have done a lot more for her if she'd only let us, but our hands are tied. She knows she has to have the nurse but she won't let anybody else into the house to help her, just shouts out of the window for them to go away. We reported it to the Council and they sent a social worker—same story, I'm afraid."

I tell Mildred how Mother has some good friends who have been taking care of her; Mildred maintains that blood is thicker than water; however, if I find things getting a bit too much for me over the coming weeks I mustn't allow myself to feel guilt or despair which is perfectly natural for caregivers; to remember I have friends down at St. Stephens, and not hesitate to ask for help!

Afterwards Mother declares waspishly how women shouldn't be priests. "It isn't natural. I wouldn't dream of taking holy communion from a woman."

"Mildred means well."

"They all do. I hate people who mean well and I don't want her here. I don't like those new people at St. Stephens, it's all changed since dear Mr. Thackeray retired. The new vicar isn't bad looking but he's one of these modern, 'with-it' types who go on television and call you by your Christian name and I don't want strangers calling me Imogene. It's most inappropriate at my age. But now you're here! You won't throw me out like rubbish, will you, Penelope! You'd *never* put me away!" Mother clutches at my hands and her nails dig into my wrist like talons.

She's come all the way from America to take care of me!
We're all so glad you've come home!

My heart lurches. Does she actually expect me to nurse her?

I think with terror of basins and needles, diapers and smells; that never before have I taken care of somebody who won't get well; that I'm not a born nurturer and would make a lousy nurse.

    Mother misinterprets my brooding silence. "Of course you wouldn't put me away! You'd *never* do that!" She hugs me close and exhales with a gust of relief which wrenches her whole body. "Oh Penelope! I knew I could count on you!"

9.

Cocktail time rolls around, and Mother, restored after her bath and draped in yellow velvet, awaits her social hour (which I've learned is a regular evening ritual) with the bright-eyed expectancy of a southern belle.

Simon arrives with a bottle of chilled Sancerre, Felicity and the Colonel with the promised soup in a Tupperware container and, minutes later, another member of Mother's court wheezes to the top of the stairs, Lord George Storey, Earl of Avon, an aged gnome in worn corduroys and Wellington boots which drop clods of dried mud on the carpet. Mother introduces me: "Dear George, this is my daughter Penelope. I do wish she wouldn't wear that blouse, don't you think it makes her look like a priest?"

Lord Storey, 92, is a suitor from Mother's debutante days. "The dear old thing always adored me," she confided once, "He actually went down on his knees and begged me to marry him, can you *imagine?*" And when I asked why didn't she say yes because she'd have been a countess, she actually giggled. "Oh darling! I couldn't possibly! He was much too short and couldn't dance! Anyway, then your father came along—"

Now, the old boy gallantly informs me that if I *was* a priest he'd certainly want to join my church, then drags me across the room to inspect Mother's portrait. "Most beautiful girl of her year! 1936—Marvellous vintage!" He rocks back on his heels the better to drink her in from the gleaming spires of her tiara to the gloved hands laid so demurely in her white satin lap. "How I hankered after your mother! Wasting my time of course, chaps around her ten feet deep, she could take her pick!" He brings his faded blue gaze to bear reflectively on me. "Taller of course—but you take after her rather!"

Nobody has previously suggested I look like Mother and she cuts through the buzz of conversation to assert how that is nonsense: "She's the spitting image of Frank! Look at that chin."

I'm the object of istant scrutiny.

"She's got your eyes, Imogene. Gypsy eyes," says Simon.

"Nonsense. They're dark, just like Frank's," Mother says. "So dark brown they're almost black."

"And your forehead."

I complain how I'm not a prize poodle to be pulled and prodded at a dog show but no-one pays any attention.

"Frank's hair," Mother insists. "So thick and curly, what a battle I'd have trying to drag a comb through it. How she'd kick and scream!"

Everyone checks the photo of my father on the night table, in which he is almost entirely bald. "We'll have to trust you there," Simon says.

"He'd sweat under his cap when he was on his ship in the tropics," Mother explains. "That's why it fell out so early. And Penelope got his eyebrows, too. You can't imagine what it took, getting her to pluck them!"

When they've all gone Mother's energy again drains like bathwater and she collapses against her pillows. As I leave the room with a trayful of glasses I catch her reaching behind my father's photo and ask: "Didn't you take a pill right before your friends came? That's only an hour ago."

"Nonsense. It was much longer ago than that!"

"Just wait a little longer."

"Why should I? Do you *want* me to be in pain?"

"Of course not, Mother—but please try."

I wash the glasses, set them to dry on the dishrack and begin to heat soup. I know Mother will have grabbed for the bottle the moment I left the room, but how can I stop her?

It's stifling in the kitchen. I fling the window open and lean out but there's no breeze, the stone balustrade is warm under my hands, the sky like tarnished brass. The phone rings in the living room and Mother's voice urges me to answer it, answer quickly, I must, must, *must!*

It isn't Johnathon this time either, of course it isn't, it's Caitlin. She would have called earlier, she says, but she's been at the marine sanctuary since dawn attending to a gunshot sealion: "How *could* somebody shoot such a beautiful animal! The poor thing is blinded now and he'll have to be euthanized."

I tell her what a shame. Privately I've often sympathized with the fishermens' efforts to protect their catch and their livelihood, but Caitlin's principles are relentless and I'd never dare tell her so.

"Let me talk with Granny!" Caitlin says and when I explain Mother's in bed and can't come to the phone is astounded—*shocked*—that there's no extension in her room. "Can't you get her a mobile?"

"Of course I can. I'll do that tomorrow," I say, and wonder why I didn't think of it myself.

"And you'll let me know right away when things start looking as if—when she—I mean, don't wait too long, is all."

"I promise."

"I guess I still can't quite believe it," Caitlin says wanly. "I thought Granny would go on forever."

"So did I."

"I was thinking—maybe I should come over and be with you guys."

"I'll let you know if she takes a turn for the worse, but right now she's—"

"I mean, right now." Caitlin pleads, "I could really help out, Mom."

I tell her no way; that school is important, that Mother could be with us for a while yet, and I have plenty of people to help.

"I'm not talking about day to day stuff like cleaning and cooking and errands. I'm talking about making it easier on you when Granny gets, you know—" Caitlin searches for the right word, then, *"When she gets on your case!"*

"I don't let her 'get on my case.'"

"Sure you do. And trust me, Granny can be majorly mean sometimes, she knows all your hot buttons, and you get all stressed."

I sigh. I've always tried so hard not to involve Caitlin in my wrangles with Mother and until now thought I'd done a reasonable job.

Caitlin goes on, "I don't know why she says some of those things when she loves you so much; it doesn't make any sense." She adds, "She cries when she leaves."

"I know she does."

"You cry too. I've seen you."

My throat tightens. I nod in silent agreement.

"So what do you think?" Caitlin urges. "I should come, right?"

"No!" And before she can object, "Of course I want you here, I really do—but not quite yet." I think of the accusations Mother has flung at me through the years, some justified, some not; of my sense that something darker and deeper lies between us; that this is my last chance for us to talk as mother and daughter, for me to understand, perhaps make amends and say

I'm sorry—perhaps for her to say she's sorry too. Finally, "I need to be with Granny alone for a little while longer. Just us."

Caitlin is silent, and I feel she instinctively guesses at what I can't quite say. How did my 20-year-old daughter grow so perceptive? "Maybe I can come over at Thanksgiving break," she says.

"That might be good timing. Let's work on that."

"Okay." Caitlin is reluctant but reconciled. Then, "Dad and I went to St. Joseph's last night after supper, to light a candle for her. It was so cool, like we were really doing something to help her, sending energy up there with the flame! They're saying a mass for her on Sunday!"

"That's kind," I say, "but do me a favor and don't tell her."

Caitlin says she respects Mother's point of view about Catholics and wouldn't think of it.

"Meantime, please don't worry about Granny and me." My voice sounds reassuring, even to myself. "Don't forget she's sick and doesn't have the energy to fight with me this time. We're actually managing very well, better than usual, and it's only going to get better. How can it not?"

"That's good, I guess," Caitlin says.

"It'll be fine," I say and, *"Trust me!"*

10.

3.00 a.m. again.

My bedroom door is limned with light and Mother's slippered feet are shushing down the passage. The bathroom door closes. I wait for what seems much too long. Would I have heard if she'd fallen? I think anxiously how she might be lying on the floor unconscious right now and fling back the covers— but then the toilet flushes, Mother's footsteps return and moments later the light clicks off again.

I plump up my pillow, lie on my back staring into darkness, think about making myself a cup of coffee, decide I might as well.

The kettle shrills; damn, I'd forgotten to remove the whistle; but Mother's room remains silent.

I return to bed and close the door.

Wish I had something to read but the newspaper won't be delivered for hours.

Sit with my knees hunched up under my T-shirt, emerald green, XXL, FOLEY CONSTRUCTION across the front in black letters, the I of CONSTRUCTION dotted with a small shamrock, and gaze thoughtfully at the cedar chest.

The next thing I know I'm setting my cup down, crossing the room and raising the lid—only to find, to my disappointment, that there's nothing inside but a stack of Mother's old family photo albums.

I sink back on my heels, disappointed and rather annoyed, she should have asked me first before throwing my stuff out— though to be fair why should she ask? Wouldn't she have decided, quite reasonably, that if I'd really wanted it I'd have had it all shipped to San Francisco years ago?

I pick up an album, glance through it, put it down and pick up another.

Of course I've seen them all before. I remember long ago rainy afternoons when Mother would turn the thick, black pages and I'd obediently gaze down upon three generations of Waterstones: at amply proportioned, tightly corseted women in elaborate hats; bundled and bonneted babies in perambulators the size of SUVs; young men wearing long white pants and v-neck sweaters brandishing cricket bats or tennis racquets.

Here, now, is my grandmother, a small, pretty woman, drinking tea on the lawn with her sister May and a heavyset, dark-haired man with a luxuriant moustache who must be the stinking-rich banker.

Two children—Uncle Theo and Mother—astride small, fat ponies.

Mother, older in tweed jacket and skirt, posing on the running board of a magnificent old car with a strap around its hood.

Caitlin, sprawled on a black sandy beach. . . . Hang on: *Caitlin?*

I stare down at the image and it's a second or two before I realize it's not Caitlin but Mother's brother Theo at approximately Caitlin's age today.

He's sleek as a seal, the water pearling on his naked shoulders, his long wet hair streaked across his face. A cigarette is jammed in one corner of his mouth, and he's squinting up through the smoke with a crooked smile.

I decide that no way does he look a sissy but confident, mocking, even a little dangerous.

I wonder who he's looking at.

11.

I bring Mother her breakfast at 8.30, a cup of tea, toast and honey. She's ready and waiting, propped on pillows. The pill bottle is nowhere in sight; she'll have hidden it, like a tigress guarding a hard-won kill.

The day is again hot and sultry, but my father's bathrobe is slung over Mother's thin shoulders and her hands are cold.

I ask, "How did you sleep?"

"Never closed my eyes. I heard the clock strike every hour."

Mother has always been rather proud of her chronic insomnia, insisting it's a manifestation of delicate nerves. She lies awake all night, she says, worrying about my father, about me, or angrily chafing over my marriage to Liam and what might have been. She recalls in detail every slight she has ever suffered, and what she could have said or done at the time but didn't and should have.

"How do you feel this morning?"

"Much better! I expect I'll get up a little later. I can't stay in bed all the time, can I."

"Have a lazy morning. Perhaps you can get up for lunch."

"Lunch!" Mother's eyes are eager. "Lunch with you in the dining room! At the table! How lovely!"

"And I found this." I place the opened photo album in her lap. "I thought he was Caitlin at first, but it's Uncle Theo, isn't it?"

Mother gropes for her glasses. She agrees the young man is Theo, that she supposes he does look rather like Caitlin, and that the picture was probably taken during that certain spring he just wandered off. "He was supposed to be at Oxford," she explains. "Mummy never knew or she'd have been furious. Not that it mattered, he never did any work and always passed his exams anyway."

"Where is he?"

"Majorca? The Canary Islands? Somewhere Spanish. I remember he was so brown when he came back, all that sun and swimming, he could easily have passed for a Spaniard."

"Who took the picture?"

"Good heavens, darling, how should I know? Theo had so many friends." She closes the album with a dismissive clap of pasteboard. "Has Mrs. Ship brought the paper yet? Could you check?"

After breakfast Mother begins the crossword in the Daily Express, ignoring the clues and inserting words at random. When necessary she squeezes more than one letter into the square. While she's thus busily occupied I call British Telecom, where I learn that not only can I have an extra line installed as soon as tomorrow but there's also a program offering free phone extensions to seniors. Perfect! However, toward the end of my productive chat with Sylvia in Sales Mother appears at my elbow, anxious and suspicious. Who am I talking to and why? A new phone line? What for? The horrid thing rings enough as it is.

I tell Sylvia I'll get back to her and try to explain to Mother that the extra phone line is for me so I can access the internet from home instead of downtown, that it will not result in more calls, and that a bedroom extension is purely for her own convenience.

"No!" Mother is adamant, "It's the thin end of the wedge," and when I ask what she means she's impatient with me, as if I'm being wilfully stupid.

I buy an inflatable bath pillow for the tub and a prepaid cell phone. In the Internet café, over a cup of dark French roast, I check my inbox and find at least 60 emails, five of them from Andy Sirvas concerning my Enraptor print copy. The Enraptor is an automobile, sleek in design and explosive with testosterone. However, the client company wants to attract a female market share targeting the young professional woman with disposable income and the name conveys, they hope, a fusion of aggression and romance.

Now, to my irritation—no, frankly I'm *pissed*—"This just won't do it for us," declares Andy's email, insisting my copy seems not only to encourage excessive speeding, but to promote drug use and gambling. "No way can I present something like this to the client! Think again and get back to me ASAP!"

Returning to the Crescent I find the door to No. 12 standing open and Mrs. Ship washing the hall floor. She squeezes her mop into a pail of grey water, coughs, and tells me her sister has sent over copies of *Hello* and *Royalty* magazines with lovely pictures of the poor Princess of Wales' funeral and she'll pop up with them later. "And how's your mum doing today?" she wonders. "Feeling the heat something cruel, I spose, not that it'd bother you, coming from America." Mrs. Ship clings to a romantic myth of film stars, gangsters, cowboys and high-speed car chases, while the sun beats down eternally on a landscape of skyscrapers and Saguaro cactus. "Won't last though," she predicts. "It'll break by tonight, see if it don't, and a good thing too. No use to anybody, this heat, not unless you're lollygagging about by the sea," although Mrs. Ship never personally lollygags and her idea of a vacation is her annual visit to her brother's pub outside Bristol where she spends her time mopping another floor, washing glasses and waiting impatiently to return to her real life in the Regent Crescent.

Upstairs, Mother is bored and picking restlessly at her quilt. She has finished the crossword and the newspaper lies crumpled on the floor. I take it away and make fresh coffee which she doesn't actually drink but inhales, enjoying the smell and the warmth of the mug which she holds stilled against her drawn-up knees.

She has decided she will not, after all, get up for lunch though she's ravenous and could eat a horse. I prepare chicken broth and a very small cheese omelette which she pushes around her plate and sighs how she doesn't know what's wrong with her but the moment she picked up her fork her appetite was gone.

I scoop Mother's plate into the garbage then settle her down for her afternoon nap. I pour myself yet another cup of coffee and open up my computer wishing I, too, could take a nap, but my appointment with Dr. Savage the oncologist is in two hours' time and there's work to do.

It's hard to concentrate. The afternoon sun is throwing an ever-widening bar of bright heat across the room and I draw the curtains. They are velvet, once dark green but now faded to beige down the outer folds and no longer quite meet in the middle. When I safety-pin them together the light glares through the narrow, hour-glass-shaped gap and glints through a galaxy of tiny holes in the fabric.

I stifle a yawn, check through the copy which must now be neutered, but my thoughts refuse to hold together and slide smoothly through my head like Mother's omelette into the trash.

I lean my cheek into my hand, close my eyes and instantly find myself standing among a cluster of neighbors outside my house in San Francisco the day the main drain blocked and the plumber fed down a probe equipped with a miniature video camera to locate the problem.

"Tree roots." He was a scrawny little guy, but years spent lying on his back working on recalcitrant overhead pipes had endowed him with the bulging forearms of Popeye. He beckoned me forward to take a look. "Trouble with these old clay pipes, see how the roots've broke through every three feet at the joins?" and I gazed in fascinated disgust at white globs like coccooned insects trapped in a spider web. "Toilet paper," he grunted; "it's only liquids can get through now."

Only liquids.

The sun jabs onto my closed eyelids through a rent in the drapes. My coffee is cold but I drink it anyway, wondering whether Mother's tumor is a web of root-like material steadily invading her internal organs, or a solid, fleshy lump?

Grind my knuckles into my eyes to force away the images.

Concentrate, Penelope!

I reflect how hard I pitched for the Enraptor account to prove I could compete with the guys; how I managed to sell Andy Sirvas on the concept that, since I've been a woman at least twice as long as anyone else in the company I possess double the insight and empathy—though as a representative of the target market I must admit I don't want a muscle car which can reach 60 mph in three seconds, that I'm not interested in making a statement and am happy with my ten-year-old Subaru wagon which reliably takes me where I want to go.

I slide in the floppy disk, gaze at the stylized hawk logo and then at the Enraptor captured at hurtling moments on a mountain road, in the desert, on the beach—and the young woman at the wheel is Mother, she's driving Theo's XK-120, her long dark hair streams behind her and I can almost hear her windblown laughter . . . . .

"I'm bored!" Mother says immediately behind me and I jerk upright in my chair. "I can never sleep properly in the afternoon. What are you doing?"

She leans over my shoulder: "*'Freedom is back! The thrill of the fast lane, the uninhibited rush, the highway a high-rolling adventure ready for the taking'*. . . What on earth's this all about?"

"It's an ad for a car. They want some changes in the copy and I need to play around with it." I delete '*rush*' and '*high-rolling*' with their potentially questionable associations. Consider the hawk logo and, as she watches, type *The dream of flight is now a reality.*

Mother stares astonished at the screen and wonders how I made the words go away just like that and new ones appear. "In the old days I had to rub out my mistakes on the original and three carbon copies as well! I wish they'd had these things then!"

I ask if she would like a computer lesson. She would.

So I sit her down in my chair and show her how to cut and paste, underline and italicize. Her hands don't shake. "What a fascinating toy!" she says. "I wish I could write something on it."

"Then why don't you?"

She's excited. "What shall I write?"

"Whatever you want. A letter?"

She composes a letter to Caitlin, her fingers flying over the keyboard, underlining and italicizing as she goes:

Darling, this is Granny typing on Mummy's computer. I've learned to do all *sorts* of things! I can correct my mistakes,

<u>underline</u>, and move words all over the place! Can you *imagine* me doing this at my age . . . . . !

When my father retired he briefly consulted for a non-profit organization which preserved historic naval sites and monuments. He was able to work from home, was allocated a small allowance for office help, and engaged eighteen-year-old Eleanor Diggins, fresh from the local business college, for two afternoons a week to transcribe his handwritten texts. At the end of each week he would count her meager wages into her pay envelope, hand it over ceremoniously when she left—I do believe this is yours, Miss Diggins—and she'd reply how it's good of you, I'm sure, Commander, and see you on Monday.

At first Mother paid little attention to Miss Diggins, a mouse of a girl in smeared glasses who always seemed to wear the same pink orlon sweater set and shapeless grey flannel skirt. As the weeks passed, however, a certain camaderie developed between boss and typist, and perhaps Mother noticed the young pointy shapes beneath Miss Diggins' sweater and how my father awaited her arrival with more enthusiasm than seemed quite necessary. One morning Mother announced, "If a silly little thing like that can learn to type it can't be so difficult," pinched her housekeeping money till it squealed, and eventually saved enough to buy a teach-yourself-to-type manual and an ancient office Royal for £3.00. She faithfully practiced each afternoon and when she reached a respectable forty words per minute Miss Diggins was fired and Mother took over. My father kept the secretarial allowance for himself and Mother didn't protest, though she did once admit to me, rather sadly, how she'd hoped for just a little of the money.

Now, she concludes: .... so enjoy *every minute* of college with **lots** of parties and fun, love, **Granny!!!!!** and turns to me with a proud smile. "How do we send it to her?"
"If we could access the internet, you could simply hit a key."
"And off it would go?"
"Just like that. But not without another phone line."
Mother presses her lips together. "Phones are like doors."
The thin end of the wedge! And now, *Doors?*
" Things can come in." Mother's eyes are wide and fearful and I sense her sliding away somewhere uncertain and dangerous inside her head. To bring her back I ask, "Do you remember Miss Diggins?" and thankfully watch the fear replaced by healthy contempt.
"Oh, *her!* Such a dull, stupid little thing. Dreadful B.O. Well, no wonder—she wore the same clothes every day, I'd have to open all the windows after she left to air out the flat, and she made so many mistakes she drove poor Frank crazy." After a moment's reflection, "He was never very good at spelling, you know. I'd correct his mistakes too, but of course I never told him!"
I feel an immense surge of love for Mother. At last we're talking to each other, easily, unselfconsciously, like the friends we should always have been. I say impulsively, "He *ought* to have paid you!"
"Of course not, Penelope. I was his wife. I didn't expect to be paid."
"But you did. You *told* me!"
"Then I can't have meant it. We were married! What was the point?"
"Because it was *your* money, you'd earned it, to spend how *you* wanted." How well I remember my father on Monday

mornings presenting Mother with the housekeeping money—five pounds for the whole week, for everything, the pound notes placed grudgingly one by one into her outstretched hand with not even the dignity of Miss Diggins' envelope—and her buying the cheapest cuts of meat; tired produce; the charity shops for her clothes and saving penny by penny for that battered old Royal, the heavy keys with raised metal rims round them which must have hurt her fingers.

Of course I know I should stop right here, we're venturing onto dangerous ground but instead, like a fool, I press on. It seems really important for her to acknowledge, just once, that my father was not quite perfect. I say, "You shouldn't have been forced to scrimp and save on that measly little allowance!" and Mother springs to his defense as always. "You don't know what it was like after the war!"

"The war had been over for years."

"There were still shortages and ration books. Sweets didn't come off ration till 1953."

I tell myself, *let it go, let it go,* but I can't. "We're talking about the *'sixties.* You can't still blame the war."

"Things don't build back up overnight. It takes years to recover from something like that. Decades. I was proud to help out with my little economies."

"He was taking advantage of you."

"Everything was so expensive, especially—"

"Especially *liquor*!" I'm hot, tired and frustrated or I'd never have said it: "All you were helping out was his liquor bill."

There's an ominous silence. The mood has turned on a knife blade. Mother whispers, "How *dare* you, Penelope!"

I'm appalled with myself. I'd take the words back if only I could. "Mother, I'm so sorry!"

"If Frank drank a little too much sometimes, so what! He'd earned the right and it's none of your business!"

"Please, let's forget it. It really doesn't matter."

"I'm damned if I'll forget it. It matters to *me!*"

"I didn't mean it. I didn't want to upset you."

"Of course you did. You always do."

"I said I was sorry." I lay a gentling hand on her arm but she thrusts it away.

"Frank *wasn't* a drunk! He could have stopped any time! He was a wonderful man, he adored me and I miss him dreadfully. Even now, after ten years, I come back from shopping with little things to tell him which will make him laugh, and he's not there. Nobody's there. I never get used to that, to nobody being there. It's a terrible thing, loneliness, but how should you know or care?" Her voice is shrill and rising. "You never loved him, even though he gave you everything! *Everything!* And now he's dead and can't defend himself against your beastly lies and insinuations."

I think despairingly, If only Caitlin was here. Or Liam—he'd settle Mother down and she'd let him do it because he's a still a man even though not the one she wanted. He'd calm me down too. He's done it often enough. "Give your dad a break," he'd say, "He went through a world war, he had his demons and got pissed every day to wipe them out. It goes with the territory. Can't you stop blaming him and put it behind you?"

Of course it isn't only my father I blame—but I can't tell Liam that because then I'd have to tell him all of it, not only what my father did to me, but what Mother did too. The memory has haunted me for almost thirty years, and the anger. How could she have done what she did and then, later, accuse me of callous abandonment when her own betrayal had been so much worse?

Most of the time I'm able to push it all safely away, the memory of that night buried deep, deep like radioactive waste in a sealed container—but any container will eventually erode and leak its poison into the ground, I know there's no escape and the hurt will be as cruel as ever, and even while I tell myself that Mother's dying and for god's sake stop it, stop it *right now* I hear myself demand, "Didn't you once, over all these years, think what it was like for *me?*"

Her mouth thins to a hard line. "You made it worse. You never tried to love or understand him!"

And I'm finally over the edge. "If *you'd* really understood him you'd have made him get help. Maybe *you* didn't love him enough!"

At once the air feels sucked from the room as if the pressure has taken a sudden and catastrophic drop. Mother is on her feet, white with rage. "How dare you! Your father was *everything* to me!"

"I know," I'm saying, "And I was nothing, was I."

Mother's eyes are a virulent, poison green; her nostrils inflate and I can hear her rasping fight for breath. She strikes me across the face so hard I crash against the wall and her rings cut into my cheek.

She gazes at me with hatred and her thin body shudders. "I gave you life, Penelope! I gave you all my love, and you threw it back in my face. You're a taker, you always have been! Go back to America, back to that lout of a husband of yours! Go away wherever you want, I don't care!" She's at the door now, her head high. "At least I know where I stand now! I realize I never truly had a daughter!"

She hit me that other time, too.

12.

Dr. Savage's office is determinedly up-beat with yellow walls, tangerine colored rug, window curtains patterned with sunflowers. A woman is leaving as I arrive, leading a bald-headed child by the hand.

The doctor is slender with a wispy ginger beard. He wears round glasses with tortoiseshell frames, a sports jacket of fuzzy brown tweed and reminds me of a gentle nocturnal animal, maybe a lemur. "How good to meet you, Penelope! I hope you had a pleasant flight over. Tell me, how is your dear Mother?"

"Holding her own. So far." I hear my voice dry and brittle as if coming from far away across a stony river bed; my stomach is a clenched fist.

I can't do this anymore. Not another day.

I'm putting Mother in the first nursing home which will take her.

I don't give a fuck whether she lives in terror of *those places*.

I don't give a fuck that she's dying, I'm getting out of here. I'm living up to her expectations and leaving her. Again. It's what I do best, after all.

"And the pain?" the doctor asks.

I touch the lump rising on the back of my head, then my aching cheek, and it's a moment before I realize he's not talking about mine. "It seems to be manageable."

"In good spirits, is she? Silly question—of course she is, now you've come home."

I want to scream, *for once and for all this is not my home!* I don't, though. I don't know whether I reply at all, and

Dr. Savage looks at me closely for the first time. I checked the mirror before I left the apartment and the angry imprint of Mother's rings flared crimson. Does it still? There are no mirrors here.

"Your eye," he says.

A black eye too? "I walked into a door," I say.

He peers at me anxiously, "I see," but doesn't sound convinced. After a moment, gently, "This is a hard time for you, Penelope" —god, does the man think I'm *grieving*— "Would you like anything? A cup of tea? Maybe a glass of water?"

"Nothing. Thanks."

"You'd better sit down," and I let him steer me to a seating area beside the window where we face each other across a tabletop piled with out-of-date gossipy magazines (the top cover features last summer's auction of poor dead Diana's evening gowns), jigsaw puzzles, children's books and three foam-rubber nerf balls in neon colors. He holds the chartreuse one in his pink, scrubbed fingers, gently squishes it and we watch it bounce back to its original shape. A distant roll of thunder registers as a deep vibration in my breastbone.

"There're a couple of matters I wanted to discuss which I thought better to do in person rather than on the phone," Dr. Savage says, "That is, if you're up to it?"

My eye throbs. "Sure. Why not?"

"For instance, your mother's treatment or, rather, non-treatment. Perhaps you're surprised that she didn't have surgery, or at least a course of radiation or chemotherapy."

"I didn't even know she was sick. Nobody told me anything."

"Very unfortunate. But now?" Dr. Savage looks wary as if, knowing I come from a litigious country, he's waiting for the other shoe to drop. "I know you'll be accustomed to more aggressive measures, but in her case we didn't have a choice. She'd waited far too long. She was sure the pain was a gas attack or a pulled muscle and would go away on its own, but Dr. Cameron was suspicious and the MRI proved her right. The cancer had metastasized and surgery would have been not only pointless but cruel for someone your mother's age. Chemotherapy would have bought her a little time, but not enough, in my opinion, to offset the discomfort of the treatment. Of course I had to suggest it, your mother needed to know all the options, but she wouldn't hear of it and under the circumstances I returned her to Dr. Cameron's care. I hope you understand?"

At my nod, "You can trust Dr. Cameron with your mother's day-to-day pain management, but please feel free to call on me at any time if you have questions."

"Thanks. I'll do that." My cheek has settled to a low-key throb and my heart is no longer tripping. Because I have to say something, can't just sit here like an idiot, I ask Dr. Savage what *he* thinks will happen when the morphine dosage goes off balance (which won't affect me since I won't be here), and he agrees with Dr. Cameron that hallucinations are possible and likely to be unpleasant; "However, as you'll have been told, the situation can usually be controlled with the right balance of tranquilizers. I believe she has prescribed valium."

I explain that Mother has used high doses of valium for at least thirty years and will have built up a tolerance; he suggests that if Mother is comfortable with valium there's not much point switching her to some other drug at this late stage and I'm sure he's right and what does it matter anyway.

I stare down at Diana's sexy, midnight-blue dress in which she danced with John Travolta at the White House. Such a beautiful girl. Life's not fair.

I ask carefully, "If the pain is controlled, and everything continues as expected, do you have any idea how much time my mother might have left?"

Of course Dr. Savage does not, since he no longer sees Mother regularly. He explains, "Biology is an inexact science and there's no underestimating the psychological factor. The whole equation has changed now that you're home and she has something to live for again, which brings me to the other point I wanted to discuss with you. Not that I imagine it's really necessary now or even, under the circumstances, imaginable—but it's important I put you in the picture."

The oncologist shifts in his chair, plainly unsure how to broach a sensitive subject. Am I sure I wouldn't like some tea or coffee, he can boil the kettle in a jiffy if I don't mind a teabag or instant, and when I say no thank you, no really, visibly braces himself before leaning forward, leather-patched elbows on his knees, voice pitched low. "You won't be surprised to learn your mother has at times been very depressed. Once, in a particularly dark mood, she warned me that if she really did have Big C—she dreads cancer, you know, won't even say the word—she planned to take her own life. Said she'd swallow some pills and wash them down with gin and she knows exactly how many to take." His ginger eyes search my unresponsive face and he lays a compassionate hand over mine. "I'm sorry, Penelope. I know it's a shock for you, hearing something like that."

Actually, it's no shock; the overdose threat is nothing new for Mother, though I doubt he'd believe me. I ask, "Under the circumstances would that be such a bad thing?"

We're venturing onto dodgy ground here. The doctor sinks slowly back in his seat clearly wondering how to respond and I'm ashamed of myself. He's a kind, good man and I'm a horrible daughter, speaking from entirely the wrong script. I say, "She wouldn't do it, though."

The room has grown visibly darker, he leans forward to switch on another lamp and I hear thunder again, closer. He says, "You can never be sure, Penelope."

"She doesn't believe she has cancer, so what would be the point?"

"Unconsciously, I imagine she knows perfectly well, which was why she waited so long before seeing Dr. Cameron in the first place." Dr. Savage takes his glasses off, polishes them, then puts them back on again and hooks them meticulously behind his ears. "Denial could be her own way of coping with a terminal illness. One might argue that her refusal to consider radiation and chemotherapy is in itself a form of suicide."

Which seems reasonable, even likely. I think of Mother watching herself grow old, degenerating into a crone with stick legs and sagging stomach. She'd never want to live like that, she'd seize on cancer as the solution even if she couldn't bring herself to say its name.

As for chemotherapy? Forget it. She'd rather be dead than bald—and despite myself I think how there's something almost heroic about that.

Outside, the afternoon sky is purplish black. Dry leaves rattle in an irritable wind and lightning flickers behind the tall brick factories down by the river.

I have to wait ten minutes for a cab.

Rather dead than bald—what a vain, vicious, brave woman. I love her. I hate her. I hate myself. I feel as I do each time when I deliver Mother to the airport after one of her awful visits and she walks away from me, small, erect, not looking back, when my relief at her departure switches to guilt, desolation and irretrievable loss, I'll think what a crazy fucking waste, cry all the way back to the city and know that, in the plane, she will be crying too.

Now, recalling this afternoon's disaster, I can't believe I could have said such things. I remind myself how no-one knows what happens within a marriage, what compromises are made and what secrets are kept.

I dread returning home. What I'll find. What she'll say. I've done damage.

I can't abandon her to a nursing home now.

I crouch in the back of the cab, lean my bruised cheek against the window, begin to cry, wipe the tears away with the back of my hand, and then we're pulling up outside No. 12 just as the first raindrops hiss onto the hot sidewalk.

"Penelope! Thank God you're back! Where have you been for so long? I've been *terrified!*"

The sky rips in two and blazes, the tattered drapes surge horizontally into the room and Mother claps her hands over her eyes with a shriek. I slam the window closed and switch on the light which she insists I turn off again or we'll be struck by lightning, everybody knows electric current draws it down. When I offer the usual cup of tea, panacea for all ills and calamities, she gives a convulsive shake of the head, clutches my hand and begs, "Don't leave me now!"

When the storm is over I sit on Mother's bed and call Caitlin on my new cell phone.

She returns to school tomorrow, getting up at four a.m. to finish loading the car, and hopes to arrive in Santa Barbara before noon. I'd been planning to take the day off and ride down the coast with her, looking forward to the long drive down the 101, just the two of us trapped among clothes, books and sports equipment, and to our first real talk all summer—but of course there'll be many chances for future talks with Caitlin.

I give her my new phone number, tell her to take care and don't forget to call when she gets there and I sense her eyes rolling back in her head as she patiently sighs yes Mom, of course Mom, doesn't she always, and can she talk with Granny now?

Mother eyes the phone with suspicion, accepts it with reluctance, "Do I hold it like this? How can she hear me with it so far from my mouth?" yells, "Have a lovely term, darling!" and thrusts it back at me as though it were red hot. "Don't make me talk on that thing again!"

As I tuck it away in my purse, "Now you know what it's like," she says with baleful intent, "When your children go away to the other end of the earth and shut you out of their lives."

I point out that Santa Barbara is hardly the end of the earth, it's close enough for Caitlin to drive home for long weekends and holidays, even to bring her dirty laundry and Mother says, "You know perfectly well what I mean! I look at other mothers, with their daughters living near them, loving them and wanting to be with them, and I cry inside. You never really loved me, did you, Penelope!"

But I don't take the bait. Not this time. Not anymore.

I can do this.

13.

It rains solidly all the next day, Mother's restless spirit is grounded by the rattle of water on the window, and she's happy to doze through the afternoon while I take another look inside the cedar chest in my room.

Now it's daylight rather than the middle of the night I find that the Waterstone albums only comprise the top layer and that my stuff lies buried beneath: old diaries, cards and letters, theater programs and a bunch of photographs including an 8 x 10 black and white photo of Johnathon and me at a wedding. Johnathon is elegant in a cutaway coat and striped pants, I'm lanky and coltish in a black lace micro-mini, and we look happily drunk, clutching champagne glasses and each other. That was the night he kissed me for the first time, stopped for a traffic light, the rain clattering on the car roof as the lights changed red yellow green yellow red yellow green and us still kissing for five solid minutes until another car pulled up behind us, hooted and broke the spell. And here's the valentine card he sent me once, still in its envelope. I kept the envelope because his hand held the pen that wrote my name and address on it and his tongue licked the glue on the flap. I remember romantically licking that flap myself and imagining Johnathon's dried spit as a second-hand kiss. I take out the card and look at it once again: an armored knight on bended knee offering flowers to his lady: "Gad how I lovest thee!" he's saying, but Johnathon couldn't have meant it. He never argued about not staying for dinner the night Mother's party, and he should have argued. He should have fought for me, like a real knight.

14.

The rain continues. Summer is washed away, the days grow cold; night falls earlier and lasts longer.

I keep the gas heater lit in Mother's room, and the window cracked open for safety. I'd like to call in an inspector from the gas company but Mother grows agitated thinking of strangers in her bedroom, the heater has survived for thirty years and will surely last through the winter.

The morphine pills reappear in the nightstand drawer and at Dr. Cameron's suggestion I create a medication chart: Monday through Sunday across the top, breakfast, lunch, supper and bedtime cross-referenced below. I instruct Mother how, each time she takes a pill, she should put a check mark in the relevant box and she nods, she understands, of course she does. She's generally calm and quiet, and although there are occasional comments about distant, neglectful daughters there are no more violent outbursts except her routinely expressed animosity toward Nurse Follis, who is oblivious, and Mr. Pye the landlord, a pleasant, pear-shaped little man who arrives one morning with a bunch of yellow daisies, whom she refuses to see.

"What was *he* here for anyway?" Mother demands. "As if I couldn't guess!"

"Just a courtesy call. He wanted to know how you're feeling."

"He wants to know if I'm dead yet." Mother eyes the daisies with disfavor—"Take those things away!" Her busy fingers worry at another small rip in the quilt. "He doesn't think I'm paying enough rent and if he had his way he'd throw me out on the street. He'll try and talk you into putting me away somewhere, you mark my words, so he can get the flat back again." She angles me a suspicious, green glance. "I bet you wouldn't mind getting rid of me, either. I can see it now, the two of you with your heads together, plotting."

"Mother, I have no intention of plotting anything with Mr. Pye."

Her eyes well with sudden tears. "Such awful things happen in those places. They steal your money, the nurses hit you and they don't give you enough to eat. Like they did to Daddy, all those tubes sticking out of him and that thing over his face—"

"That was an oxygen mask so he could breathe." I perch on the bed and hold her hands before she tears the hole any wider. "You *know* they were good to him there. He was perfectly happy," which I'm sure was true and in his final weeks, contentedly detached, he'd drift between the present, which clearly meant increasingly little to him, and early days with old navy colleagues, which just as clearly did. "Wouldn't he have told you if someone hit him?"

"He wouldn't have dared. He'd have been too afraid of what they'd do to him when I wasn't there. They wouldn't give him his pain pills. They'd torture him—"

"Don't you think the doctor would've had something to say about that?"

"They're all in it together. And Daddy died, didn't he."

"Of course he died. He had pulmonary fibrosis. His lungs were like stones!" And I think how ironic it should be his lungs which let him down because he never smoked.

Mother says, "So if you're thinking of sending me to One of Those Places you can think again. And you can tell that Pye creature he's not forcing me out."

"He can't do that anyway. You're a senior citizen, a sitting tenant, and it's against the law."

"How would *you* know about those things, coming from America? Oh," she cries, "If only Daddy were alive, he'd know what to do!"

15.

"Scottie and I would be pleased if you could take tea with us at four this afternoon, provided Imogene can spare you. We feel it's time we were better acquainted . . . ."

Bethany lives in a sprawling basement apartment behind the Crescent, accessed by a steep flight of steps and a stone-flagged patio in which a few tubs of spindly shrubs struggle for survival. Clearly she's not a gardener.

"Welcome to our humble abode!" She ushers me through a dark, chilly living room crowded with file cabinets – she's not much of a housekeeper either—into a screened-off nook over-filled with chintz armchairs, bookshelves stacked with vintage American thrillers, and a card table upon which she has assembled tea things and a plate of Scottish shortbread. I produce the chocolates I have brought as a gift and her eyes gleam. She politely offers them to me first and when I decline closes her eyes, wanders her thick fingers above the upper layer, pounces upon a rum-raisin cluster, *"Oh goody, my favorite!"* then tosses a raspberry cream to Scottie who catches it with an efficient click of teeth.

We indulge in cheerful, nondescript chat; she offers to read my cards at a special 'friends' rate which I accept for an unspecified later date; eventually she gets down to business, saying heartily as she fills my cup, "Jolly nice to have you all to myself, gives me a chance to talk about Imogene to my heart's content!"

I smile encouragement. Rather than a librarian she reminds me, both in appearance and her use of outdated slang, of a boisterous girl-scout troupe leader from the 1950s.

"Bet you're wondering how your mother and I came to be such chums," Bethany says.

I tell her that, being neighbors, I'm sure they run into each other all the time.

Bethany agrees. "I'd see her out and about of course, striding around the Crescent, her head held high, her back so straight, what wonderful posture your mother has, she studied ballet, didn't she, when she was a girl and it shows, even at her age, but I never dared talk to her. But then," as if awed by her good fortune, "*She* came to *me!* She saw my little advertisement in the paper for private readings. 'How wonderful to find somebody like you just around the corner!' she said, and came over that same afternoon. So kind and gracious, and how she loved dear Scottie! She'd ask advice from the cards about you, you know. She'd say, 'If I can only break through that wall Penelope throws up between us! Sometimes I feel she almost hates me.' It's presumptuous of me to tell you this," Bethany colors faintly, "and of course it's not true, anyone can tell how much you love your mother and what a shock it must have been to hear about her illness, but I thought you should know her *deep* feelings. And then she'd ask when she'd see you again. She trusts the cards implicitly, you know, and is quite open to the power of suggestion. I'd tell her it would be soon but that she must be the one to take the initiative, so she'd go all the way out to America and always have such a wonderful time—" and I close my eyes with remembered pain although, by then, Mother had probably convinced herself it was true.

"She's a particularly loving person, your mother." Bethany adds, "In my personal opinion, she's almost a saint!"

I observe how, when thinking of saints, I don't get much beyond sackcloth and martyrdom and can't quite see Mother in the role, and Bethany is at once indignant. "Is there any rule that says a saint can't be beautiful and give pleasure? Just *think* about your mother's life! Growing up beautiful and popular, a handsome husband who adored her, a long happy marriage and a healthy child—how easily she might have taken it all for granted, how arrogant and selfish she could have become! But no, Imogene's a giver. Always goes out of her way to be kind, especially to people who aren't so fortunate as herself." After a brief pause she confides, "I've never told anybody of course, but if I could die and come back as anybody I wanted, quite frankly it would be as Imogene!"

I rock backward in my seat. "Have you told her that?"

"Good Heavens' no! That's not the kind of thing you tell somebody, is it, Penelope! Promise me you'll stay absolutely *mum!"*

I assure Bethany her secret is safe with me, whereupon she confesses, the words tumbling: "I was never pretty, you see, and much too serious. Rather plump too, my clothes were always wrong and I never knew what to say. I longed to be glamorous and witty and have men fall in love with me but they never did. I'd sometimes be asked to parties when I was young, but only when it would have been rude not to invite me. I'd pretend to be having a good time, but I wasn't—none of the boys asked me to dance, only peoples' fathers because they felt sorry for me."

I think of poor, plain Bethany bravely smiling in her corner while the lithe, laughing girls like Imogene were swept around the floor for dance after dance. "It's rough being a teenager," I say. "I'll bet a lot of the other girls felt the same as you."

"That's exactly what *she* said! You're kind, just like her!" Bethany's voice gives a tiny wobble and she blinks back a surreptitious tear. "Do you know what else she said? That if only she'd known me back then, she'd have been proud to be my best friend! Though of course she wouldn't have. Known me, I mean. She was twenty years older and from quite a different social circle, but it's just the kind of sweet thing she would say. And now you must run home again, so you can be with her. You mustn't waste any more of your precious time on me!"

16.

  The days pass. I fix tiny meals on trays and clean them up again, tidy Mother's bed, attempt to monitor her pill intake, shop for groceries, entertain her guests.
  Having heard nothing from Andy for a full week about my revised Enraptor copy, I suddenly learn from another source that my original version was used in the presentation after all and the client liked it. Andy's agile mind is now convinced he'd approved my copy all along, do I have any idea when I'm coming back, they're pitching for a new account, a charter jet leasing company, and he thinks we'd be a good match.
  Liam calls from his mother's house where the family has gathered after Sunday mass—Granny Foley, Liam's older brother Paul the priest, his two brothers-in-law, his sister Deidre, and his sister Maureen, pregnant again with her sixth. I imagine the massive slab of pot-roast, the potatoes and the pie to follow (berry or apple), the Foleys happily crowded together in that cramped little room complete with the two family icons: the flickering votive candle before the bowed and veiled Virgin, and the enormous new TV on which, after lunch, Liam will watch the 49ers game with the guys while the girls wash the dishes. He sounds cheerful as he shouts above yelling children and the NFL pre-game show. Things are going well, he tells me: a big project he'd bid on months ago and written off suddenly looks as if it might come through after all! I'm happy for him.

  Caitlin calls from Santa Barbara to report on the new fall quarter. It's a tumbling reminder of another world: of issues with room-mates; classes and professors; she's planning to cut her hair short; whale migration; her latest volunteer project reducing oil seepage from the beaches.

Mother complains, "Ringing, ringing, *ringing!* If it's not one damn thing it's another! *Do* tell them to stop!"

17.

Noon-time sherry with the Colonel and Felicity; my social calendar burgeons.

I admire the new greenhouse, the vegetable garden, the Colonel's neatly built compost heap, and the fall flowers bright against the mellow stone wall.

"No chemicals," Felicity maintains proudly; "We plant garlic around the edges of the beds, spray the plants with onion juice and the ladybirds eat the aphids. You can buy them, you know, a thousand to a box. You let them out after dark, so they go to sleep and don't try to fly away home!" They both chuckle at her small joke and I envy them their happiness.

We drink our sherry and nibble on home-made cheese puffs on the terrace, sitting on decorative but fiendishly uncomfortable wrought-iron seats which will leave an engraved pattern on my behind. Felicity explains how they don't like to waste a minute of this lovely sunshine, it'll be winter soon enough, and I tuck my cold hands into my armpits.

I thank them for their kindness to Mother, and Felicity says how she's only too grateful to have a chance to help. "Imogene's been so good to us and we owe her so much!"

"Marvellous woman!" the Colonel agrees. "Only just moved here, didn't know a soul, and she came right up to me the street, made no bones about it, said, 'I've seen you out walking with your pretty wife!' and invited us to tea right then and there! Took Flee under her wing. Introduced her round. Flee's always been shy about making new friends, haven't you, Pet," and I think how strange to see Mother through other eyes, as herself, out of my father's shadow.

Felicity nibbles abstractedly at a fingernail and blurts, "Frankly, I've always wondered why someone like Imogene would bother with me!"

"Don't be a silly billy, Pet!"

"She's so glamorous and interesting, not at all like me, but I feel I can tell her anything, more than I could ever tell my own mother. She says she thinks of me almost as her own daughter, with you so far away, Penelope, living your own life and not needing her anymore." Then, stricken and coloring, "of course she doesn't *mean* it about me being like a daughter. She loves you so much. She's so proud of you, doing all the things she never had a chance to do—but of course you know that!"

18.

Mother has one of Mrs. Ship's sister's *Hello!* magazines open across her lap at a double-page photo-spread of Princess Diana's funeral. She's frowning deeply. "I wish you hadn't stayed away so long, Penelope. The phone was ringing again, all afternoon. Maybe it was important. Perhaps it was your young man."

I tell her not to worry and I'll call Liam later.

"I don't know anybody called Liam. I mean Johnathon, of course. I can't imagine why he hasn't rung before, surely he knows you're back." She rustles the magazine. "And isn't this dreadful! So sad, what a criminal waste."

I agree, yes indeed, and only thirty-six years old.

"Just lying there rotting! Millions of pounds worth—" which is when I realize Mother's not talking about the slaughtered princess but the acres of floral tributes. "Penelope, when I die there mustn't be flowers!"

"Not if you don't want them." I eye her warily, thinking how never before has Mother acknowledged that she may not live forever.

"No wreaths either. Put something in the paper about it. And don't you dare bury me, suppose they made a mistake and I was still alive after all! It happens, you know. They find scratches inside the coffin lid. Have me cremated and scatter me somewhere lovely. Just save a little pinch of me to be with Daddy, and throw the rest off a cliff into the sea."

I sit on the bed and take her hand. "How's your tummy today?"

"Not too bad really."

"What does it feel like when it hurts?"

"Sort of a grinding, like when you have the curse." She takes my hand and places it gingerly on her abdomen. "It stabs me right here—but we won't worry about it, like they said, it's only a tumor. That other doctor, that specialist man, tried to tell me I had Big C and I should take those chemicals that make you sick and your hair fall out, but he was only trying to scare me. He was after the money of course, they're all the same, but he had to give up in the end. I said I don't want to see you ever again so he fobbed me off with that young girl. What's her name?"

"Dr. Cameron."

"That's right. She's only National Health but she must be quite good because I haven't had a *real* pain for ages. Did you know she's pregnant? I don't see how she can go on being a doctor when she has a baby. I know exactly what she's in for. Her daughter will grow up and walk away and leave her. But she wouldn't believe me if I told her so what's the point. She'll find out for herself soon enough."

For lunch Mother has a cup of bouillon, and tiny smoked-salmon sandwiches which I've cut in triangles with the crusts removed so they look like cocktail canapes. Even though she doesn't eat them she will at least enjoy playing with them— but it does nothing to improve her mood. She's tired and querulous, complains her feet feel sticky and her hands smell of fish. She says crossly, "You shouldn't give me fish to eat! I wish I could have a bath. I feel so dirty but that wretched nurse creature won't be back for days. I *hate* feeling dirty."

On the days between Nurse Follis' visits Mother takes what she calls a strip-wash when she balances unsteadily at the bathroom sink, hanging on with one hand, swiping under her arms with a soapy sponge. I've offered to bathe her myself but she's adamant: "Don't be ridiculous, Penelope, I'm your mother."

I urge now, "Couldn't we give it a try? Then you can stay in the tub for as long as you like!"

"No, *no!*" She says at once. "I'd feel funny."

At teatime, "About that bath, Penelope. Do you think you really *could* do it? Are you *sure?*"

I attach the rubber pillow to the back of the tub, run the water, drop in scented bath crystals, check the temperature with my elbow the way I used to when Caitlin was a baby and in what is clearly a gesture of appeasement, Mother makes a dramatic entrance wearing the scorned yellow robe.

She clings to the side of the tub and peers inside. "Oh Penelope, bubbles! What a nice idea!" She casually shucks the robe. Underneath she's naked as a jaybird, her skin dry and chalky, stretched tight over jutting bones. I can't help but notice she has almost no pubic hair—because of the disease, or does one automatically lose body hair in old age?

I'm both shaken and saddened by the ruin, the vulnerability, but also the iron majesty of Mother's nakedness. This is what we all come to. This is what it means to be human. I feel something crumble inside me, a hardness I didn't even know was there as I help her heave her legs over the side, one and then the other, and lower her into the fragrant froth. She's surprisingly heavy, for a moment I'm afraid I'll drop her, but I manage to settle her safely, then squeeze the sponge over her shoulders and stomach and rub gently at her papery skin.

Mother closes her eyes and sighs with pleasure, then, "For goodness sake don't just dab at me!" She snatches the sponge from my hand, briskly soaps her chest and flat breasts and splashes the water like a child. "How heavenly," she cries,

"I'm going to stay in here for *hours!*" However, she quickly tires, gives a sudden groan and complains her seat bones feel as if they're pushing right through her so I haul her out again, settle her on a chair and pat her dry. It's warm and steamy in the bathroom but she's already beginning to shiver. There isn't an ounce of spare flesh on her body and I think how fall is already here and winter just around the corner.

At cocktail time, "I'm lovely and clean," Mother announces proudly to Simon, Bethany and Lord Storey. "Penelope gave me a bath! I never thought I'd live to see the day! I must confess I didn't like the thought of having my own daughter bathing me like a baby but it all seemed quite natural after all, Penelope didn't turn a hair, now I can have a bath every day and I don't have to have that horrid nurse!"

Everybody is pleased for her, rewards me with smiles of approval, and I can't imagine why I haven't done this before.

What a simple way to give pleasure. Tomorrow I'll buy a rubber mat so Mother can't slip, and a pad to sit on to ease her poor bones. I'll see about having a handrail installed.

I feel out of reason happy and know that whatever she does or says now, nothing can spoil this moment.

The next day, for the first time in ten years, I see Johnathon again.

19.

Previously, Price and Williams occupied a graciously proportioned Georgian townhouse which, with its wood panelling, Adam fireplaces, crystal chandeliers and elderly clerks in striped trousers and black cutaway jackets, could have been lifted directly from a Dickens novel.

Now, with Johnathon as senior partner, the firm has outgrown its historic quarters and moved to a brand-new building in the center of town. The typewriters and telex of the 'eighties have been replaced by computers and fax machines, the furniture is sleekly modern, the ageing clerks have been pensioned off and I'm escorted up in the elevator by a stylish blonde in a charcoal pin-stripe business suit beside whom I know I appear to disadvantage: middle-aged and dishevelled (it's windy out), wearing jeans, baggy sweater and raincoat.

Johnathon's office, however, might have been transplanted intact from the old building with the same antique partners' desk, leather furniture and mansion-sized Persian rug. He hasn't changed much in ten years either, still trim around the waist, impeccable from his neatly-barbered brown hair to his glossy black shoes, and so closely shaven his cheek would feel smooth as a baby's. I remember that smoothness.

He springs to his feet at once. "Pen! How grand to see you, though I wish it was in happier circumstances. You're looking very fit!"

We briefly embrace. He smells faintly and cleanly of soap and Old Spice.

"Thank you for fitting me in," I say.

I'm here to arrange for Power of Attorney.

"The electric bill? The water? But I just paid them," Mother insisted, peering at the threatening red capitals, PAST DUE, stamped across the top of the envelopes. "They can't possibly want more money already!"

"You paid them in June. It's October now." I placed the filled-out checks on her breakfast tray and handed her a pen, but her hand was shaking too badly to sign.

"I can't even hold this damn thing! Are you *sure* we're not paying these too soon?"—and when I said I was quite sure, immediately panicked that the utilities would be cut off and we'd freeze to death or that Mr. Pye would throw her out into the street, whichever came first. "Can't you sign them for me?— Why not?— What will we do?" and, a familiar refrain, "If only there was a man to help us!"

Now, Johnathon inquires politely after Caitlin, remembering her name, and I ask in turn after his boys, ashamed I don't remember theirs; hear they are doing well as is Rosemary his wife, busy as usual with the garden, her horses and her various charities. While we chat he signs the documents, passes them to me for my own signature, then stamps and notarizes them: four copies of the power of attorney, one of which he retains, and three for me which he slides into a manila envelope. It's all very efficient.

"It's certainly a good thing you're here to take up the reins," he says. "How long do you plan to stay?"

"I suppose for as long as it takes."

"And will your husband—Liam, isn't it?—be joining you?"

"Maybe later."

"If there's anything I can help with in the meantime, you've only to say the word. For instance—" Johnathon steeples his elegant fingers and regards me over the top—"What about nursing homes? Do you have a place in mind?"

I tell him not yet, remembering how, such a short time before, I couldn't wait to stash Mother away somewhere, *anywhere*, but not anymore. It's strange how something as simple as giving a bath can change everything.

"Don't wait too long," Johnathon advises. "She'll need professional nursing and pain management sooner rather than later;" and points out, as if I didn't know, that the best places will have waiting lists.

I tell him there's been too much else to think about. "And anyway, she hates the idea and won't discuss it."

"Well of course she hates it," Johnathon says, "Most people do, especially an independent soul like Imogene, but she'll adjust faster than you'd think. My own father—you remember Pa?—put up no end of a struggle but he was happy as a lark once he got there," although, as I recall, the elder Price, unlike Mother, was adrift in gentle dementia, convinced he was fly-fishing on his favorite trout stream and would have been content in a coal mine.

Johnathon opens a drawer of his desk. "Just in case," he says, "I put together a list for you." He takes out a sheet of embossed, cream-colored stationery with four names and addresses neatly centered. The writing is small and black (he always used a fountain pen and black ink) and still familiar after so many years. "At least look them over."

I thank him, promise to do that, fold the paper in half and put it in my purse with the power of attorney, after which there seems nothing more to say and we rise together.

He smiles at me, such a well-cut mouth, such a warm, professional smile. "Give Imogene my love and tell her I'll be up to visit one of these days. Rumor says she holds court at six o'clock?"

He walks me to the door, a friendly hand on my shoulder, and I have what I came here for, and more besides, in less than fifteen minutes.

I think how smoothly impressive he is, fitting me into his crammed schedule at a moment's notice and easing me back out of it again, and realize that, although I might have meant something to him once, there's nothing left now, not a glimmer.

Had I secretly expected him to cry, "Pen, I've never got over you, I've never forgotten you, I still love you!" and sweep me off to some discreet, dark boîte in which, over an expensive bottle of wine, he'd kiss me passionately, confess his marriage was a mistake and a sham as mine must surely be too, and that we must seize the moment?

What an outrageous idea, I'd thought no such thing! But, *"Liar!"* black-lipped Satan whispers in my left ear. "Fool yourself all you want, but don't think for one minute you can fool me! You've been comparing the two of them, and that rough tough husband of yours is starting to come up short beside Mr. Lawyerman with the baby-bottom cheeks!" when I think, to my shame, how Mother's relentless disparagement of Liam, even if angrily and constantly denied, might wear anyone down over time like water dripping onto stone.

"You're back early," Mother observes, surprised. "What happened?*"*

"I have power of attorney and I've lodged it with the bank. I can sign checks for you now. You don't have to worry about a thing."

But she's no longer interested in checks or bills. "I wasn't expecting you for ages. I'd have thought Johnathon would at least ask you to lunch!"

I remind her it was a business visit not social, and she sighs crossly how it served me right and she'd told me to wear a pretty dress.

20.

By four o'clock the afternoon drizzle has turned once more to driving rain and the wind is rising. I offer a bath but Mother turns me down; her stomach is hurting again. She's tired and cantankerous and I call to cancel Simon's visit; so far as I know he's the only guest we're expecting tonight.

My rough tough husband, calls at 8:00 p.m., his voice taut with excitement. He cries, "We got it, Pen!" and when I don't immediately make connections, "That job in Presidio Heights I told you about?"—which indeed is great news. It's a seismic upgrade and remodel of a turreted, 12-bedroom mansion on Pacific Avenue which will metamorphose into an exclusive boutique hotel. He'd never expected the job to come through, he knew his bid was by no means the lowest—"But it was realistic" said Liam at the time, who always maintains that cost trimming and undercutting are false economies leading inevitably to extra expense, poor relations with the client and bad publicity. "Better to be up front and honest with no bad surprises down the pike," he says, and his policy seems to have paid off because the deal was finalized yesterday, he's signed the contracts and his grin of triumph is reflected in his voice.

Then he says, "The only downside is there's no way now I can take the time off to get over there. I'm real sorry, Pen."

"It's Okay. There's nothing you could do here anyway, except be moral support."

"I could hold you. That's better than nothing."

"It sure is, Oh believe me—" But if I'm honest, I'm relieved he won't be coming. In Mother's eyes Liam will forever be the usurper who isn't Johnathon, and even if, by then, she *had* been removed to a nursing home, even if I hadn't told her he was here, she'd still somehow intuit his presence and her current fragile equilibrium would be destroyed. I remind him, "Even if I was back home I wouldn't see you much. Not with the new project starting. You'll have to focus on that."

"I guess that's true," Liam agrees. And, "I'll make it up to you. This is big. It's really going to do it for us."

"You mean, next time Mother says I'm married to a stinking rich builder it'll be true?"

"Not so far off. And Pen? It's gotten me thinking."

"About maybe a luxury world cruise?"

"More like about Maureen."

For a moment I simply don't get it.

"You're only three years older than her," Liam says.

"I know," I agree. "So?"

"So there's time for us yet," Liam says.

And I think, *Oh my god!*

The thing is, I know he's only half joking. Even now, with me closing in on menopause, with a twenty-year-old daughter, I know he'd be delighted to welcome a new little brother or sister for Caitlin into the world. Holy shit! But I keep it light. "I'd never get maternity leave after this trip!"

"It's time you gave up work anyway, and that guy Andy is a jerk."

Well, of course he is, but I guess I think of him as *my* jerk. And although I regularly complain about my job I find myself resentful when Liam suggests I give it up because it's *mine!* It's something *I* built up against a lot of resistance and now, with the corporate jet account perhaps coming my way, I realize I *do* want it, I want it badly.

"You've worked hard all your life," Liam says into my silence, "And don't think for one moment I don't appreciate it;

I'd never have gotten where I am without you. But that's behind you now. Hopefully it'll all be downhill from here. You can relax!"

I think, Relax? Forty-eight years old with a new baby? Who does he think he's kidding?

I tell him, in what I hope is a neutral voice, "We'll talk about it later. I have to go now. Mother's calling."

It's the first time I've cut Liam off.

I can hear the Devil laughing.

21.

Mother goes to bed earlier than usual and I retire to the living room, carrying a chicken sandwich and a glass of wine, to watch TV and not think about babies. This was a gracious room forty years ago when the walls were freshly painted, the carpet new, the floral slipcovers on the sofa and two armchairs clean and unfaded; like a garden, Mother said. Now, used less and less, it seems dreary and barren and the shadows puddle deep in the corners. I don't come in here often; perhaps because my father spent so much time in it. He loved television, not for what was on the screen so much as the mindlessly annealing spell it cast; he'd shut himself in here at night with his bottle and watch until very late with the sound switched off.

Now, as the screen brightens far too slowly to a faded purplish-grey, I realize this must be that very same set, still receiving just the four channels available back then. Faced with the choice of sheep dog trials on a Scottish moor, a re-run of the X-Files, a Doris Day movie from the 'fifties and a tableful of long-faced economists discussing the IMF bailout of a beleagured country in the Balkans, I settle on the sheepdog trials since those heather-clad moors are naturally purple and I can almost persuade myself the color control still works.

By now the rain is hurling itself against the window like handfuls of nails. I pull the drapes closed, assemble my supper beside me on a card table, stretch out in one of the arm chairs where the webbing has given way so my bottom sinks almost to the floor, and take a large slurp of wine. I suddenly recall that the last time I drank wine in this room was the night of Mother's party. Squeeze my eyes shut and don't open them because if I do

I'll see my father leaning against the TV's walnut veneer casing longingly fingering the knobs while, in his other hand, he grips a bottle of cheap Yugoslav Riesling like a club, as if he'd like to hit someone over the head with it. He never drinks with company present and I know he's counting the minutes till the door closes on the last guest when he can dart into his office, pour his first shot of vodka, and begin the serious business of the evening.

I briefly open my eyes to see a mauve and black border collie slithering on its belly through the wet heather, then close them again. Mother is circulating with a dish of cheese straws, casting triumphant glances toward the window where Johnathon and I (three piece suit, starched blue shirt, striped tie; Pucci print minidress, white vinyl boots, eyeliner like a raccoon) talk together with quiet intensity.

Mother just *knows* that tonight's the night, that Johnathon will pop the question, she can *feel* it! She has invited Johnathon to stay for dinner after the party. The invitation is politely conventional—"You've been to the Prices so often, Penelope, and never invited him back, it's only right!"—but anticipatory of celebration, with the table laid with the best glasses, clean napkins and newly polished silverware.

I can almost hear our voices, though I don't need to strain my ears, I can recall that conversation word for word:

Johnathon: "Why *can't* you come home more often? Why must I always go to London if I want to see you? Don't tell me you can't afford it, I'll *give* you the fare!"

Me: "Because I don't *want* to! I hate it here."

I've lived in London for two years now. Mother wanted me to stay at home after completing my typing course, not least because of the proximity of Johnathon—but staying at home was unthinkable.

I have a job as a trainee copywriter at Young and Rubicam which, if I'm lucky and work hard, might lead to a real career, and I'm two chapters into a novel focussed on a young girl's experiences in swinging London, currently stalled for lack of time. My life is an exciting montage of parties up and down the King's Road, art gallery openings, discos, and adventurous expeditions to pubs in rough neighborhoods which are longer no-go areas because the tiresome old class and sexual barriers are breaking down. Everything's breaking down. Everything is changing. I don't wear mere clothes, I wear costumes: 1930s silk negliges from vintage shops, belted with Indian scarves or mens' ties; caftans in wild colors and unusual fabrics; gladiator sandals; go-go boots. I smoke marijuana and sometimes do a line of coke for the rebellious danger of it.

"You'd like it if you gave this place a chance," Johnathon says and, meaningfully, "You'll have to get over it sooner or later."

So Mother is right, all I need do is look him in the eye and demand *why* must I get over it, *tell* me, and Johnathon will say he wants me to come home for good, marry him and have his children and most girls with a particle of sense would cry yes, YES!

But I'm not most girls.

I think, with sad envy, of those dinners with Johnathon's family, his distinguished, greying father, his kind-faced mother, pretty sister and her fiance the landscape architect. Of three well-cooked courses with appropriate wines, and civilized chat about books, fishing, gardens and local politics.

Then I think about our dinner tonight.

We'll sit around the dining room table, Mother and I facing each other across the middle, Johnathon at the far end. We'll admire the cooling pie and the wilting salad. "Daddy will be coming any minute," Mother will assure us brightly while I listen to the unpleasant sounds from the bathroom followed by my father's unsteady, approaching footsteps.

He'll fling the door back so hard it hits the wall, then collapse into his chair, mess with his food and spill his water glass onto his plate where it will mingle with the gravy and drip on the rug. He'll be alternately tearful and combative—"Nobody gives a fuck for the poor old bugger who pays all the bills. Who in hell were those arseholes drinking my booze?"

So far his drinking is a well kept secret, Mother makes sure of that. But Johnathon's family is prominent. His father was mayor once and our wedding will inevitably be a big event (who will pay for it?—I dare not think), it will be photographed and written about and, soon enough, everyone will *know*. Of course Johnathon, a true gentleman, will do the honorable thing and people will say how marvellous of him to marry Penelope even though her father's a hopeless drunk—and I can't let that happen. I've decided to drive Johnathon away. Not for myself, not for my father (certainly not for him) but for *her,* for my mother, because I can't bear the thought of her humiliation.

So I give a derisive laugh, feeling sick and noble at the same time. "Don't tell me you're planning to spend the rest of your life stuck away down here!"

"Where else?" Johnathon's grey eyes are puzzled.

"You'd be satisfied with a small country law practice?" I raise weary brows. "I'd be bored out of my mind."

Johnathon stares at me, perplexed. He rubs at his immaculately shaven chin, then takes his silver cigarette case from his inner pocket, snaps it open, offers it to me, takes one himself and lights us up. "You never talked like this before."

"But I've thought it."

"You always seem to have a pretty good time when you're here."

"I'm a good actress. Actually I loathe the country."

"*Actually,* this is a fairly large town."

"It's country to me. So bloody provincial. Everybody knows everybody else's business. It's like living in a fishbowl."

He narrows his eyes against the smoke. "What's wrong with you, Pen?"

"Nothing's wrong with me. It's this *place*. Nothing happens, there's nowhere to go, it's all so *dull*. So *dead*. You should have been at this party I went to last week down by the docks—" which I invent on the spot and populate with the most obnoxious of the so-called 'in crowd' including the current Parliamentary prostitute, a drug dealer who supplies the Rolling Stones, even the Kray brothers (an infamous pair of Cockney criminals who've inexplicably been taken up by society) who showed up at 3.00 a.m., after which the party really got going. I point out, "Nothing like that happens here!"

I'm not sure I haven't overdone it because Johnathon's shapely mouth gives a slight twitch. He says, "Thank god for small mercies!" And, gently, "Must you pretend to be so tough?"

I almost break down then; but I manage to drain my glass and shrug.

After a moment, "If that's the kind of person who interests you, you've lived in London far too long." Johnathon adds politely, "If you ask me."

"I'm not asking you. I love London. I can be myself."

"Why can't you be yourself here?"

"Because I just *can't!*" And I tell Johnathon I don't want him to stay for dinner after all.

His eyes lock on mine. He stubs out his cigarette. "What are you really saying?"

"I made a mistake."

"You mean about us? You and me? The future?"

"*What* future?"

"But I thought—!" He's at a loss now. He doesn't know what to do, what to say, he's only twenty three. "You're quite sure?"

"Quite."

"I see." His eyes don't change, but I sense an invisible steel shutter drop between us. He replies with dignity, "In that case, Pen, I'll be saying goodbye. Have a wonderful life in London."

He leaves me beside the window and I watch him first thank my oblivious father for a pleasant evening and then my mother, in turn startled, disbelieving and dismayed, who lays a restraining hand on his forearm and cries "But you're staying for supper! Of course you are! The table's laid and everything!"

As if Johnathon's departure has been a signal, the other guests begin to trickle away. Perhaps they've also been waiting in excited suspense and now find no reason to stay. Mother is bitterly upset with me not only for spoiling her party but for ruining my life and hers, and my father doesn't even come to the table but shuts himself into the living room and stays there until very late watching television in the dark.

I don't think about what happened after that.

22.

I open my eyes on tangled wreckage and flashing lavender light, the sheep dog trials are over and this is either a cop show or the ten o'clock news.

I'm cold and stiff. I switch off the T.V. (a fifteen car pile up in fog on the M1 Motorway, three dead and the northbound lanes closed until further notice), finish the dregs of my wine then check on Mother who lies still and silent under the covers. Her quilt has slid to the floor; I rearrange it over her and tuck it in.

The wind howls eerily down the chimney, the windows rattle and I fall asleep listening to the building groan and creak like a ship laboring in heavy seas while outside something metallic (a garbage can?) rolls maddeningly back and forth in the street.

Sometime in the night, however, the wind must have died so it's all the more startling when I'm jerked awake by a wild pounding on my door. *"Penelope! Will you* **please** *answer the phone!"*

Mother is standing in the passage, shivering, wringing her hands with distress. "Don't just stand there! *Answer it!"*

I dash to the living room which is cold and silent as a vault.

"Well of course it's stopped!" Mother cries. "You took so long! I can't imagine how you didn't wake up ages ago. It's been ringing all night. I haven't slept a wink!"

I lead her back to bed, explaining how it's either some lonely drunk random-calling from a bar somewhere, or a fax machine set on redial for the wrong number ("What on earth's a fax," Mother wonders). Then, recalling the gruesome images of the car wreck on the news, I think of Caitlin in Santa Barbara, of a Friday night party, mangled bodies strewn across the freeway and somebody trying urgently to reach me. Remember it's still early evening in California, not yet prime time for mayhem, just as Mother complains, "And what about all these people? I wish they'd go home."

I rub my tired eyes. I gaze from Mother's tumbled bed to the armchair where Simon usually sits when he visits; to the bedside table crowded with photographs, flowers, tumbler and juice pitcher; to the empty stretches of soiled white carpet. Ask, "What people?"

"Are you blind, Penelope?" Mother's finger stabs impatiently. "Her. Him. Those two, over there. Make them go away! I don't want them here."

And I suddenly get it. It's happened at last. Mother is haywire and now I must walk her through it.

I try my best and purposefully circle the room. "Imogene's tired," I tell the chair, the bureau, the space in front of the closet, "She needs her rest. It's time to go." Beckoning toward the empty corner, "You too."

Mother is relieved as I herd my invisible group out of her bedroom and down the passage, hoping I haven't missed anybody. I reach the front door and raise my voice loud enough for her to hear: "Goodbye! Don't come back, it's getting late."

I slam it behind them for good effect. Tell Mother, "It's all right. They've gone."

She's gracious. "Thank you, Penelope! I knew I could count on you."

23.

I lie in bed on my back, eyes wide, staring up at the dark ceiling.

Is this the new normal?

And what *about* that ringing phone?

Caitlin . . .

An accident can happen any time of day, not only late at night after a drunken party, perhaps somebody *was* trying to reach me—the police? A hospital emergency room?

I call her mobile with no luck, then her apartment when I talk with a young man called Alan who seems never to have heard of her. "Caitlin?" he says doubtfully, "Caitlin Foley?" then with dawning recollection, "You mean Seetee?"

For a moment I think he's referring to some obscure Hindu goddess, then recall that Caitlin's middle name is Theresa after Liam's mother.

"Yeah, sure I'll tell her," Alan says, but I don't believe him.

I call Liam, who is reassuring and eminently sensible. "There's no reason why a cop or a hospital in Santa Barbara would call you in England. Your mother's phone number isn't on Caitlin's emergency list. They'd be in touch with me, wouldn't they!"

Of course they would.

In the morning Mother is full of the night's excitements: "Ringing, ringing, ringing! Who *could* it have been?"

"Mother, how many pills did you take last night?"

"Just one." Righteously, "You know that's all I'm allowed, even if I do have to suffer."
"Are you sure?"
"Of course I'm sure. I only take a pill when I'm supposed to. Don't keep on about it, I'm not a *child!*"

Dr. Cameron is not surprised about the hallucinations, both visual and aural, although, as she points out, last night was turbulent with rain and wind and by my own admission I was deeply asleep down the passage with my bedroom door closed.
"I'll leave my door open tonight," I say. "But what if she swears the phone rings and I know it doesn't?"
"You must be more vigilant with her medication, Penelope."
"I try, but she says the morphine is too slow. She's frightened of the pain. She'll accuse me of rationing her pills because I *want* her to suffer."
"Then perhaps this will do the trick." The doctor writes a prescription for a fast-acting codeine-based drug which Mother can keep at her side. When I suggest she's likely to double up on those too, Dr. Cameron says in effect that it's no big deal, Mother will only feel groggy and sleepy. She writes another prescription for valium to take care of any lingering anxiety. Says, "You know what you need to do, don't you, Penelope. Things aren't going to improve—please don't wait too long."

I've forgotten to buy chicken so I re-heat Felicity's soup for lunch. Mother complains it's a funny color, there're things floating in it like tiny eyes, and they're frowning at her.
"It's only grains of barley, Mother. Trust me."
"I don't know about that," Mother says, peering into her bowl. "*Can* I trust you?"

It's raining again, the sound is gentle and soothing, my broken nights are catching up with me, I stretch out on my bed and close my eyes, but sleep doesn't come.

I get up again, sit at the dining room table with my laptop, click into 'games' and begin to play hearts against myself. Half an hour later I hear Mother's footsteps in the passage but by the time I've gotten up to check she's back in her room and the door closed.

Later, in the kitchen to fix her tea, I find a hunk of cheddar cheese on the counter and stare, perplexed, at a double row of tooth marks. "Well, I was hungry!" Mother complains, "you didn't give me any lunch!" and later, when Felicity and the Colonel stop by, "Penelope only gives me this rubbishy soup with eyes in it! I was forced to pull some cheese out of the fridge with my bare hands and gnaw like a rat and I'm so hungry now I could cry!"

My cell phone yodels from my pocket.

Caitlin says, "Hi, Mom! Dad said to call, sorry I didn't earlier, I didn't want to wake you last night and I had an early class... Yes, I'm fine, of course I'm fine, why wouldn't I be?"

Mother cries, "Tell those beastly people, whoever they are, to stop ringing me up all night and to leave me *alone!*"

24.

"I want to have Holy Communion today," Mother declares in a take no prisoners tone of voice.

It's the next morning after a thankfully quiet night; coffee time, the half-filled mug, the trembling.

"Of course I know I can't get up and go to church while I'm like this, but when Daddy was ill, before he went to That Place, the Vicar used to come up to the flat and give him communion right here in bed. He'd bring his silver chalice for the wine, make a little altar on top of the dressing table, with a candle and a white cloth spread out, and I'd put our crucifix in the middle. He's such a dear. You must remember him. He gave Daddy such a beautiful funeral. What *was* his name?"

"Mr. Thackeray." I remember him well, a craggy old man with thinning white hair and huge but tender hands, a soccer fan in whose sermons the battle between good and evil was routinely compared with the World Cup Final with God captaining the winning team.

"So it was," Mother agrees. "Could you fetch the crucifix for me, Penelope? I've been thinking about it all night! I want it back in my room now."

"You want the crucifix? In here?"

"You needn't repeat everything I say! Go and get it for heavens' sake—it's on your bureau."

What should I do? Remind Mother she donated the crucifix to St. Stephens almost ten years ago? That her old friend is long retired?

"Frank would be so happy knowing this comes to you," she said when, the week after the funeral, Mr. Thackeray arrived to pick it up and stayed for dinner. She had gone to a lot of trouble with the table arrangements, and installed the crucifix as centerpiece where it looked quite at home flanked by candles and a bottle of wine in a silver coaster.

When the vicar left, his prize carefully swaddled in bubble wrap, I asked Mother, "won't you miss it?"

"Of course," she said, "but I don't need it anymore."

I'd wondered at the time what she meant.

"Do give Mr. Thackeray a ring, Penelope," she's urging now, "Go on! What are you waiting for?"

So I call the office at St. Stephens and, with Sunday morning services in full swing, cannot reach a live person although I receive a recorded message including times of worship, upcoming festivities, parking suggestions and voice-mail menu.

The Vicar's name is Dr. Reed; Press 1.

"Dr Reed?" At first the name means nothing to Mother, then her brows draw together in annoyance. "Oh for goodness sake, not him! He's the new man. Haven't you been to St. Stephens yet, Penelope? It's all changed. A lot of the older people have dropped away, they don't like this craze for calling you by your first name, all that bobbing and bowing and jumping for Jesus, and Peace Be With You in the pew. Maybe it's awful of me but I just don't like shaking hands with every Tom, Dick and Harry and pretending to be friends when I'm not. Perhaps you young people do, I wouldn't know, and it's getting so high church they'll be using incense next. Ring back and ask for Mr. Thackeray—but first bring me the cross! Daddy gave it to me, you know; he found it in an antique shop on Milton Street and bought it for me just like that! He always took such good care of me. . . . !"

I buy myself some time washing coffee mugs.

How do I go about tracing the old Vicar and what should I do if he hasn't retired locally? Decide a creative lie won't hurt, and mentally dispatch him to a spiritual retreat in the far north of Scotland. Mother is vexed. "But I want him to come today. Did you talk to him personally? Did you tell him *I* wanted him?"

I explain how one cannot interrupt a retreat; that it must be Dr. Reed after all. I remind her it's Sunday and he'll be conducting services, "But I'm sure he'll come as soon as he can."

"I *won't* have that man!" Mother's look of disdain leaves no question of her opinion of Dr. Reed.

"There's always Mildred."

She doesn't deign to respond. With a sigh, "I'll just have to wait then, I suppose. And what about my crucifix?"

Another lie: "I've taken it to be cleaned. It was so tarnished—" and count on Mildred, a Christian woman, to lend it back to me.

"When will you pick it up?"

"I'll go down tomorrow morning first thing."

Grudgingly, "I suppose that will have to do."

"Where would you like me to put it?"

"I think on the mantlepiece, below my picture. Then I can see it from my bed even when I'm lying down and those people will see it right away from the door and won't come in."

Those people. I ask, "You mean the ones who came the other night, who I sent away?"

Mother considers. "They seemed to be all right."

"You're not talking about Follis? Or the social worker?"

"Good lord no. I mean the *others,* Penelope. The ones who came into your room—only of course it was my room then."

I feel a ripple of alarm. "When was this, Mother?"

"Years ago, after you left for America. It seemed a shame not to use such a lovely big room, so sunny and warm in the afternoon, and Daddy snored, you know, terribly loudly, I swear you could hear him all through the house. I think now there's some medicine you can take, or some kind of *apparatus* to fit over your nose so that—"

"And those others weren't all right?"

"No, not at *all.*" In a matter of fact voice, "They'd come to take me away—so of course they had to kill me first. That's why Daddy bought the crucifix and had it blessed for me specially."

I'm shocked. Why has she never said anything about this before? Or *did* she tell me and I dismissed it as her overwrought imagination?

I begin a circuitous course toward the bed, as if stalking a skittish horse, only instead of a handful of oats I collect Mother's hairbrush on my way because she has never been able to resist having her hair brushed. I prop her against the pillows and begin, my strokes slow and very gentle because her hair is so thin that her scalp shows through, not pink but chalky white as if I'm seeing through the flesh to the bone.

"Oh yes!" Mother purrs, "That's lovely!"

"Did Mr. Thackeray bless the crucifix?"

'Good lord no!" And Mother tells me, to my astonishment, that my fiercely anti-Catholic father sought the help of Father Diarmid at the Church of the Most Holy Redeemer, a working-class parish down by the river.

"Father Diarmid? Are you sure?"

"Daddy said he needed a *real* priest."

"Why should a Catholic priest be more real?"

"I suppose he thought they'd have more experience and—how do you young people put it?—more *clout*. They believe in the devil, don't they, so they should know how to deal with him. Personally I think that's a lot of hooey but Daddy was quite superstitious." Mother picks another hole and begins to worry out a feather. "Of course what he really wanted was an exorcism."

My hand falters. "He thought the room was haunted?" "He wasn't taking any chances. He wanted to protect me."

"What actually *happened?*"

But Mother will not be hurried. "So he rang them and they said no, they don't do exorcisms these days. Isn't that hypocritical, they say they believe in the devil but won't do anything to get rid of him but there you are, that's Catholics for you! But Father Diarmid was quite happy to do a blessing instead which he said ought to do the trick. Such a nice young man even though he was Irish, bright blue eyes and a lovely voice, not a day over thirty, so masculine, what a crime they can't get married. . . . ."

I cut in, "Did it work?"

"It must've, mustn't it, because they didn't come back."

"Tell me about them." I resume brushing, my strokes slow and rhythmic while Mother works on her feather. It's a big one, she rips the fabric wider and tugs.

Mother says, "I never saw actually them. I was lying on my side, facing away from the door. I didn't hear it open, but I could sense them coming in and standing round me. Tall shapes without faces."

I put the brush down and very gently begin to massage her scalp. "How do you know if you couldn't see them?"

"It was odd because in some way I *could.* Not with my eyes but inside my head. I can't explain but it seemed quite natural at the time. Oh yes, do go on darling, that's bliss."

"Was it dark?"

"Oh no; it was in the afternoon, bright and sunny. And they talked to me."

"Were you frightened?"

"Not then. Their voices were so lovely, you see. The most beautiful I'd ever heard. I *couldn't* be frightened."

"Were they mens' or womens' voices?"

"Maybe women? I remember thinking they sounded the way angels would talk but they aren't supposed to have a sex, are they. Do you suppose they have both sets of, well, organs—or nothing at all and smooth all over? I've often wondered, I know it's blasphemous of me but—"

"What did they say?"

"How easy it would be, and how happy I'd be with them! They spoke very softly but as clear as a bell, and their voices seemed to be coming from all around me, even from inside me. 'Don't think about it', they said, 'Just do it!'"

"Do what?"

"For heavens' *sake,* Penelope," Mother snaps, "Do I have to spell it out for you?"

Dr. Savage says Mother knows exactly how many pills to take and I believe him. She has many uses for pills beyond those medically indicated: to gain attention, to protest, to manipulate. Surely that was what happened all those years ago, knowing my father would expect his afternoon tea and find her in plenty of time?

Mother is saying, "So those lovely voices told me all I have to do is open the window and jump. It would be like flying. 'Come on, Imogene', they said, 'You know how unhappy and lonely you are, you can change all that, it'll be easy,' and I was so tempted. They said, 'Why not? What else is there? Your husband doesn't love you, your daughter hates you!'"—a pause, a glance like a knife, but I refuse to be drawn. "Then their voices suddenly weren't beautiful any more, they were horrible, jeering and cawing like crows: '*You see? Nobody wants you. Nobody loves you! You have no choice!*' I could feel them bending over me, any minute they'd touch me and I couldn't move a muscle. I was terrified."

I set the hairbrush down, cross to the window, stare down at the wet grass across the street where flocks of seagulls are poking about for worms and open the window wide to let in a gust of fresh air. It carries a clean, salt tang even twenty miles inland. I think about the valium Mother has always hoarded, and how she must have been stoned out of her mind.

I say, "It was just a bad dream."

"I wasn't asleep, Penelope. I told you. It was broad daylight."

"Of course it was. What happened then?"

"They touched my face, their hands were so cold they burned. I felt myself falling and was sure I'd gone out of the window after all. I thought I was dead. Later on, Daddy found me lying on the floor. He helped me up and asked what was that mark on my face? I said what mark and he said look at yourself in the mirror and sure enough there was this great red welt across my cheek. Here." Mother presses two fingertips against the spot. "There was no way I could have got something like that, just lying there."

"You must have been lying on a fold in the bedspread before you fell off."

"But I wasn't! And it took weeks to go away. *They* did it. I know they did. And they'd come to take me to hell."

"What did the doctor say about the mark?"

"The doctor?" Mother seems astonished I should ask. "Why should I have seen a doctor?"

"But *surely* —"

"We didn't want people poking their noses in. Who knows what they might have thought? All sorts of odd things perhaps. Anyway, after a bit I was quite all right again. Just horribly shaken and I couldn't sleep because I was always waiting and listening. So Daddy bought the cross to stop them coming back and they never did."

I turn away from the window to find her blowing tufts of down from her fingers. I ask carefully, "These people in your room the other night, the ones I sent away—did they have faces?"

"Oh yes, but I don't think I knew any of them."

"Was my father there?"

"Heavens no."

"But they were good people?"

Mother considers carefully. "I'm fairly sure, but just in case I'd still like the crucifix, I think I need it again now" and I decide that, no matter what, it will be returned to her tomorrow.

She pleads from her bed, "I really don't care if it isn't shiny!"

25.

There's a darkness inside her, a burden she's carrying, old and heavy and secret.

As I hand over the evening morphine, the valium and the glass of water, "Mother, can you tell me *why* you think you're going to hell?"

Her denial is robust and immediate. "What are you talking about? I said no such thing!"

"But if you *had* said it?"

"I wouldn't have. I don't believe in hell."

There's no point in pursuing it; she'll either tell me or she won't. I say encouragingly, "My best friends are sinners; I can't think of anyone I like who'd make it into heaven. It'll be boring there."

"You can leave the bottle beside the bed," Mother says.

Instead I place it in reassuring sight on the bureau, and the codeine on her night table with the cap removed. "If you have a pain, take one of those. Dr. Cameron says it works faster."

"I haven't got a pain."

"But if you do."

"If I do." Mother nods obediently. "One of those."

"Remember you should never take more than four morphine pills in one day. It's bad for you and makes you see things that aren't there. It's important."

"If you say so."

"It's not what I say, it's what Dr. Cameron says that counts and you trust her, don't you!"

I check on Mother again before I take my bath, find her lying on her back in semi-darkness, her face a sculpted mask of shadows. Her eyes are partly open, I can see a wet strip of brightness beneath her lashes, but she makes no sign she knows I'm there. She's gazing toward the mantle where tomorrow, with a bit of luck, the crucifix will stand and I wonder, a sudden coldness between my shoulder blades, whether there's anyone else in the room apart from the two of us.

I've bought more comforts for the bathroom: a heated rail which I load with fresh new towels, a fluffy white bathmat with rubber backing, and a hand-held shower hose with rubber cups which fit over the faucets. The water heater runs twenty four hours a day and it's the warmest room in the house.

I run a deep tub, add foaming salts, sink down into the water until I'm almost submerged except for my nose and chin. It's the first time I've relaxed in days.

The sounds of the building come to me hollowly enhanced through the ancient water pipes: the far-off flush of a toilet; a slammed door; echo of running feet. Somewhere music is playing: a faint choir of richly beautiful voices ascending and descending the scale. They could be Mother's angels—or her demons in treacherous disguise.

Oh, poor Mother.

I'll get her crucifix back for her tomorrow come hell or high water—an unfortunate expression for the circumstances, but apt.

I sit up to shampoo my hair and the sounds and voices shut off; when I slide under the water again they resume, compounded now with muffled hammering (home handyman at work?) and a doorbell which rings repeatedly before settling into a long, sustained peal, surely a full minute, whoever it is should have guessed by now that nobody's home.

I raise my head from the water—and at once am *assaulted* by sound. It's *our* bell, at *our* front door! Have they no consideration? *Shit*—Mother must be scared out of her mind—

until it occurs to me there's been an accident, or the house is on fire and I'll somehow have to manoever her into her bathrobe, all drugged and confused, then down three flights of stairs and out into the cold.

I leap from the tub, wrap myself in a towel, run down the dark passage— no smell of smoke thank God—and fling open the door.

Miss Bannerman stands outside. She's the retired principal of a girls' grammar school, small, chunky and reclusive, and lives in the apartment immediately below. One arm is raised, finger still stabbing at the bell, her other arm supports Mother who wears nothing but my father's undershirt and is bare from the waist down. "Well!" cries Miss Bannerman bitterly, "At last!" She gazes accusingly at my towel-clad figure. "I found her all the way downstairs trying to open the front door. She said she was going shopping. Like that!"

"Wasn't I silly!" Mother sounds amused. "All the shops are closed. This person reminded me. And I'd forgotten my basket. Wasn't it kind of her to bring me home! I can never remember her name."

I lead Mother down the passage towards her bedroom, Miss Bannerman close on my heels. "Wants a tip," Mother confides with a backward jerk of her head. "Better give her something. Sixpence should be enough."

"It's extremely lucky I heard her." Miss Bannerman's lips compress into a pale line. "I'd just finished watching *National Geographic*, and switched off the set. And you're also lucky she didn't fall and break her neck. She needs to have responsible supervision in a proper nursing home. You can't always rely on other people."

I tuck Mother back in bed while Miss Bannerman hovers outside the door, understandably ruffled.

"Dreary old cow," Mother remarks with disastrous clarity, "I bet she's never had a man!"

26.

I pass the night with my bedroom door open and the hall lights on, the front door locked and the key under my pillow. Each time I close my eyes I jolt awake again as Mother pitches over the stair-rail and falls sixty feet onto stone, finally deciding it wouldn't be such a bad end—a second's wild plunge, no time for fear, then a sheet of white light inside her head, warm darkness and no more pain. That's when I drop into a dreamless pit from which I'm aroused by the blasting of the doorbell again. 8:00 a.m. and broad daylight. I unlock the door and peer warily out, half expecting to find Miss Bannerman once again supporting a sparky and unrepentent Mother.

Instead it's Mrs. Ship, wearing a man's overcoat over her house dress and an expression of severe affront. "That Miss B! I can think of another 'B' word as suits her better!"

I hustle her into the kitchen and start to brew a pot of tea strong enough to stand a spoon in it the way she likes and, while waiting for the kettle to boil, prepare Mother's juice and the toast she won't eat but still demands because she's always had toast for breakfast.

"Pops out of her door like a Jack-in-a-box as I come up the stairs!" Mrs. Ship is wrathful. "Said as it's a disgrace about your Mum getting out and wandering about in her skivvies and no knickers and she's going to call the Council. I said she'd better bloody not—Oh yes I did—we don't want that lot poking their noses in here again and anyway Mrs. Sayle's daughter is home now to look after her and she says well she'd better start doing that then, hadn't she. I told her you'd do as you thought best and it's none of her business. She says as how I'm to remember my place and mind my manners and tried to slam the door in my face but not before I said as how Mrs. Sayle is a *real* lady, unlike some as I could mention . . ."

I've opened a package of chocolate cookies but Mrs. Ship is too high on her horse for a cookie . . . "And in future if she wants her letters and paper in the morning she can bring them up herself 'cause I'm not lifting a flipping finger!"

I pour the tea and point out that Miss Bannerman had had a bad fright and was justifiably upset, but Mrs. Ship is unmoved.

The atmosphere doesn't lighten until I ask whether she'd like to carry in Mother's tray while I call the doctor, when she's flattered and pleased to be of service and Miss Bannerman's perfidy is shelved, at least for now.

"Good morning, Madam."

"Why, good morning, Mrs. Ship! How very kind of you to bring my breakfast, I think Penelope must have overslept."

"How are you feeling today?"

"Actually, I think I'm feeling a little better."

"I'm ever so pleased to hear that, Madam."

"Are we going to see the sun later on, do you think?"

Most people I know in California, or anywhere else for that matter, would find this exchange between two old women who've known each other more than forty years not merely inconceivable but the stuff of a comic skit, but Mother and Mrs. Ship are from an older time and don't believe in overstepping boundaries. Their relationship remains a formal one and respects their different stations in life which is utterly reassuring to both. Mother would never invite familiarity, and in her turn Mrs. Ship would neither expect nor welcome it.

Finally, after an exchange of ceremonious pleasantries which has a salutary effect on both of them and gives me a chance to pull on some clothes and call Dr. Cameron's office, Mrs. Ship returns downstairs, equilibrium restored and her rage at Miss Bannerman transmuted comfortably to contempt.

Mother herself has no recollection of last night's exploits. "Of course I'd never go shopping in the middle of the night, are you mad? And what on earth do you mean, Miss Bannerman brought me back? I haven't seen her in months. Don't have anything to say to her when I do. Such a dull, plain little person!"

Dr. Cameron finally appears around noon, just as I'm beginning to worry she isn't coming at all and Mother is demanding the crucifix for the tenth time.

The doctor wears a fawn duffle coat, sweat pants, and purple Nikes with white swooshes; she's flushed with exertion and looks about fifteen. She makes a thorough examination of Mother's abdomen, "Does this hurt? Any twinges? How about here?" while Mother grumbles about cold hands, says well yes she supposes it does ache a bit, and complains the codeine pills make her feel sick, they're too big, they hurt on the way down and have given her a runny tummy.

I leave the house at two p.m., lock the door and take the key with me.

Though Mother appears quiet and drowsy I worry about her becoming agitated, wandering around the flat searching for me, growing cold, trying to light the gas heater by herself and an explosion. I daren't leave her alone for long.

I stop first at the drug store, which in England is called a chemist shop, to fill the new prescription for Immodium.

Next, the florist where I buy a gold crysanthemum in a pot for Mrs. Ship and an African violet as a gesture of appeasement to Miss Bannerman.

Finally, St. Stephens to pick up the crucifix.

"Looks lovely, doesn't it," says Mildred; "Mrs. Amory polishes it every week. It's a shame to keep it in here, it ought to be on the altar really but you can't take chances nowadays and we have to keep the church locked between services. Of course we never used to lock up, people were free to come in and wander round or sit quietly and pray."

Mildred and I are in the vestry. This part of the church was destroyed by bombs during World War II but has been faithfully restored to its original Victorian effulgence and now, observing the elaborately carved panelling, fluted pilasters and gaudy stained glass, it's impossible to imagine it as a pile of rubble overgrown with ragweed. It even manages to smell old, of mustiness, mildew and mothballs, though perhaps the odors linger in the ceremonial robes which date back for decades and are not cleaned often enough, in the Vicar's roll-top desk with its dozens of dusty cubby holes, and the piles of crumbling prayer books set out for repair.

"It's drugs of course," Mildred is sighing, "And wouldn't it be awful if it was stolen to sell for drugs money. They'd take it to London, or it would be over on the Continent in a couple of ticks. Melted down and gone forever. We'd never forgive ourselves, would we."

She has checked with Dr. Reed who is happy for Mother to have the crucifix back for as long as it will bring comfort (he's a good man even if he has infused the parish with the frisky modernity she hates) and I stare at it in awe where it glimmers at me from the Vicar's desk top, appearing, thanks to Mrs. Amory's dedication, to be wrought of solid gold.

At least one of my lies has turned out to be nothing but the truth.

I'm not so far out regarding Mr. Thackeray either, who is indeed on a retreat, but a lot further away than Scotland and of infinite duration. "Carried off in the flu epidemic two years ago," Mildred says. "The poor old thing was quite frail and didn't have much chance when it turned to pneumonia. There was a very nice memorial. Hundreds of people came; I'm sure your mother was there."

"She doesn't remember."

"Yes, well," sighs Mildred, "we're none of us getting any younger."

I return home across the park where I sit down on a wooden bench flanked by Mrs. Ship's crysanthemum, and Mother's crucifix wrapped and taped, to Mildred's embarassment, in a black plastic garbage bag since there were no appropriate wrapping materials in the vestry.

I extract Johnathon's list from my purse. Of course he's right. Miss Bannerman is right. So is everyone. Mother needs more support and better care than I'm qualified to give.

Anyway, I don't think I can go on much longer.

I read:

Shelby Lodge
Priory Gardens
Beech Grove
Prince of Wales House

Names of such cloying respectability as to leave little doubt as to their function.

Wonder how to break the news. Imagine Mother's shocked face and betrayed eyes: "You said you'd take care of me, not throw me away like rubbish! You *promised!"*

I feel like Judas, but I have to do this.

So, which will it be?

Shelby Lodge, where my father died, is out of the question.

Priory Gardens, terminal home of Johnathon's father, is too far out of town.

Beech Grove, a mile away across the park, is a possibility.

Prince of Wales House, just minutes from the Crescent in a pretty, tree-lined street, seems ideal. Of course, considering its prime location, there'll be little or no chance of a vacancy, and I call with little hope. However, to my great surprise, a large private room has become unexpectedly available on the second floor, they can take Mother within the week and, with a conviction that this was meant to be, I make an appointment with Miss Vine, Director, for tomorrow afternoon at three.

Mrs. Ship is polishing the brass mailbox to its customary blinding shine. Chrysanths!" she exclaims with pleasure at my gift. "That's ever so kind, you shouldn't have. Lovely color too, quite the ray of sunshine! Yes, dear, just leave them there, then I can enjoy looking at them while I work!"

I don't ring Miss Bannerman's bell, I'm a coward, and place the African violet outside her door with a grateful note tucked between its leaves.

Mother is still safely in bed. I unroll the black plastic and place the crucifix proudly in place beneath her portrait.

"That's not mine," she says.

"Of course it is. Didn't Mrs. Amory do a lovely job?"

"Who on earth is Mrs. Amory?"

"The cleaner at St. Stephens."

"It still doesn't look like mine! But of course, if a *cleaner* says it is I suppose it must be . . . . "

The crucifix seems to have retained its power and Mother passes a quiet night. Me too, far too good. I wake to a flood of sunlight and leap up in a panic—but Mother is calmly in bed shredding feathers as she waits for her breakfast. "It's a very special day today," she declares and, after a good night's sleep and Prince of Wales House in my future, I couldn't agree more.

I spend an energetic morning scrubbing the bathroom and kitchen, vacuuming the rugs, ironing to a radio station I've found which plays non-stop 'seventies hits. "My goodness you're in a good mood," observes Mother.

After lunch I change into black slacks and camel hair jacket, smart but understated, appropriate for interviewing directors of nursing homes, and the doorbell rings at 2.45 just as I'm about to lock Mother in.

Sue with the laundry. I'd forgotten.

"Hello, Mrs. Sayle. How're you getting on today?"

"Very well, thank you, Dorothy. Come here. I want to show you something." Mother is wearing her yellow velvet, and bright lipstick which she has erratically applied herself. She cradles my father's photograph and touches his face with a reverential forefinger. "The most handsome man in the Navy! And today is our anniversary! Do you know, we were married more than fifty years!"

Sue heaves a romantic sigh. "That's lovely. An example for us all!"

Mother was actually married in May, but I don't say anything and make a mental note to stop on my way back from Prince of Wales House and buy flowers for her anyway. A bouquet of golden roses might cushion the blow.

She's saying, "I didn't know him well before we got engaged, it was like that in those days; you didn't sleep with your boyfriend before you were married. You haven't slept with your young man, have you, Dorothy. You're not that kind of girl."

Sue remarks comfortably how there's more to a relationship than just sex, isn't there, "And shall I do the sheets now, Mrs. Sayle?"

I help Mother out of bed and settle her in the arm chair by the window, still dreamily reminiscing: "Frank and I met in

London during the war. He was a naval officer and I was his chauffeur when he was posted to the Admiralty. I'm a very good driver you know; they didn't take just anybody. Theo—my brother—taught me. He had a Jaguar sportscar, we'd go all over the country and have lunch in pretty little pubs. Don't ask me how he got the petrol, but Theo always managed these things. He said I had good hands; I was a natural; Frank would tell me I drove much too fast, 'Slow down,' he'd say, 'This isn't a racetrack, we're on Whitehall!'"

I rush off to the bathroom to collect the towels, damn, I'll be late for my appointment with Miss Vine.

Mother is saying, "He asked me to marry him, out of the blue, when we were going round Piccadilly Circus. I was so surprised I'd have hit the statue of Eros if they hadn't taken him down for the war. It wasn't like Frank to be . . . . " She breaks off in mid-sentence and stares me up and down. "You're looking smart, Penelope. What are you up to? Are *you* having a special day? Are you meeting Johnathon?"

27.

I suppose Prince of Wales House had sounded way too perfect to be true, and I fear the worst the moment I step through its deceptively welcoming door with the white paint and polished brass into a long, dark hallway painted chocolate brown to shoulder height and an institutional beige above. I want to turn right around and walk out again before anybody sees me but it's too late, a pear-shaped woman wearing too much make-up and a peach nylon blouse over a black bra is already bustling up to me with outstretched hand. "Mrs. Foley? Hello there, I'm Eleanor Vine!"

She stands too close and I take an automatic step backwards. Her hand is soft, damp and too warm.

I apologize for being late and she cries how it doesn't matter a hoot, she didn't have any other appointments.

I follow her down a hallway lined with doors which all stand open so we can look in on the old people, some of whom sit nodding in wheelchairs while others lie in bed and stare vacantly into space. Each room has two beds, a rug between them on the linoleum floor, two washstands, two bureaus, two chairs, everything tidy. The rooms must be clean enough to pass health inspections, but a dingy film seems to lie over everything and there's an underlying sweet/sour odor. At the end of the hallway the more ambulatory guests—not *patients*, as Miss Vine ("*do* call me Eleanor") insists—are parked in a wheelchaired semicircle watching television. One elderly gentleman, wearing a duck-egg blue bathrobe over grey flannel trousers and formal black shoes, holds a yoghurt container in his lap and very slowly feeds himself with a plastic spoon.

"This is Mr. Johnson," Miss Vine says brightly, "He's a very special guest, he used to be the managing director of a bank you know, been with us ten years already, haven't you, dear!" but Mr. Johnson's eyes are fixed on the television screen where Big Bird and a red fuzzy creature with pop eyes and a tambourine are singing a soulful song about sharing toys. I watch Mr. Johnson miss his mouth and a blob of pink goo slide slowly down his chin and splash in his lap.

I feel light headed and grasp the back of the nearest wheel chair to steady myself; stare down into the thin white hair and pink scalp of an old woman in a yellow terry bathrobe exactly like the one I bought for Mother.

"I say!" exclaims Miss Vine—*Eleanor*—"Are you Okay?"

I gulp a mouthful of hot, stale air; give a speechless nod.

"You looked a little pale for a sec. It'll be the heat. We have to keep the temp up high, they feel the cold so, and visitors find that trying sometimes. Shall we go upstairs to our nursing floor and see your mother's room?"

Mother's room. *Here.* God. I shake my head, *"No!"* Belatedly realizing I'm being unbearably rude, "I mean, no thank you! Excuse me. I can't— I made a mistake."

Miss Vine – *Eleanor*—trots after me down the hall saying she knows just how it is when the time comes to put a loved one away, it's quite natural to have qualms, she thinks the more of me for having them, I should go home and come back tomorrow.

I fling the door open and draw in deep gulps of lovely fresh air which I know actually smells of exhaust fumes and the clogged drain on the corner while she insists how happy Mother will be at Prince of Wales House, that they're all one big happy family, and I think of her lying in her bed, yoghurt puddling on her chest, as she stares at Big Bird and sucks on her empty spoon.

28.

A mud-splattered Range Rover pulls up to the kerb ahead of me; the window winds down, a man waves and I've almost walked past before I realize it's Simon.

"Pen!" He's out of the car now, confronting me. "I saw you coming round the Crescent. Thought I'd —" He looks at me with concern. "What's the matter? You're white as a sheet. Don't tell me Imogene—"

"She was all right when I left her half an hour ago."

He slams the car door and takes my arm. "Come in the house for a minute. Have a quick cuppa."

I shake my head. "I've got to get back."

"Just for a minute. You don't want her seeing you like that." His grip tightens as if he's afraid I'll fall. "Trust me!"

I nod, "Okay then, thank you," guessing I must look really bad, knowing that Mother, whose instincts are preternaturally sharp where I'm concerned, will demand "*What's wrong,* Penelope? *What have you done?"* and extract the grim details within minutes.

He steers me through his front door then down a long, stone-flagged hallway. I have a quick impression of light and space, glossy furniture, flowers, and gilt-framed paintings, half hearing his flow of soothing commentary, how this place was a dump when he bought it, chopped up into horrible little bed-sitting rooms, endless pantries and cellars, mouldy plaster, smelly and dark, you wouldn't believe, and when I tell him he must have wrought miracles he shrugs and reminds me that ruins are his thing.

The kitchen in back of the house is huge and airy with exposed stone-work and beams, and overlooks a walled garden.

Simon dislodges two Siamese cats from the cushioned bench one side of a pine refectory table and pitches them onto a window seat where they rearrange themselves gracefully in the sun. He parks me in their place on the warm pillow, hangs up my jacket, pulls off his Wellington boots and roams the room in bright yellow socks. He boils the kettle while chatting about his afternoon checking out a derelict Elizabethan pigsty which in due course will metamorphose into a three-bedroom cottage with medieval charm and twentieth century plumbing for which some American will fork out a bundle, then collects a pair of mugs from a dresser filled with bright pottery, asks, "sugar and milk?" and without waiting for my reply says "of course you do" and pours in an ample supply of both.

    I sip gratefully.

    "That's better," says Simon. "Got a bit of color back now. You were looking pretty rough back there. Want to tell me about it? I don't want to pry, but it mightn't be a bad thing to unload on somebody."

    He's right, unloading would be wonderful, but Simon is Mother's best friend. He was the one who agreed, when she collapsed in the kitchen, that an ambulance should not be called nor the authorities involved.

    However, "It's all right, you can trust me," he says again and so, against my better judgment, I do. He listens quietly and it's such a relief that the tears are suddenly pouring down my face, I had no idea I could hold so much water. "It was *horrible!* I couldn't bear to think of her being in that place. I *couldn't* do that to her."

    "It's Okay, Pen." Simon strokes my bent head with a kindly hand as if I'm one of the cats, then reaches into a cabinet behind him, grabs a bottle of brandy and pours a large slug of it into my tea.

The liquor hits my stomach with a burning wallop. Simon tears off a couple of paper towels and hands them over, I mop up my streaming face and blow my nose; gasp, "Sorry, I don't usually just lose it like that." The stale, sweet smell of Prince of Wales House clings to my clothes and my hands feel greasy. I wipe them obsessively on my knees. "I need to wash."

"Down the hall on the right," he says, and I return feeling better for hot water and lavender scented soap from Provence. I've even scrubbed my nails.

"POW must have gone downhill," he says (POW— Prisoner of War—how nastily appropriate). It was a bit gloomy and old fashioned, but I don't remember it being as ghastly as you say."

I tell him it probably isn't so bad as such places go, the inmates—*guests*—are obviously well cared for but I *cannot* allow Mother to spend her last weeks or months trapped in a place like that.

"Of course not," he says, but points out, quite reasonably, how Prince of Wales House is the first place I've seen. When I tell him there were only four possibilities to begin with, that two are now off the list and the third is far out in the country he reminds me of rental cars, taxis and buses—"And who knows, Beech Grove might be ideal."

"Suppose it isn't? Suppose I don't find *anywhere* Mother would like?"

Simon is matter of fact. "You won't, because no such place exists—at least not from Imogene's point of view."

He sits across from me in companionable silence while I cradle the hot mug in my hands. I ask whether he's faced this situation with his own parents and he shakes his head. "My father was killed when I was fifteen—broke his neck out hunting, just the way he'd have wanted to go—and my mother's still going strong; she's eighty-five now but a tough old bird, she'll see us all out probably."

"Are you close to your mother?"

"We tolerate each other." He confides, "She once told me she was glad Father was dead and thus spared the disappointment. That's when Heather and I filed for divorce and I told Mother I was gay. She refused to believe me at first. Morley men were generals, judges, or country squires—*manly* types. She said Heather and I were just going through a rough patch, it happened to everybody one time or another and I'd get over it, perhaps I should go up to London and find myself some clean young man and get those urges out of my system—yes she truly did, I swear—So, no, we're not close, but we're polite and we observe the amenities. I go home for family gatherings, always alone and not for long. To do her justice, Ma's respectful of what I do professionally, I suppose she's thankful for small mercies—at least she doesn't have to tell her friends I'm a hairdresser or running a flower shop—and my brothers have provided endless grandchildren so the name won't die out. I might even end up as the favorite son when Ma's ready for the nursing home and they're the ones who have to put her there. Distance makes the heart grow fonder; all that stuff. Family dynamics are *so* complicated. Now I'll tell you a secret—" he pours more brandy—"I've sometimes wished Imogene was *my* mother!"

"Really?" I gaze at him in slight alarm, because that's not at all how Mother likes to be perceived by an attractive man. "I hope you've never told her that."

He chuckles. "I'm not a total fool."

"How did the two of you meet?"

"Bumped into her in the street a few years ago." And I can see it as clearly as if I'd been there, Mother running full tilt (by accident or design?) into the New Man in the Crescent. "We chatted a bit, she said she'd love to see my house now I'd finished it because she was sure it would be gorgeous, so naturally I asked her in. A couple of days later we ran into each other again and she invited me up for a drink."

"And one thing led to another."

"Thank goodness! Your mother's great fun you know, lots of style, and innocently outrageous like a character from a Noel Coward play. Such a relief; they're a stuffy lot round here. The first time I took her out to dinner she flirted with me quite naughtily all the way through till the coffee came when she leaned across the table, very serious, and tapped me on the arm. 'What a *shame* you're gay!' she said; 'I bet I'd have changed all that nonsense if we'd met when I was younger!'"

I'm fascinated. "What did you say?"

"I told the absolute truth: 'If anyone could have done it, Imogene, it would have been you!'"

29.

Mother has hidden her pills again, her midnight visitors have returned and this morning, returning from a quick trip to the grocery store, Mrs. Ship was waiting for me in the hall to report that Madame was took queer, banging on the door and shouting. "I got her back in bed and watched for you, Penelope. I didn't like to leave her . . . ."

Mother accuses, "You're *never* here when you're needed!"

Now, I can't get her out of here fast enough, before something dreadful happens.

30.

It's two days later and an all-over grey afternoon when I set out for my appointment at Beech Grove. Simon has volunteered to babysit so I can take my time. He has unearthed the pretty gold-rimmed tea set which Mother hasn't used in twenty-five years because it's Spode and only for best occasions and I leave him carefully washing the dusty cups and saucers.

I cut through the north end of the park, pass the golf course and Shelby Lodge, find myself in an area of Victorian urban sprawl where tall, grey houses not quite big enough to be mansions loom both sides of the street behind high walls and know at once, with jarring déjà vu, that this is where Mother and I were walking in that dream which I'm sure is no dream but a memory. I even find myself reflexively trailing the tips of my fingers along the rough stone and jerk my hand away.

Where were we going? Why?

And where is the garden with the fountain and the statue of the little boy?

The air is laden with moisture, it's so deathly quiet I can almost hear it settle on my hair and shoulders, and although the street and houses haven't changed the trees are much taller and form a dense, dark canopy over the sidewalk. They're Victorian favorites: cedar, yew with the poisonous red berries. Graveyard trees.

I walk on.

The afternoon is fading into a dim, misty evening and I'm starting to think I'll wander for hours and never find Beech Grove at all, which by now I'm picturing as a sinister mansion from a Charles Addams cartoon—but then, round the very next corner, a sign points up a driveway to the right, I follow, and it's like walking out of a black and white movie into full technicolor.

Beech Grove is comfortable and rambling, its walls covered with blazing Virginia creeper. An emerald green Volkswagen bug is parked in the driveway and a young woman in jeans is opening the passenger door for a small girl in a hot-pink parka.

They're mother and daughter, here to visit Granny. And who have I come to see? I'm looking for a place for my mum? Well, I couldn't have picked anywhere nicer!—and it turns out they're quite right. The interior smell is of freshly brewed coffee and lemon furniture polish. The public rooms are attractive, there are floral arrangements on nearly every surface and flower prints on the walls. The director is a jolly Scot called Robin McQuarry with a rosy, round face and red curls whom I can more readily see in some brisk, outdoorsy career such as P.E. instructor or country vet.

Best of all, again, there's no waiting list. This must either be an exceptionally healthy town, or people are dying like flies. McQuarry shows me two available rooms, both south-facing and cheerful with private bathroom, white walls, blue carpeting.

Surely not even Mother could be unhappy here!

Simon has had a busy afternoon. In addition to washing the cups he has unearthed Mother's ancestral silver teapot, polished it until it's incandescent, and used real tea instead of teabags. "And just look what this dear man brought for me!" Mother gloats; "My favorite chocolate biscuits from Fortnum and Mason! Penelope, why don't *you* ever buy us nice things?"

I walk Simon to the door, give him a 'thumbs up;' he nods, smiles and squeezes my shoulder, the door closes behind him, and I'm on my own.

There's no good way to tell her.

But I put it off for later because Lord Storey arrives clutching a bouquet of overblown roses which he presents them to Mother with a flourish just as the last petals drop onto her quilt. "Damn wind. Started falling apart as soon as I got out of the car," he grumbles. "All right when I picked 'em; pretty color too."

"For heavens sake, they're beautiful!" Mother says. She hands me the bundle of stalks, sends me to the kitchen to find them a nice vase as if they're the grandest floral offering she's ever received and I suddenly love her so much I could weep.

When I return, the rose stalks nicely augmented by a few left-over ferns, he's sitting on the bed holding her hands and gazing silently into her gaunt but still beautiful face and I leave them alone together.

31.

Three a.m. again. Mother at my bedside, gripping and shaking my shoulder: "Penelope! Wake up! It's back again! It won't stop ringing. For god's sake *make it stop!*"

32.

Next morning I sit on Mother's bed after breakfast, tell her it's important we talk, and she knows at once what I'm about to say. Her face grows rigid, her eyes narrow, and she tucks her trembling hands under her armpits. When I come to the end of my practised spiel—how her medication is out of control, how demeaning to ration her pills, how I can't leave her alone in case she hurts herself—she doesn't say a word, just leans against her pillows and stares over my shoulder at her radiant young self in the portrait.

"It's a very nice place," I say bracingly, "More like a good country hotel."

The silence drags out for a full minute.

Finally, "Was that why Simon was here yesterday?" Mother asks. "Don't tell me he's in on this too."

I cannot, in all justice, include Simon in the blame. I shake my head.

"Of course not," scoffs Mother, "He'd rather shoot himself."

"At least look at their brochure." I lay it on her lap. In full tempting color, the photographs feature active seniors chatting on the sun porch, playing croquet, or watching T.V. in a typical sunny bedroom, personal knick-knacks strewn about as in a real home. Mother closes her eyes and thrusts it away. "What's the point? You've made up your mind. I'll be seeing the place for myself soon enough won't I. I'll have to see it for the rest of my life. However long that is. I wonder why they have *two* vacancies. I suppose the people died."

When Robin McQuarry stops by in the afternoon to meet Mother, for she likes to meet all future inhabitants of Beech Grove, Mother's attitude is that of a duchess interviewing a potential housemaid. She does not offer tea and when the formalities are complete she remarks, her eyes at their greenest and most virulent, "I've always so disliked the Irish. When my husband visited his friend in Dublin wearing his naval uniform they actually spat on him."

McQuarry remarks how those must have been touchy times and doesn't point out, as I foolishly did once, how it was tactless, not to say dangerously stupid of my father to flaunt his hated English navy uniform so soon after the Troubles.

"They're sly," Mother insists, "They never say yes or no, have you noticed that? They say, 'I will,' 'I will not,' and 'I did so.'"

I pointedly ask McQuarry where her family is from in Scotland. Aberdeen, she replies.

"And during the war," Mother continues relentlessly, "When we had strict food rationing here in England, they ate as much butter and bacon as they wanted and let the German U-boats use their harbors. . . . . "

She asks later, "What did that Irish woman say I could bring with me to that place?"

"Whatever you want. Pictures. Small pieces of furniture. Photographs. Your clock. You can make your room just like home."

"No I can't. It'll be a horrid room. You know I get claustrophobia. And I don't want to take anything. What's the point? I'm only going there to die, like everyone else in that place."

I point out that people also go to nursing homes to recover. Or to have a rest.

"Eternal rest!" snaps Mother. "When are you throwing me out? Tomorrow?"

"You're booked in for next week."

"Why wait so long? Might as well get rid of me as soon as you can."

I take a deep breath. "Actually, you'll find it's not so different from living here but warmer, with your own private bathroom and loo."

McQuarry has said, "We try to give them a little treat every day, something to look forward to," so I list all the coming attractions: the hairdresser, the manicurist, and the jacuzzi which has a fork-lift attachment to lower Mother up and down so there'll be no more perilous climbing over a high metal rim.

She's unimpressed. "What does all that matter when I'll be in prison, locked away with a lot of old people. I don't like old people."

"You don't have to see anyone you don't want, and the staff are all young. And of course your friends will come and visit, I bet they'll be over your very first day. They can park right outside and now poor Lord Storey won't have to climb all those stairs."

"I shan't want them to see me in a place like that."

" Don't you dare say you don't want Simon or Felicity or Bethany to stop by—"

"And how about you? Where will you be?"

"Right here of course."

"Nonsense. You'll put me away like an old dog nobody wants and go straight back to San Francisco. To that awful husband of yours. You'll never come home again. You'll leave me, just like you always do."

I tell her I'm not going anywhere but she doesn't believe me.

We drag through the final days, Mother keeping up a relentless litany of objection: "The food will be horrid; will they make me eat it? I suppose I've got to wear nightdresses. I don't like things dragging around my legs in bed. Am I allowed to wear my bedjacket?"

The phone rings constantly, which further upsets her: the bank; the ambulance company; the City Council; Mildred (when would Mother like her to bring the sacraments and perform the Holy Eucharist? *Never!* snarls Mother); and Mr. Pye who by some occult process has learned of my decision to put Mother in the nursing home almost before I make it myself and plans to send round painters and electricians to give estimates for work before the place goes on the market. Perhaps she has been right all along about Mr. Pye.

"I don't want a phone in that place," Mother says. "Must I have one?"

"Nobody's forcing you to do anything you don't want."

She says, "*That,* Penelope, is the stupidest thing you've ever said. Just think about it."

As if to prove there's no need for a nursing home Mother is now remarkably lucid with no more nocturnal lapses, while my own nights become ragged with nightmares. One recurs with horrid regularity: I'm lying in Mother's bed cold to my bones, my body a cellophane envelope of bad news. My hands rest side by side on the quilt, they have the bluish translucence of non-fat milk, when I push at the skin it wrinkles into dry pleats and stays that way which is when I realize they aren't my hands after all, they're Mother's hands and I'm in Mother's body even though I'm not the one who's dying.

Since she so definitively rejected the nightgowns, I buy Mother half a dozen new men's undershirts and several pretty bed-jackets for when her yellow velvet is cleaned, although in her present mood she'll probably refuse to wear any of them.

I pack a box containing her little brass clock, hand-mirror, make-up and photographs.

She wants nothing else. "What's the point?"

On the night before she leaves I kiss her papery cheek and she says, "Good night, Penelope, I hope you sleep well, you're killing me, you know."

Sometime before dawn I open my eyes to find Mother in the bed beside mine, nose pointing toward the ceiling, bloodless lips drawn back from pale gums. Her eyes are wide and dusty and reflect no light.

I stare in horror as her dead body stirs beneath the quilt with a rustle of bed linen, her grey-purple face creaks slowly towards me and I'm helpless to move, can only lie there and wait for those blind eyes to lock accusingly onto mine—then I'm awake, my heart crashing in my chest and there's nobody in the room but me, it's dark and so quiet the far-off clatter of shunting freight trains is as clear as if from the next street.

I'll never be able to fall back to sleep now, it's almost six o'clock and will be light in an hour.

I go quietly to the kitchen to make coffee, my breathing still ragged and, although it's cold in here, heave the window up for the fresh air.

The wooden sash gives a tearing screech and I wait with indrawn breath—but there's no sound from Mother's room.

I lean out, watch the breath smoke from my mouth and nose and look up and down the Crescent. Realize, as if I'm seeing it for the first time, how truly beautiful it is, how classic the symmetry of its curve, the stone balustrades, the columns framing the slumbering windows while, beyond the frosty lawn and the noble chestnut trees in the Victoria Park, the lights of the city lie spread out like a carpet of jewels.

I think of Mother watching this view through all weathers and seasons for over forty years.

She knows every inch of the neighborhood; she loves to walk, always longs to be outside. This summer was unusually warm, according to Simon, and she'd lie on the lawn all afternoon and into the evening, once till after eleven o'clock—"If I hadn't gone out there and told her to come in she might have stayed there all night," he said.

The kettle shrills; I snatch it off the burner, fix my coffee and drink it still leaning out the window, seeing the view through Mother's eyes.

Think of her lying in the grass staring at the sky, her solitary walks, her garishly patched quilt, her gypsy soul—then trapped in a small room which might indeed be bright and warm but which isn't hers and whose window overlooks a concrete parking lot.

Two young women present themselves at the door punctually at eleven o'clock. They wear navy uniform trousers, shirts and official ties, one is tall, gap-toothed and cheerful, the other is short, chunky and dour. Mother demands, "How are those two supposed to carry me out of here and down all those stairs?"

The morning has passed smoothly enough, her manner has been distantly civil, she's packed her washing things and seems resigned to her fate but now she's bitter. "You'd think they'd send men!"

The tall one says, "It's Okay dear, I promise we won't drop you!" but Mother is not amused, especially when she sees the small seat with slings and poles in which she will ride downstairs. "I expected a stretcher; why do I have to sit up?"

"You want to see where you're going don't you?" says the short chunky one, but Mother doesn't deign to reply.

Down in the street her nostrils quiver with insult as she regards the waiting minivan and I can read her mind precisely. If she *must* go it should be with style, loaded from a stretcher with a male attendant at each end into a real ambulance with flashing red lights and a siren.

It's as well nobody she knows is around to see this, only Mrs. Ship, cigarette drooping from the corner of her mouth as she sweeps the front steps, who is probably the only person in the world Mother can bear right now.

"Good morning, Mrs. Ship."

"Good morning, Madam. A bit on the raw side today."

"It is, isn't it. I expect we'll have some rain later on."

Into the van now, Mother buckled up. I sit beside her and don't even think of trying to talk.

Mrs. Ship resumes sweeping and doesn't wave, just as if this were no big deal and Mother out for a brief excursion. Nor does Mother look back but straight ahead, stone-faced as Marie Antoinette in the tumbril. She wears my father's bathrobe over his old undershirt, determined to make as derelict an impression as she can on the staff of Beech Grove whose brochure she has long ago ripped up and tossed in the trash.

It gets worse.

We enter through the wheelchair entrance in the back of the building which I haven't yet seen, a brown linoleum ramp, dim and dreary, the walls in need of a paint job.

Nor is McQuarry anywhere in sight; instead we are greeted by an attendant I haven't seen before either, a grey-haired woman with a cast in one eye.

Our grim procession wends its way past the living room where, instead of virile sixty-somethings playing bridge, two crones in bathrobes hunker beside the radio, fluffy white heads nodding gently to a recording of *Amazing Grace*.

"It's exactly how I imagined it," Mother says in triumph and I cringe with dismay at my terrible mistake. Beech Grove must only have seemed bright and attractive in contrast with Prince of Wales House and how could I have mistaken those plastic flower arrangements for the real thing?

It doesn't matter that Mother's room is cosy and bright, that the sun really does come out for a moment, that a pretty young aide bustles in with a tray of coffee and little cakes and that McQuarry herself appears, apologising for not welcoming Mother in person but she'd been on the telephone.

I unpack while Mother maintains a derisive silence. I place the photographs of my father in strategic places, her brushes and cosmetics on the bureau top, and on her nightstand the card Caitlin has sent, a pretty coastal scene with sailboats.

"I'll never see the sea again, will I," Mother says.

I nibble distractedly on one of the cakes which tastes sour and leaden – wouldn't you know it, the food's awful too—and hang the yellow bathrobe from a hook on the back of the door. Mother stares at it with hatred and hugs my father's old brown one tightly across her chest. "You might as well go now," she says, which is when I become aware of the high ringing in my ears, the cold heaviness in my stomach, my clammy hands.

I reel from the room and collapse in an armchair placed strategically at the head of the stairs.

The aide reappears and pauses, concerned. "Are you all right?"

No, I'm not all right at all.

There isn't even time to close the bathroom door.

I fall to my knees, grip the toilet seat and vomit with such violence I clutch my stomach to hold myself together then collapse in exhaustion on the floor.

When I finally haul myself up on trembling legs and cling weakly to the sink my reflected face is the color of putty and my eyes peer out from dark pits. I look older than Mother. I think about walking over a mile back to the Crescent and know I won't make it.

McQuarry helps me outside. I hear myself muttering about taxis but she drives me home herself and I drop fully dressed onto my bed, sleep all the rest of the day and through the night and this time I dream of nothing.

PART II

1.

Morning again.

My body feels scoured and achy and it's almost unthinkable to move but it's 9.30 already, it's late, late, Mother will have been calling for an hour, I must ask how she slept, straighten her bed, bring her tea, make her toast—which is when memory takes hold and fills in, faint to bright like a developing polaroid photograph:

I don't have to do it any more. It's over.

Mother is gone. She's safe. I no longer need to lock her inside the apartment, nor worry that she might fall, hurt herself or burn the place down.

She will no longer be pounding on my door in the middle of the night.

The shameful relief washes through my mind in soft, cottony waves and I fall again into drowned depths from which I'm abruptly wrenched when the doorbell rings: Mrs. Ship with the mail and newspaper who tells me I look terrible, I must have picked up this nasty stomach bug going about and a poor little baby died of dehydration on last night's news.

I drag myself to the bathroom, gaze in the mirror and quickly away, lean woozily against the sink, splash my face with cold water, then wash my acid-grating teeth.

I'm back in bed and almost asleep when the bell rings again, Felicity this time, buttoned up in a scarlet peacoat and bearing a thermos of chicken bouillon. "You poor thing! I came rushing over as soon as I heard! I tried to phone but the line was busy. It'll have been the nervous tension, you would have been feeling so guilty about putting poor Imogene in the home!"— followed by the usual crumple of distress, "Not that I'm *in any way* criticizing your decision! You couldn't have done anything else. *Please* don't think for one *moment* that I'm—" and on and on while I sway in the doorway and swear I've taken no offense.

When she finally leaves I wobble back to bed and belatedly check in with Beech Grove. Learn that Mother has passed an Okay night with no disturbances or delusional wanderings. Tell McQuarry there's no way I can visit today, she says it'll do Mother no harm to have some time to herself and they're readjusting her medication, so I drowse without guilt until evening when I drink a bowl of Felicity's soup, eat six crackers, take a long bath, wash my hair, and sleep for another twelve hours.

"Penelope! At last!" It's eleven o'clock the following morning and Mother is waiting. She's in reasonably good spirits, her face is made up and her hair brushed, she wears her yellow velvet and is surrounded, as usual, by flowers. She eyes me up and down, avidly curious. "I must say, you aren't looking at all well! That Irish woman told me you'd had a nervous breakdown! She said you were so sick you brought everything up in great big chunks!"

I start to explain it was only a violent stomach bug not a nervous breakdown (what was McQuarry *thinking?*) and that I'm improving hourly, but catch myself mid-sentence. If it makes Mother happy to believe me prostrated by remorse, then by all means let her continue to think so. I admire her flowers instead and, happily diverted, Mother tells me how Simon brought the yellow roses, and that dear sweet girl and her funny old husband sent over the white ones, she can't remember their names but there's a card somewhere, while I decide my first impression was correct after all, this *is* a nice room, particularly now the sun is casting a cheerful glow across Mother's floral offerings and the pristine whiteness of her blanket.

However, greetings over, she's full of complaints. "I hope I don't have to stay here too long. The food is dreadful. They bring me far too much at the oddest times. Who on earth can eat dinner at five o'clock? When I told that Irish woman I didn't like my dinner before seven-thirty at the *earliest* she said the kitchen staff all go home at six. I ask you! How ridiculous to put the servants' needs before ours but I suppose one can't expect anything better in a place like this."

I don't attempt to reason with her. Instead, I reassure myself about the bathroom which is also as I remember, immaculate with glistening white sink, shower stall, stack of fluffy towels and strategic safety rails. It could be a bathroom on a luxury cruise ship. "Your own bathroom just a step away!" I exclaim with genuine envy, "*And* a jacuzzi! How grand!"

"That stupid thing?" Mother is not impressed. "A man has to come to mend the jets. There isn't a real bath to lie down in properly so I've got to use the shower, a nurse has to be with me all the time in case I fall, and there's hardly enough room to swing a cat."

"I'm sure they'll fix it soon." I exit the bathroom and close the door. Notice the chart hanging on the back. She weighs 37kg. In a space marked 'comments' someone—MacQuarry? a nurse?—has written, '*at risk.*' Has Mother seen it? Would she understand what it means?

She adds, "And the demon's back in the phone."

"A demon? In the phone?"

"You don't have to repeat everything I say, Penelope. It's terribly annoying."

"But you don't even have a phone."

"It was here when I came. I told you I didn't want one but you weren't here to stop them, were you. It was watching me and listening to everything I said, and it made the phone ring all night so I couldn't sleep. It was a nice white one with little buttons on it but I told the nurse to take it away. I told you this was a bad place."

2.

Back in the Crescent, late in the afternoon, I venture into Mother's bedroom for the first time in two days. It's barren and depressing in there without her photographs and flowers, and smells of dust and stale face powder. I notice the darker patches on her vanity top where her bottles and jars used to stand, the grimy traffic patterns in the once-white rug and find, when I lift a corner, that the ancient rubber pad beneath has melded to the floor. Her bed is as she left it, blankets pulled back to reveal threadbare, stained sheets and her quilt is flung carelessly over a chair-back, no longer flambuoyantly gypsyish but a tattered relic a bag lady would reject. Mother's portrait with its ostrich plumes, satin and pearls seems absurdly out of place in this dreary barrack, as does the crucifix, bravely glittering on the mantle below. . . .

The crucifix! How *could* I have forgotten it?

I set it beside the front door to take to Beech Grove first thing in the morning, close Mother's door against the chill and the gloom, and spend the next hour moving everything I could possibly want or need into the dining room.

I place the most comfortable armchair in front of the fireplace, together with the old leather ottoman from my father's office on which to rest my feet. Collect my favorite paintings from around the apartment—a seascape with blue sky and sailboats, a Peter Scott print of wild geese flying over a marsh, and an exuberant oil of Rio de Janeiro at sunset which for some reason has always hung unseen behind my father's office door. I bang nails recklessly into the wall, hang them in a cluster so I can look at them all together without moving from my chair, and with a physical effort which leaves me panting, drag in the cedar chest from my bedroom so I can go through the contents in warmth at my leisure. Then, energy not merely spent but overdrawn, I collapse with my feet up, gaze at the incandescent sky above Rio's Sugarloaf mountain and ponder the mechanics of closing down a lifetime: what to keep and what to discard among Mother's clothes, furniture, drawers, boxes and closets all crammed with *stuff.*

It's quiet save for the gentle hiss and sputter of the gas heater. The drapes effectively block out traffic noises and the phone doesn't ring. Then I remember I left it off the hook the morning Mother left for Beech Grove—no point upsetting her any more than she was already—and that my cell phone is still switched off too.

It's tempting to postpone rejoining the world quite yet, but I must and I do and find my voicemail full, mostly from Andy Sirvas and Liam. I'll deal with Andy tomorrow, tell him I'm bursting with thoughts about JetShare and I'll fire them off soon (I can stall him for a week or two) but I should respond to Liam's progressively anxious messages tonight.

Then I hear my choice of words and wonder at myself. *Should* respond? To Liam, my husband whom I love and miss like hell? Who loves me? What's going on here—and why am I relieved when I don't get directly through to him?

I listen to my voice telling his voice it's been a frantic few days; wiped out by a stomach bug; fine now but really tired, going to bed and call you tomorrow—and think how, if anyone overheard me, they'd assume I was talking to a distant acquaintance or a business colleague I was trying to avoid.

I don't understand myself and don't try because I know I won't like what I find.

3.

"Can you imagine me, *at my age*, being bathed by a young man?"

The Jacuzzi is fixed and Mother is simultaneously amused, thrilled and scandalized by her new experience. "His name is John. He sponged me all over, even *down there*! He's so nice, and quite good looking. I thought he must be queer, you know, to be so kind, but not a bit of it, he's got a girlfriend who works for a bank. Can you believe it? I said you shouldn't be doing this kind of work it's not right but he says why not and being a nurse is well paid and they want to get married and buy a house and anyway he enjoys it. I said, lifting old ladies in and out of the bath? How can you? And he said he doesn't think anything of it, one person's body is just like anybody else's"—with an amused headshake—"Just as if he was a *real* nurse!"

I place the crucifix on a small table at the foot of Mother's bed, and flank it with Simon's roses and a pot of michaelmas daisies from Bethany. It looks quite at home and authentically liturgical and now, with her medication doled out at the right intervals by an authoritative person in a white coat, Mother must surely feel safer.

However, nothing can be done about the phones ringing in other rooms. "Such a busy, *noisy* place!" Her eyes flit from the door to the window and finally to the closet. With a sideways jerk of her head, "She's gone in there now, you know."

I open the closet door. There's hanging space on the right, occupied by the despised yellow bathrobe; shelving to the left with its tidy piles of unused bedjackets, underwear, and her lavender scented sachet of hankies. I step back so she can see. "Look—only your own things. Nothing else."

Mother peers inside, then anxiously scans the room. "Are you *sure*, Penelope?"

"I promise."

"That's because it's daytime now and she's asleep. But she'll come back tonight, stand beside my bed and stare at me. An old woman with no eyes. She'll take me away soon."

Who is she really?

Again I feel the darkness building inside Mother—a nameless fear, or an ancient, unspoken grief?

I sit on the bed and take her hands in mine. "Of course she can't. Mrs. McQuarry and I won't let her. The crucifix won't let her."

"She climbs in through the wall. There's a door in the back of the cupboard."

"Nonsense!" Then I recall the infamous closet in *Rosemary's Baby,* and the witches in the neighboring apartment. I take the bathrobe out, and hold the door wide open so she can see. Rap my knuckles against the plaster in back. "It's quite solid. See?"

"Stop that!" Mother cringes against her pillows. "You'll wake her up!"

She orders me to take the bathrobe away with me when I leave; "I don't want it anyway. You keep it and wear it. Surely you need a new dressing gown?"

4.

"Beastly for you catching that bug," Bethany says, "but I'm not surprised with all the emotional stress over poor Imogene. It's hard to think of her gone from the Crescent, those big, grand rooms suited her so well, but it had to happen."

We're drinking tea again at her card table. A Mickey Spillane paperback lies open on the bookcase; Scottie is draped, snoring, across her feet. Bethany says, "Such a pity I can't take him to see her. We rushed over to Beech Grove on her first day when you were ill, we hated to think of her all alone, but dogs aren't allowed and the poor thing had to wait outside in the cold. Isn't that ridiculous! Everybody knows animals have healing powers. It's all over television these days, those programs about pets for the elderly and children and people in prison. I really must take it up with that director woman."

But I have not come here to commiserate over the insult to Scottie, bred for northern moors but overindulged in overheated rooms, I'm on quite a different quest, and break determinedly into her tirade. "I need your help!" and Bethany, who longs to be needed, at once sets her grievances aside. "Anything!" she cries. "Fire away!"

I tell her about the demon which has taken up residence in Mother's closet and awaits the chance to carry her away to hell, and Bethany is profoundly shocked. "The *poor* darling, Imogene of *all* people, I can't bear it! Such a generous, good person and, now she's near the end, so unbelievably *humble*. The very *thought* of her going to hell would be ridiculous if it wasn't so sad."

I consider telling Bethany about the sinister beings who flung Mother to the floor during what I can only assume was a bad drug reaction, but hold back. Say only, "It's all in her mind, of course, and the side effects of the drugs, but she's become obsessed."

Bethany's jowls quiver in sympathy. "I normally wouldn't suggest this, it would be hypocritical because I'm not what you'd call a believer, but if this is a spiritual crisis would it comfort Imogene to talk to a minister? Perhaps somebody from St. Stephens? She thought highly of them there."

I explain that, with Mr. Thackeray gone, there's no-one left whom she trusts.

"What a sad situation! I'd do anything to help, anything *at all!"* Bethany sighs. "But apart from regular visits to keep her spirits up, and flowers of course though everybody brings those and Felicity's are so much prettier, there's nothing I can do."

"But there is!" Walking back from Beech Grove in the eerie dark, the yew branches dripping on my shoulders, I'd had an inspiration. "Would you consider giving her a Tarot reading?"

"A reading?" Bethany is puzzled. "With so little time left?"

"Not a *regular* reading. Something special." I remind Bethany of Mother's deep respect for the occult (Bethany readily agrees, adding that she's always guessed Imogene was gifted that way herself), that Bethany herself has admitted Mother's suggestibility, and how, with specific cards displayed in a certain order and appropriately interpreted, Mother might be led to believe the demon vanquished.

While speaking, I watch the expressions chase each other across Bethany's ruddy face from confusion to understanding to dismay. When I finish, she blurts in unconscious Spillane vernacular, "You're suggesting I stack the deck!"

"Isn't it worth a try?"

An emphatic shake of the head. "Impossible."

"Why?"

Bethany raises an obdurate chin. Scottie whines beneath the table but for the first time I've known her she ignores him. With utter sincerity, "Because in certain circumstances I become a conduit to outside powers. I open up my mind and they enter at will. It's a gift—and one should *never* abuse such a gift."

"But it can't be abuse when the intention is good."

"It's not as simple as that."

"Won't you consider it?"

"I can't, and please don't ask me again. The powers don't take kindly to manipulation." With surprising force, "It's not a *game,* Penelope!"

I'm impressed despite myself. I have drastically underestimated Bethany's dedication to her calling and she probably now considers me a cheap cynic. However, in for a penny in for a pound as they say and, hating myself, "It's always seemed to me that Mother was led to you for a purpose!"

Bethany now looks as if she could cry and I feel worse than terrible. "I like to think so too, I really do, *believe* me, but not for this! You don't understand, Penelope. The Tarot is a sensitive tool and there could be unexpected consequences. Improper use could backfire and do a great deal of harm."

I almost ask what could be more harmful to Mother than dying in expectation of hell, but bite back the words in time.

"I'd do anything else," Bethany pleads; "Anything at *all!*"

"Maybe I'll take you up on that."

"Promise!" She throws me an anxious smile, clearly longing for me to leave, so I stand, gather my things, thank her for my tea and climb the steps towards the cold and the light.

As the days pass, however, the demon seems quiescent. Perhaps I have indeed managed to convince Mother there's nothing sinister inside her closet, which I keep almost empty so she can see for herself.

It could be due to the new regimen of drugs, to Mother's renewed faith in the crucifix, or simply that she's comforted by the routine of Beech Grove as Johnathon promised she would be. Her bed linen is changed regularly and she has always enjoyed the sensuous smoothness of clean sheets. She's warm and fed. She's bathed and her hair washed. Her toenails, uncut for months and grown hard and yellow like little hooves (I've studied them in despair during bathtimes) have been soaked in a special solution, softened and trimmed. She enjoys the young nursing staff who provide a new and admiring audience for her stories while her friends visit faithfully with flowers and cards and bottles of wine. "I do miss my view though," she complains. "Am I going home soon?"

5.

Mother's desk is crammed with old bills and checkbooks. She seems never to have thrown away a letter in her life.

There are letters from aunts and uncles and friends and cousins.

Letters from me: she's even kept my cold, sparse notes from early days in California, duty notes to keep her updated on my current address, into which little warmth creeps until after I meet Liam. She owes him that much, at least; "Of course you must write her, she's your *mother!*" he'd say. But for my father, nothing; no acknowledgement of his existence, and no word on his birthday or Christmas. Punishing him; punishing her. I'm not proud of myself. I bundle them up and drop them in the trash among coffee grounds, old tea bags and fruit rinds.

And then there are dozens of letters to Mother from him, my father, tied with faded silk ribbons, written through long periods of wartime and post-war separation and periodically thereafter until 1949, the year before I was born.

I open one at random, from June 1945; read, *"My darling little girl"*—and thrust it back in the envelope as if it scorched my fingers.

Love letters. Unimaginable. Disgusting, actually. Whatever should I do with them?

Burn them? Take them to Beech Grove? If Mother is still able to read, will she find them a comfort?

And then it occurs to me that this may be my only chance to discover what went so fatally wrong in their lives and what bound her to him, to the exclusion of anything and anyone else, even me, her child, beyond an outdated sense of duty.

What they did.

What she did.

Isn't it my right to know the truth?

So I resolutely take the letter out again and smooth it carefully on the table top:

"*My darling little girl:* . . . . *It was nice to hear good old Bunkie say he thought we could be happy together. I think he even said 'wonderfully!' And why not? But has it ever struck you to count up the actual number of hours we have spent together? I have, and it's less than fifty, even including when you were driving me around London. I counted every minute, you see!*"

I feel a little sickened but force myself to read one more:

July 17, 1946: "*My Enchanting Witch:*. . . . *I'm frightfully attracted by that snap you gave me last week, the one on the lawn at your Aunt May's house. You are bending slightly forward and your hair is straight and longish which is when it looks its prettiest and is hanging down and looking ruffly and I think you've got bare legs.*"

Then a third:

December 10, 1946: "*My dearest Love:* . . .. *I live only for you. It was thinking of you waiting for me the other side that brought me safely through hell. How can I bear the thought of you looking at or speaking to another man, even the postman or a taxi driver? It's you. It's you. It's you . . .*"

I stare bemusedly down at the elegant, faded writing.

Such eloquence, from *him*. His heart at her feet.

I can't bear to read any more. Not yet. Maybe not ever.

I stack the letters in a pile, gentle with the envelopes, so fragile with frequent handling, and wonder how often she read them to herself and remembered.

My father's desk drawers have remained untouched since his death.

I find records from his earliest years in the Navy including his officer's Commission from 1919 personally signed by King George V; yellowed newspaper clippings relating to sea battles; a sketchbook from his much-travelled youth, complete with notations. He draws fortresses, monkeys, palm trees and parrots; a squatty little man wearing a lampshade hat and pyjama bottoms; a brown lady with huge bosoms drinking out of a bottle with a caption reading, 'Delia gets squiffy again!'

There are albums filled with formal photographs of uniformed men seated at long dining tables or standing at attention on the decks of war ships (I search for my father with a magnifying glass but the faces are curiously alike and I can never be sure); snapshots of young men posing with self-conscious grins in front of Hindu temples, awkwardly atop camels, or hamming it up at cafe tables in foreign ports.

My father is never featured because he was taking the pictures and I think how his face will appear in other long-forgotten albums in photos taken by his buddies; how perhaps at this very moment some other middle-aged son or daughter might be sorting through them and puzzling over what to keep and what to throw out and who are all these people anyway; deciding it really doesn't matter because they're likely all dead.

Now, suddenly, here's a picture I recognize, the names printed below in white ink upon black: Bunkie, Swifty and T.J. (*It was nice to hear good old Bunkie say he thought we could be happy together*), arms companiably linked, laughing at my father behind the camera and suddenly I can hear his voice, in this room, at this very table: "Look, Penelope, they don't have any shadows. Why's that, d'you suppose?"

I must have been eight or nine, sensible and scornful. "Because the sun isn't out."

"But it is. It's glaring bright. It's hot as hell."

"Frank!" warned Mother.

So it was a trick question. I carefully studied the photo again, announced triumphantly, "Yes they do have shadows, they're on their feet!"

"Well done!" And my father explained the picture was taken at noon in Colombo, Ceylon (now Sri Lanka), which is on the equator so the sun was immediately overhead. "You're a clever girl, Penelope!"

For the first time I could remember he smiled at me with spontaneous approval, I felt a window flung open to reveal someone young and laughing who loved me after all and I tentatively smiled back—but the window closed and never opened again.

The following afternoon I revisit my father's yearning letters to Mother.

I can't help myself, my need to know easily trumps their privacy, and finally perhaps my search is rewarded.

February 1949, married four years now: *"My dear Imogene"* (no more beautiful darling or enchanting witch, not any more)—*"I do like to be taken seriously, and if you've been impressed by nothing else I have said I hope you've thought deeply about this child question...."*

I think, she wants a baby and he's saying no.

I shove myself back in my chair, stare at Rio de Janeiro, thrust my hands deep in my pockets and remember that first afternoon back in the Crescent, lying in the heat, dreaming of a long ago, equally hot afternoon and Mother's voice: *He even asked me to sign a paper promising I'd never have a baby ... I had to fight for you tooth and nail for years..... Oh, what I had to do to get you, Penny ...*

Poor Mother. How could so passionate a lover deny her a child? Did he feel a child would come between them? Was he already jealous?

I read further: *"You asked me once who gives in if we are both strong minded about something? Well, there isn't any question about my giving in on this . . ."*
Did he believe that would be the end of it?
I hustle through the next three months; scan, set aside. Scan, set aside. The baby issue is not raised again, at least not by him (though of course I'll never know what she wrote back) and the tone of his letters, though no longer angry, is restrained until May 31 when his ardor resumes full blast:
"My very own darling: . . . by the end of next week, God willing, we'll be docking in Portsmouth, and soon after that you'll be back in my arms. Be a good girl till then and remember you're mine, you're all I ever wanted, just you and your loving smile!"
It would seem, then, that Mother had given in to him.
But—and I make a quick calculation—she was pregnant five months later.
What I had to do to get you!
What *did* she have to do? And how?
I mentally scan through possibilities.
I see Mother waiting impatiently for my father to leave the house in the morning then pouncing on that box of French letters (of which he used two each time), and deliberately puncturing every one of them.
Or, upon his return in the evening, greeting him in her yellow velvet bedjacket and nothing else, *"Darling, I thought you were never coming home!"* and a bottle of champagne and two glasses beside the bed.
But I'm convinced by neither scenario. In those days well-brought-up girls were not merely sheltered but kept purposely ignorant about the mechanics of sex, and it would never have occurred to Mother to sabotage his condoms.

Nor can I see my father, however powerful the temptation, giving in recklessly to animal impulse.

The only other possibility is that she did it the old fashioned way and took a lover—but I discard that notion at once. My father had just returned from sea, he was living at home, he was a jealously possessive man, and the logistics of arranging an assignation —most likely more than one—would have been daunting if not impossible.

Anyway, she loved Frank Sayle as passionately as he loved her.

And I'm his spitting image, aren't I.

6.

Mrs. Ship brings up the mail next morning and there are two actual letters among the bills and junk mail.
One, written in graceful copperplate script, is from Miss Bannerman inviting me to tea on Friday at 4.00 o'clock.
The other is from Mr. Pye. He'd like to bring to my attention that upon vacating the flat Mother is liable for restoring it to rentable condition and encloses copies of estimates from three different painting contractors, ranging between £8,000 and £10,000 which seems to me an awful lot of money.

"The lease for the flat?" Mother is vague. "I expect Johnathon's got it. Which reminds me, Penny, where are you living now? I ought to know but I've forgotten."
I tell her I'm still in Number Twelve and she's happy for me. "Why of course you are! How well I remember that dear flat"— as if she left it years ago rather than weeks.
By now Beech Grove is becoming her whole world, merging in her memory with the grand houses, hotels and cruise ships she frequented in her youth when there was still money. She's effortlessly re-assuming the mantle of privilege while I find myself elevated to the status of favored visitor or fellow traveler.
"Penelope," she'll cry, "What a lovely surprise! I'm so glad you could come, what are you doing today? Who are you seeing? Are you having a lovely time?" And to the nearest available staff member, "Please bring my daughter a hot cup of coffee! She's come to see me all the way from America!"
Dr. Savage stops by. Mother forgets she took him in strong dislike and assumes he's some long-lost beau. "Such a

dear, kind face and gentle voice. I offered him a gin but he was in a hurry and couldn't stay."

Mother's attitude to McQuarry has also undergone a radical shift, perhaps on account of her kindness during my 'nervous breakdown.' Now, McQuarry is no longer referred to with scorn as 'that Irish woman' but with affection as Dorothy.

Dorothy again.

"Such a dear little person!" says Mother. "She takes such good care of me!"

A clue: to Mother, the modifier 'little' does not necessarily refer to size but can relate to a person of lower status who is held in some degree of affection, as in 'my little sewing woman,' or, 'that nice little man who fixed my vacuum cleaner.' But I don't recall anyone named Dorothy, of whatever social standing, in Mother's past.

"She'd do anything for me," Mother says now, "*Such* things!"

I'm arranging her latest floral offering, a mixed bouquet of tiger lilies and gorgeously colored leaves and berries. We're running out of vases and space. I ask, "What sort of things?"

"I can't tell you," Mother says.

I don't know whether she refuses to tell or it's the literal truth and the memory inaccessible, and I don't have a chance to find out because Neela the pretty Indian aide appears carrying a huge arrangement from the ladies of the local Conservative Party Association, there's no container remotely large enough, and I'm sent downstairs to the kitchen pantry to find one.

When I return, Mother is entertaining a visitor. "Penny darling! *Look* who just walked in!"

Johnathon sits in the armchair beside Mother's bed, the lamplight gleaming gold on his smooth head. He wears a charcoal pinstripe suit, a light grey shirt with crisply starched white collar, and the pale-blue-and-black striped tie of his exclusive boarding school.

He rises at once and takes my hand in his warm grip. "Hello, Pen. I hoped I'd find you here." He opens his briefcase. "I've brought the lease."

"Do sit down again," Mother says. "Penelope will get you a gin. Unless you'd prefer a whisky? I think we've got whisky?"

I've wondered whether there are rules about liquor in patients' rooms but if so they are certainly not enforced. Her friends, bless them, continue to visit at cocktail hour bearing gifts, and by now Mother's bureau top has become quite a well-stocked bar.

Johnathon accepts a small Scotch, relinquishes the armchair to me, takes one of the three folding metal chairs which are stacked in one corner to accommodate Mother's extra visitors and manages, as only he can, to appear elegantly at ease upon it. For the next ten minutes he and Mother chat comfortably on her favorite topics such as local weddings and the Mayor's upcoming cocktail party. When he prepares to leave Mother announces firmly, "Penelope has to go too, would you be an angel and give her a lift home?"

I protest but Mother, patches of color flaring on her cheekbones and energized as I haven't seen her in weeks, will have none of it. "No, really, Penelope! I'm *awfully* tired and I simply *have* to rest now!"

I tell Johnathon he mustn't feel obligated, that I was planning to walk and need the exercise but he says certainly not, it's cold and dark and the Crescent is directly on his way. He helps me on with my coat and holds the door for me. And then we're outside in the driveway, the vapor of our breath mingling as Johnathon unlocks the passenger door of his Rover sedan. The interior is leather and walnut and smells rich, Vivaldi plays softly on the expensive sound system and I think about what it must be like to be Rosemary; that *I* might have been Rosemary.

He sits beside me in the dark.

There's a plushy armrest between us, I lean my forearm on it, curl my naked fingers over the end, half hoping he'll place his hand on top of mine and half dreading it because what would I do then, but his eyes are fixed on the road ahead and both suede-gloved hands are squarely on the wheel, clearly he has no intention of touching me, which is just as well because if he did I'm sure I'd lace his fingers with mine and crush them against me, demand he stop the car, fling myself into his arms and weep in a disabling upwelling of loneliness and hunger for a man's strong body on mine.

Stop it, Penelope!

So I clasp my hands tightly in my own lap, glad he can't see my face even if he happened to be looking at me, which he's not.

I wonder whether, if I invite him upstairs to No. 12 for a drink, he'd accept. Don't we need to discuss Mr. Pye and his demands, which Johnathon has agreed are unreasonable? Of course we do.

We're pulling up. Because this is Johnathon, there's a parking space right outside the front door, and I think how he's a man for whom there'll always be a parking space, an empty taxi on demand, the best table and an instantly attentive waiter.

But he leaves the engine running and declines my invitation; he has to hurry home, a city councilman and his wife are expected for cocktails, he'll put me in touch with his associate Millicent Parker who's a whiz with landlord/tenant disputes, and when I ask if he might deal with Mr. Pye himself he tells me that he could, naturally, but this is Millicent's area of expertise and she has much lower billing rates. When I say I'll come down to the office so he can introduce us he says there's no need, he'll brief her tomorrow, she'll be expecting to hear from me and we can communicate by phone and fax. I give him one last chance and suggest a quick lunch together for old time's sake but, sounding genuinely regretful, he's snowed under right up until Christmas. What a shame. And talking of snow, he's taking the whole family skiing for the holidays. "Have you been to Courchevel, Pen? It's beautiful, not far from Chamonix and you can see Mont Blanc from the top of the lift..."

 Johnathon is a gentleman and watches to make sure I get safely inside the front door.
 I climb three flights of stone stairs, alone. Light the dining-room heater, pour myself a huge glass of vodka, collapse into my chair and stare once again at Rio whose sunset lights twinkle cheerily back at me. Take a large swallow of my drink and feel very grateful to Johnathon for saving me from doing something really really dumb.
 What was I *thinking?*
 And the answer is that I was not thinking, I was reacting as I have always reacted to Mother and her romantic ideal of Johnathon, just as I've reacted to her on-going disparagement of Liam as the coarse workman with the sprawling blue-collar family whom it's rather easy for people like Mother and me, in our perceived superiority, to patronize.
 I decide I'm worse than she is, actually, because at least she's honest about it.
 And now I've bought into it all over again and, for a few shameful moments, allowed myself to share Mother's dream.
 What if I'd married Johnathon?
 And, *what if* I'd never gone to California?

Which leads by natural process to the night of Mother's party and *what if* it had been Liam instead of Johnathon whom I was trying to drive away.

"Don't be a goddam fool, Pen," he'd have said, "I don't give a fuck for that phoney London shit and neither do you. I don't know what's going on with you right now, what this is all about and where your head's at but something's wrong and we'll deal with it together."

Liam would never have let me walk away.

He'd have fought for me.

"So your father drinks," he'd have said; "I'm not marrying *him*."

I'm a fool. I don't deserve him.

I call Liam and get his voice mail.

Wonder whether, seeing my name on his caller ID, he's choosing not to answer.

Knowing better because he doesn't play silly games.

Tell myself, get smart, Penelope! He's working his ass off on this project, he can't talk, and he'll get back to you when he can. He'll be on-site eyeballing dimensions for panelling (he can compute to the hundredth of an inch), comparing the merits of various hardwoods, figuring a location for the four-storey elevator. He could be tearing out mouldy plaster and plywood and three generations of crappy renovation, right down to the studs to be bored and threaded with brightly sleeved wiring and miles of copper pipe. He'll be creating order and function from chaos.

Liam is a builder. He builds things. He *creates,* and I'm proud of that.

It's a beautiful thing when a project runs smoothly, he says, *it's like music!*

I think of his powerful, calloused hands, so deft with tools and materials; then of Johnathon's hands, so smooth and manicured, which hold golf clubs, padded steering wheels, papers to push across desks.

"Leave a message and I'll get back to you" says Liam's voice mail.

"Call me," I tell him, "I'm here, I love you."

7.

"I must say, you don't resemble your father at all!" Miss Bannerman leans forward and stares so intently I shift in my seat with discomfort. "No doubt about it, you're your mother's daughter through and through."

Her living room overflows with a mix of Victoriana and far-flung colonial artifacts. Ormolu clocks and stuffed owls under glass jostle for space with Burmese gongs and ebony elephants while, above the fireplace, a pair of crossed native spears is flanked by faded and foxed watercolors of the Scottish highlands.

The African violet thrives in a brass filigree pot from some Eastern bazaar and occupies pride of place on the coffee table between us. "So good of you," Miss Bannerman says, "And a lucky choice, I happen to love African violets. Do you take milk and sugar, Penelope? A slice of lemon?"

I accept the lemon, Mrs. Bannerman wonders politely about Mother and how is she settling, I tell her as well as can be expected and she murmurs a polite "jolly good" but, as I quickly realize, she's indifferent to my mother's situation; what she really wants is to talk about my father.

"I got to know him quite well, you know, after you left for America. He used to visit me every day at five thirty and stay for one glass of sherry. I'd leave the door open for him, and he'd walk right in and make himself at home. We had some excellent talks; he had a fine mind."

I can't even begin to imagine it. "What did you talk about? If you don't mind my asking?"

"Books and literature—he was a great reader—but mostly art of course. He always wanted to be an artist. You never knew? It was his dream, but in those days, coming from a Navy family, it was unthinkable he'd do anything but follow tradition." She gives a philosophic shrug of narrow shoulders. "Your father never questioned his duty; he was an honorable man. And it all worked out for the best; I'm sure he was happy enough" and I can't help but think, with a stab of pity, how suitable an epitaph for a life half lived.

"Anyway," says Miss Bannerman with complaisance, "I think he was grateful for the conversation and the company—as was I. He gave me this beautiful book," and places in my lap a massive and clearly expensive coffee table tome entitled *Canaletto's Venice*. It is inscribed in my father's distinctive handwriting: 'For Jane on her birthday, 9th March 1978, with warm appreciation, Francis' and it occurs to me, in sudden revelation, that she was in love with him.

I try not to stare. Miss Bannerman has pouched cheeks like a hamster and her greying hair is pulled behind her head into a severe bun. She wears a navy-blue pleated skirt with matching cardigan, dark stockings and sensible lace-up shoes. It's hard to guess how old she is; she has probably looked much the same for most of her life.

"I was extremely fond of your father," Miss Bannerman says, "Though it was perforce a one-sided relationship. He always came down here to me, I was never invited up there. Your mother had little time for me; I'm afraid she thought me dreadfully dull. I'd hear her on the stairs sometimes, 'What on earth do you find to talk about?' she'd say; then give that little laugh, you know how she does, as if it was unbelievable anyone should even want to speak to me, let alone spend time with me on a regular basis," and I have an awful image of poor Miss Bannerman lurking on the landing hoping against hope that one day my father would speak up for her; declare that "Actually, Jane is perfectly fascinating and a highly intelligent woman."

"So," I venture, "you called him Francis? Not Frank?"

"Francis is a beautiful name, why reduce it to the commonplace? He was Francis, Francis Sayle!" repeats Miss Bannerman, luxuriating in the sound of it, while I think with bemusement that this man she invokes with such intensity is my father, selfish bastard, tender lover, squalid drunk and, now, hopeful artist for whom, upon his death, I never cried.

I say, "I didn't know he painted."

"He gave it up after he joined the Navy, he couldn't have borne it just as a hobby. He always sketched, though. He kept diaries of his travels on the ships and he'd illustrate them with little drawings of the people and the things he saw from day to day. He'd show me, and tell me all about them. I always longed to travel." Miss Bannerman's eyes grow misty as she gazes into far and exotic distances. "My father's people were missionaries and lived all over Africa and then in China—but I grew up in England, then the war came and I hardly ever went abroad again. Francis' sketches brought all those places alive for me even more than a photograph would have done, though he was a keen photographer too and quite good. There was one particular sketchbook; I wonder if your mother kept it? I do hope so but of course I'd never dream of asking her."

I tell her I have it safely upstairs, and think with dismay how I'd considered throwing it out. "I'll bring it down for you. In fact," in a flash of inspiration, "Would you like to have it? I mean, to keep, to remember him by?"

Miss Bannerman is shocked. "I couldn't possibly, Penelope! You must treasure it!"

I tell her my father must have treasured his times with her and he'd want her to have it and for a moment I'm afraid she's going to cry.

I escape upstairs and pour myself an early drink.

Poor Miss Bannerman! Was her undeclared love for my father the only romance in her life?

And how did he feel about her? I hope as more than a mere convenience. Decide he must have done or he wouldn't have given her such an expensive gift (*for Jane—with warm appreciation*).

And what about Mother, with him going downstairs every day to find the schoolteacher's door always open and sherry and intelligent conversation waiting for him? I'm sure Mother never for one moment considered Miss Bannerman as a potential rival but the idea of Frank Sayle paying attention to any woman other than herself was unthinkable. Remember how speedily she got rid of Miss Diggins?

For the first time I wonder how my father spent his time during Mother's annual visits to me in California and whether Miss Bannerman might have taken advantage of those visits, regarding them as her great chance?

Did he still go downstairs for his glass of sherry? I suspect he did not. I can see him, rather, like a dog abandoned at the kennels, watching and enduring beside the door hour by hour, day after day, drinking vodka in his brown bathrobe and mourning his loneliness while, below, Miss Bannerman waited in vain for the sound of his footfall on the stairs.

Did he clean up his mess before Mother returned (because she always would return, there was no question) or did he leave a pile of empty bottles in mute reproach? How was that first night of her homecoming? Did they curse or love each other? What did they talk about? Did they talk at all?

8.

32 kilos. At great risk.

McQuarry calls me into her office, "I'm sorry to burden you with this, Penelope, but we must talk." She has her back to the window, it's an unusually warm, sunny day but her face is in shadow and I can't read her expression. "It's time to make plans for your mother."

For an instant, with a plunge of apprehension, I think she's telling me that for some reason or another Mother must leave Beech Grove.

"For when she passes," McQuarry says gently. "I'm sure you've noticed her condition is deteriorating and we need to be prepared. I'm not saying she could go tomorrow, maybe not for a few weeks, but at this stage anything's possible."

"Your mother would expect Woodhouse's, they took care of your father," says Johnathon when I call for advice. However, I have walked past the dignified facade of Woodhouse & Sons, Funeral Directors, Est. 1875 countless times over the years and, perhaps unjustly, created an image in my mind of dim, hushed rooms and unctuous, clammy-handed flunkies in dark suits.

McQuarry suggests an alternate in Hargreaves, relative newcomers (1983) but of perfectly sound reputation for all that. They're located in a new building in the lower part of town, the offices are light and airy with modern furniture and Mrs. Peabody, the funeral director, is a stout matron in a bright blue cardigan.

Of course the product is inescapable but that's not her fault.

I study the catalog of caskets, each model named for a British county: the Buckingham, the Lincoln, the Bedford - with the Argyll and the Pembroke if the end-user happens to be, respectively, Scottish or Welsh. They are very grand, built of oak or mahogany, insect treated, satin lined, brass handled and I'm simultaneously fascinated and repelled. "What a waste," I can't help but exclaim, "When it'll be all burned up!"

Luckily Mrs. Peabody is neither shocked nor insulted as I suspect Woodhouse's would have been. In her comfortable West Country burr, "You'd be surprised how there's always some who want all the trimmings and hang the expense, and how many start with certain ideas and change their minds. You can never tell, so I have to show you everything, don't I."

In the end I choose something in blonde pine which is both reasonably priced and quite handsome. It's upholstered in rayon, which looks close enough to watered silk, and the handles could easily be brass. It's called the Northampton. "Very nice," approves Mrs. Peabody, "Quite appropriate, if I may say so," as if I'm choosing a hat for a garden party, while I stare at the casket in the photograph and imagine Mother inside it wearing my father's undershirt.

Mrs. Peabody now raises the question of urns. "There's rather a lot of residue, several pounds in fact. Most people prefer to scatter a symbolic sample and preserve the rest."

Several pounds? I had no idea. I remember Mother in the Memorial Gardens, pausing beside a bed of richly-perfumed apricot roses which drooped in blowsy full bloom—"He always bought that color for me, he knew it was my favorite"—opening the little box Mr. Thackeray had given her and tossing a pinch of my father across the flowerbed; but if that was just a sample, what happened to the rest of him?

It all seems increasingly unreal, I stifle a hysterical and highly inappropriate urge to giggle, dutifully consider my options which range from something in ceramic like a Chinese ginger jar to a chased bronze number with pedestal solid enough to survive any cataclysm short of nuclear holocaust, and try to think of Mother inside. I can't. I tell Miss Peabody, "She'd hate it, it would be worse than a coffin" and Mrs. Peabody says in that case they'll just package the cremains (a peculiarly ghastly word) in a stout cardboard box and I can make my own arrangements.

She walks me through the rest of the procedure starting from the initial phone call from Beech Grove. "We pick her up right away if we can or, if it's at night, first thing in the morning and bring her back here for storage"—when I think involuntarily of morgue scenes in TV cop dramas and Mother sliding in and out of a freezer on a steel tray, particularly since, as Mrs. Peabody explains, "With a cremation, we have to keep them five days in case there's evidence of foul play. So silly when you think of old, ill people like your mum dying perfectly naturally, but it's the law."

Five days. I shiver in sympathy and we move briskly on to the viewing. "You'll want to pop in and visit, won't you. And perhaps some of her friends and other family might like to say goodbye too. We can make her look ever so nice with a touch of makeup," and there's Mother lying in state with her bright red mouth, her semi-circle eyebrows, her dyed black hair combed out on her rayon pillow when to my dismay, having survived this far, cremains and all, I sway in my seat while the color drains from my surroundings and leaves me sweating in a landscape of greys. I mutter, "I think I'm going to be sick."

"Put your head down a minute, dear, it does get to you. Here, have some water."

I sip from a paper cup. I'm cold and shaky but the nausea is fading. I hear myself say, faintly but firmly, "No lipstick."

And here again Mrs. Peabody is in full agreement. "Oh much better not. I never recommend a lot of makeup, especially not for the older ladies. We'll just use a clear foundation and a tiny dab of rouge so she looks more natural . . . ."

I'm still cold when I get home clutching Hargreaves' thick grey folder with the picture on the front, appropriately, of an apricot rose.

Everything is now arranged: hearse, coffin with four bearers, two hymns, no flowers.

I slump in my chair and stare at the boats and the silvery glitter on the River Thames, and then at Rio de Janeiro in the sunset, so warm and lush and golden and far away both in distance and time. I've never felt so alone, nor yearned so intensely for a sister, brother, even an uncle or aunt at my side. For kin.

But I don't have to feel alone.

It's 5.00 a.m. in San Francisco, not too early for Liam to be up and doing, I reach him at once and he's comfortably matter of fact as I knew he would be—"I went through all that when Pa died, choosing the casket and all, remember?" and I certainly do, also that old Mike Foley's casket was top-of-the-line mahogany the family could barely afford.

I confess to choosing cheap pine for Mother.

"Don't forget Pa was buried," Liam says. "We had him done up fancy for Ma, for the viewing and the wake and all, and it was money well spent, it was important for her. But if you're asking me, I think it's a crime to waste good hardwood on a cremation. Caitlin would say the same. She loves her gran, but a mahogany casket still means one tree less in the rain forest."

I say, "It won't be long now. Caitlin had better come soon."

"I'll have her there by the end of the week."

"Let me know exactly when and I'll meet the plane."

"I could come with her, just for the weekend," he offers once again. "I know you didn't think it was such a great idea, and yes, I'm busy as hell but if it's any help to you, Pen, and now Imogene's in the nursing home . . . . ."

"It wouldn't work. She'll still know you're here. Even *dying* her radar still works. Anyway," I blurt, "It's not Mother I'm thinking about; it's *me*. Please, please don't take this wrong but you bring out the worst in her, all her pettiness, rudeness and cruelty—and I can't deal with it. Of course I should have stopped her years ago when we were first married. I should have stood up for you, told her to cut out that crap or go home—or to hell—but I always thought she'd eventually get over it, and she'd had such an unhappy life with my father I was sorry for her. But that was no excuse. And all the time I'd listen to her bad mouthing you and I'd *hate* her. And that's not how I want to remember her. I want to remember the good times. I want to remember loving her. Can you try and understand?"

9.

Mother is sleeping. She wears a white angora sweater I've never seen before and lies flat on her back with my father's bathrobe spread over her feet. It's at moments like this, when she's quiet and still, that I can almost watch the flesh sink away and the bones press up beneath her skin.

When her eyes flicker open, "Hello, Mother. It's me. Penelope."

She frowns in concentration, I wonder where she has been in her mind and who with, then, "Penelope! Of *course* it is!" She smiles her hostessy smile, pats the bed and invites me to sit down. "What have you been doing? Are you having lots of fun?"

I take her hand and summon a cheery smile as I tell her of course I'm having fun while, in my head, Bethany is laying out her Tarot cards only instead of the Sun, the Tower and the Magus, each depicts a different grade of casket: the Argyll; the Buckingham; the Northampton.

"That's good!" Mother closes her eyes, seems to fall back to sleep, then opens them again looking more alert. "Darling! You're really here! How lovely! You're not just a ghost."

"Of course I'm not!" And I beg her please not to feel she must always try and entertain me. "Why don't you take a little nap? I'm happy just to sit here with you."

"Don't be silly, darling. How can I possibly relax if I know you've come to visit?"

"Forget about me. Go back to sleep."

"I don't want to sleep. These days you hardly ever come down to see Daddy and me, I want to make the most of it, and if I go to sleep you might leave again."

"Of course I won't."

"Yes you will. You always do!" Mother plucks in agitation at her quilt but, lacking feathers, is reduced to pleating it between her fingers. "And what about Johnathon? I've been dying to hear about your date the other night. You still haven't told me. You looked so radiant."

"We had a good time but let's not talk about him now." I admire her sweater and try to ignore the stains down the front.

"Isn't it pretty!" She strokes her flat breasts with a sensuality that's disturbing to watch.

"Where did you get it?"

"The nurse gave it to me because I didn't have anything to wear. Wasn't it sweet of her?"

"But of course you have things to wear. What about those new bedjackets I bought you?" and when I show her, "Oh yes," Mother says without interest, "Those," and strokes herself again with a secret inner smile. "Isn't this lovely? So white and soft, just like your baby shawl, you used to wake up over and over again in the night, you were such a bad sleeper. I'd pick you up in my arms and walk you back and forth, back and forth across the floor." She makes a cradle of her arms and rocks them. "I'd go Sh-*sh*. *Sh-sh*. For hours. I'd be so tired I could cry. Then at last you'd be quiet and I'd put you back in your crib again and you'd look up with those great big eyes of yours and laugh at me. Oh you horrid little thing! The doctor—what do you call the baby doctors, I never can remember?"

"Pediatricians."

"That's quite right! And he was such a nice man, such a kind face—he said you simply weren't getting enough to eat. You said of course she's getting enough, she gets six ounces every feeding but she goes to sleep before she finishes and that other one, what's his name—that Irishman—he said the holes in the teats are too small, she has to work so hard to suck it wears her out so of course she goes to sleep and he heated up a needle on the gas stove till it was red hot and stuck it in and made the hole much bigger and she went glug, glug, glug and slept right through the night."

"That was Caitlin. And it was Liam who stuck the needle through the nipple on her bottle."

"Well, of course it was, darling, and I remember as if it was yesterday."

10.

Mrs. Ship asks, "when's your daughter coming home, then?"

"The day after tomorrow."

"Bet you're looking forward to it. Where're you putting her to sleep?" And answers her own question, "in the Commander's room, I suppose."

I'd imagined Caitlin occupying the other bed in my room, but we might both prefer privacy and my father's old office is small and easy to heat.

"William's over, dinnertime," Mrs. Ship says. "I'll send him round to help you move the bed."

I don't know who William is but it's a safe bet he's one of the numerous grandsons and greatnephews who hang out at her brother's pub. I start to protest how the bed's not heavy and I can manage on my own but Mrs. Ship will have none of it.

Mother demands, "Why does that door keep slamming? It's so irritating. I keep telling them not to make so much noise but they don't take any notice."

I listen carefully but hear nothing.

"There it goes again," Mother complains. "Slam, bang! It's driving me quite mental!"

It began again last night, McQuarry tells me, the banging doors and the telephone ringing in her room.

"The hole's still there for the wires," Mother whispers fearfully. "You see? They can come in through there." She has lost confidence in the crucifix. "They'll punish me whether it's there or not."

"If your mother was a Catholic," McQuarry says, "I'd suggest you called in a priest."

For the briefest moment I consider calling on the Church of the Most Holy Redeemer, as my father did long ago, then imagine a handsome young priest arriving, Mother caressing her fluffy breasts and demanding why he never married. Instead, I call Mildred, explain Mother's need, that she's too old and traditional to approve of female ministers and Mildred, a genuinely good person, says she quite understands and will send along a male clergyperson as a matter of urgency.

I return home at lunchtime to find a sandy-haired, drayhorse of a lad waiting patiently on the front step. He's wearing a battered leather jacket, greasy jeans, enormous work boots with inch-thick soles of rippled crepe and must be Mrs. Ship's nephew William. I'd forgotten that in England working people eat dinner at lunchtime and tea in the early evening. I guess I've been in America too long.

He bounds springily upstairs, picks up the mattress under one brawny arm, carries it down the passage to 'the Commander's room,' and returns for the box spring and frame. He could easily have carried the whole thing at once if it hadn't been for getting it through doorways. I try to get him to accept money for his trouble but he won't take anything.

Bless his heart.

I then have a busy afternoon.

I dust and vacuum, fling the window open and spray air freshener.

Raid Mother's room for her vanity table, a lamp, a mirror and an armchair; the living room for the sheepskin rug beside the fireplace; make up Caitlin's bed with grateful thanks to Felicity who has lent a white goosedown duvet with broderie anglaise trim.

I buy a replacement sweater for the nurse which is almost identical save for three little pearl buttons at the neck; a lightweight but potent heater, and three boxes of 30-amp fuses to go with it.

Finally I collect the rental car, a Ford Escort painted a garish metallic lavender which the clerk informs me is trendy, drive a couple of practice left hand laps of the Victoria Park without hitting anything and continue on to Beech Grove where Mother is restless and anxious and wants me to take away her hand mirror: "Something's got into the glass, Penelope. A bad face. I told you that cross was no damn good!"

Mildred really comes through for me and it's no obscure curate who billows into Mother's room the following morning wearing full clerical regalia but the head honcho himself, Dr. Reed, tall and undeniably handsome with laser-blue eyes and a mane of hair the color of iron-filings of which I sense he's very proud. He greets Mother in his carefully classless accent, "Imogene, my dear girl, how *good* to see you!" He's extremely smooth and I understand at once why she doesn't care for him, just as I'm sure he's very good on television. "And this must be Penny! My dear, I've heard all about you from Mildred!" He takes my hand between both of his and exerts just the right pressure for the correct amount of time.

He unpacks the tools of his trade from a black bag a physician might carry—flask of wine, silver cup, two candlesticks and the pyx containing the holy wafers—and arranges it all on the table top; then he shakes out his sleeves with a starchy flourish, takes Mother's hands between his, tells her with all sincerity how much she is loved by Jesus who gave up his life for her and how above all he wants to bring her comfort and set her mind to rest but Mother's eyes are fixed on the closet door and she's not listening.

Dr. Reed invites me to join the service and I accept although I haven't taken communion in years. Wonder whether I should kneel beside Mother's bed or sit in the armchair? Settle for standing in the corner by the window, hands clasped at my waist when I murmur along with Dr. Reed, "Our Father, who art in Heaven, hallowed be thy name . . ."

Mother's lips move sporadically, she appears to be listening to something only she can hear and I know that for her, despite his vaunted charisma, Dr. Reed's clout is negligible. If only he spoke with Mr. Thackeray's upper class drawl or, like that handsome young priest, operated from the security of a ritual Mother can't understand.

The Vicar however, happily oblivious to his dismissal as social upstart, breezes through the service at a fast clip.

He captures Mother's restless hands, cups them to enclose the holy wafer, guides them to her mouth, "Take and eat this in remembrance that Christ died for thee" and Mother objects loudly how she can't possibly get that piece of dry cardboard down her throat because she doesn't have enough spit.

Dr. Reed is equal to the situation and my opinion of him as a professional climbs rapidly. He takes the wafer from her hand, touches it to her lips, places it on top of its container and I can't help wondering what he'll do with it later.

Moving on now, the goblet held steady, "The blood of our Lord Jesus Christ," when Mother grasps its base with shaking fingers, knocks the rim against her teeth, chokes and spews dark ruby wine onto the white sweater.

She's absolutely furious. Roars, "that poor nurse! She'll be so upset. It's all your fault, how *could* you be so clumsy!"

"Dear Imogene, it was my fault, do forgive me." The Vicar finds a washcloth in the bathroom to wipe Mother's face while I take her hand and assure her that the winestain will come out at the cleaners.

He asks gently, "Shall we go on?"

"Certainly not!"

So he sketches a sign of the cross in the air before Mother's face. "May the Lord bless and keep you, the Lord make his light to shine upon you and give you peace, now and forever, Amen."

"*Amen!*" snaps Mother. *"Goodbye!"*

I walk Dr. Reed to his car, thank him again for coming and apologize deeply; surely such a thing has never happened to him before.

He tells me that all kinds of things happen to him all the time, I have no idea, and I'm not to worry.

I ask what he'll do with the used wafer, now wrapped in a tissue in his bag, because it's consecrated, he can't throw it the garbage, can he? and he explains it simply goes back in the ground from whence it came.

"You mean you bury it?"

He agrees that yes, a truly devout person would literally bury it; "But I prefer to recycle." He smiles. "It'll go in the bird feeder in my garden and find it's way from there. It's all the same in the end!'

11.

Bethany is pleased to see me until I fling myself almost literally upon her mercy. I tell her how the demon is still in Mother's closet; that phones ring and doors slam without ceasing; that a sinister face has appeared in her mirror and that, now, a prominent minister of the Anglican Church has probably made matters worse.

I beg Bethany to please reconsider a Tarot reading for Mother. I remind her she only sees Mother in the evenings when she's at her social best, and has not experienced, as have McQuarry and I, the dark times when the visitors are gone. "I swear I wouldn't do this if I could think of any other way," I beg, "but I don't know what else to do or who to turn to."

Bethany is silent for quite a long time. I hold my breath. Finally, "When did you have in mind?" she asks.

"Now," I say.

"Oh dear god," she says.

We don't, of course, rush over at once but spend several hours evaluating the major and minor arcana of the Tarot deck, eventually choosing five cards by appearance rather than actual significance because Mother will never know the difference. Bethany rehearses her spiel in front of her bathroom mirror. She feels like a huckster at a fair and warns me once again that no good will come of this.

We arrive at Beech Grove at 3.30 p.m. Bethany ties Scottie's leash to the wooden bench in the porch, leaves him with his favorite chew toy and follows me, with dragging feet, through the door and up the stairs.

The door is closed. I knock gently. "Mother?"

The drapes are drawn, the light is dim and my first impression is of a dark bundle of old clothes thrown on her empty bed until I see she's curled on her side beneath my father's bathrobe.

Bethany is whispering, "We shouldn't have come, she's taking a nap, they always close her door when she's sleeping, we should have waited—"

The bundle stirs and Mother raises her head. Her eyes are bleary and blinking and crusted at the corners. "Penelope? Is that you? I can't see properly. Who's that with you?"

I tell her, "It's Bethany."

"They shouldn't have let her in. The servants know I take my rest now."

Bethany says, "Penelope has hired a car and we took it for a little spin. We thought we'd drop by to say hello on our way home."

Mother says, "At least you didn't bring that beastly little dog."

There's a numb silence until Bethany asks, bewildered, "Surely you can't mean – you're not talking about *Scottie?*"

"We left him outside," I say.

"Thank god!" says Mother. "That creature's disgusting the way it farts and stinks, though I suppose if you must feed it all that rich food it can't help it."

Poor Bethany's face crumples. "But Imogene, I thought— I mean, I was *sure*—that you *loved* Scottie! He's like my child!"

Mother snaps, "An animal is *not* a child. Though women who've never had one will make up for it any way they can and go all sloppy over their pets. I think it's quite revolting."

Bethany stands frozen in the middle of the room, as if she's blundered against an invisible wall. Her right hand is still outstretched toward Mother, her brown velvet Tarot bag droops from her left index finger like a dead rat.

I say urgently, "It's the medication. She doesn't mean it."

Mother says, "Of course I mean it."

There's a light tap on the door; Valerie, the Jamaican aide, with the tea tray. "Here you go, Mrs. Sayle. Want me to bring in extra cups?"

Bethany begins, "I don't think—"

I say, "Thank you. That would be lovely!"

The aide pours Mother's cup half full, sets it back down on the tray, places the teapot safely on the dresser and says, "Back in a jiff."

"We ought to go," Bethany says.

Mother demands of me, "What's that in her hand?"

"Her Tarot deck."

"What for?"

"For a reading."

"A *reading?* For *me?*" Mother's thin fingers gather the edge of her sheet into an accordion of nervous pleats. "What's the point? I don't have a future so I can't have a fortune. No future, no fortune. If she doesn't understand that, she's half-witted."

Bethany throws me a glance which combines resignation, dread and gloomy triumph at being proven right but tells Mother, just as we've scripted, "I wouldn't think of it exactly in terms of a *fortune*, Imogene. More of a—a testimony. Or an affirmation."

Mother snorts, "Bloody rubbish!"

By now I've realized Bethany has been right all along and this will be a disaster. "More of a reassurance," I say. "It was my idea in the first place, but not a particularly good one. I'm sorry, Mother. We don't want to disturb you. We'll come back later."

"No, stay since you're here." Mother seems to have tapped into a hidden source of energy and her eyes glow as if lit from within by dark light. "I have no idea what you two have been hatching up together but you might as well get it over with."

We clear the clutter from the bedside table, move the flowers to the dresser along with the teapot, Mother's pitcher of water and drinking glass and sit down beside the bed.

Bethany lays out the cards and, with fingers which tremble worse than Mother's, turns up the first one, the Five of Cups, a bowed, cloaked figure, face averted, gazing into grey distance and says, "This is the influence now past."

Mother complains, "I can't see it properly. What is it?"

"An evil old woman who's been making your life a misery, especially at night, but she's gone now."

"How do you *know* that?"

"She has turned away from you. She'll leave you alone now. You're safe."

The next card reveals the Heirophant, bristling with authority on his papal throne. "This is the current influence dominating your life, a tall, fine, religious man. He's been here very recently, in this room, and scared her away, his power is much stronger than hers, he has real clout;" but Bethany is unnerved and upset and doesn't sound convinced.

Mother scoffs, "The only man in here today was John to give me my bath. He isn't tall and religious. I shouldn't think he has any clout either."

"This man is a—a priest. His influence is still in the room around you, so you needn't be afraid anymore."

"Oh *him!* He spilled wine all over my new jersey. I wanted the other one. The old man."

Bethany struggles on, it's awful and all my fault. She stammers, "Well anyway, he'll make sure that old woman won't be back!" then turns up the card representing Mother's immediate future: a pretty boy in tights and a floppy hat who could as easily be a girl. He is holding a rose, his designation is the Fool, and he's about to step over a precipice but Mother will never notice. Bethany says, "Someone you love very much, and who loves you too, is coming here from far away."

Mother says, "that must be Penelope coming back from America but you're lying about her loving me. She doesn't love me. Never has."

"It could even be tomorrow—I—Of course she loves you, Penelope's your daughter."

"She doesn't behave like a daughter. She's hard and cold and shuts me out of her life. She ran away to America and left me all alone. I ask you, what's the use of having a child if they run off to the other side of the world?"

"Imogene dear, you're getting too excited. And you've got it all wrong. Why, of *course* she— "

"I'm *not* wrong! Penelope hates me! I gave her everything, I ruined my own life to have her and she threw it all back in my face. She does whatever she likes and if she hurts me in the process that's just too bad!"

"Please, hush now. Here—some water—I'll hold it for you—"

Mother knocks the beaker away and the water spills in the bed. "She could have stayed at home and married Johnathon, but he was the one *I* wanted for her so she walked out on him too and hooked up with this common workman just to spite me, then she went back to school, that's what she said, *back to school*—as if the school her father and I sent her to, which cost us a fortune, wasn't good enough for her—just to learn how to write cheap advertisements. It's a wife's job to take care of her family. It's why women are put here on earth. That's what my own mother told me, and what I've always believed in." Mother's face twists in rage. "I *lived* for my husband and my child! I never ran away, I stuck it out to the bitter end, it's what one must do—but not her. *Oh no.* She's selfish, selfish to the bone!"

The aide appears in the doorway with two teacups and a small plate of cookies.

I tell her, "not now."

Bethany says, "but we're not talking about Penelope, it's your *granddaughter* who's coming to see you, it's *Caitlin*—"

"She broke my heart!" Mother bursts into noisy, wrenching sobs. "She was such a sweet, loving little girl and I loved her so much, *why* did she turn against me? Can you *tell* me?"

Bethany shoots me an appalled glance and I don't know what to do, I try to take Mother in my arms to comfort her but she thrusts me away with surprising strength. Luckily McQuarry appears, quietly efficient as ever. She holds Mother's shaking hands, soothes her unkempt head and manages, with consummate skill, to give her a shot of something which quickly calms her—but not before Mother has fixed Bethany with a basilisk stare and told her that in her opinion that horrid little dog should be put down.

Bethany stares straight ahead through the windshield, clinging too tightly to Scottie who struggles whining in her lap.

I say, "I can't begin to tell you how sorry I am about all that."

"The things she said to me! How could she! And I thought she loved Scottie."

"Try to understand, it wasn't her talking, it was the drugs."

"But drugs let out the truth of what people are thinking and feeling underneath. Oh Pen, it was horrible!"

"You were right. I should have listened to you. I'm so terribly sorry."

"And the things she said to *you!* I'd never have believed it. Never!"

"She's not herself. Please trust me—she'll forget all about it. She always forgets."

"I don't think I can face seeing her again," Bethany says. "Not now."

"Don't say that. You can't give up, she needs you."

"Do you really think so?"

"I know she does."

Before I drop her off Bethany begs to come in to No. 12, just for a minute. "I'd love to look at Imogene's portrait one last time."

It's the least I can do for her. I pour us each a large drink and we carry our glasses into Mother's room. It's shiveringly cold in there, the lamps each side of the bed are gone and the high ceilings drain the remaining light but Bethany seems neither to notice nor care. "This is how I want to remember her, when she was young and radiant." She gazes up at Mother's face then lowers her voice and glances sadly around the stripped room. In a low voice, as if afraid to be overheard, "Sometimes in bed, when I'm half asleep, I pretend I'm living back in the 'thirties and I'm Imogene Waterstone as the dazzling girl she was then. I'm being presented to the King and Queen at Buckingham Palace and one of the young princes falls in love with me. Or I'm waltzing at a ball on a ship somewhere in the tropics and there's a moon and the handsome ship's doctor cuts in. I suppose you find that pathetic."

I tell her I don't find it pathetic at all. "You're picking up on Mother's aura."

"That's exactly right. Imogene casts such a *spell* . . ." But Bethany's voice is sad and the magic is slipping away through her fingers. "I'd better go," she says.

I don't think she wants to. I'm sure she'd like to stay, have another drink with me, and another after that while she mourns. She deserves it, she's gone against her beliefs and better judgement and paid the price and of course she's entitled to sit in the warm dining room, knock back a couple of straight scotches and become satisfyingly drunk and maudlin, but I don't make the offer. It's unkind of me, but I couldn't stand it. "I have a lot to do," I say, walking her down the cold passage to the door; "I have an early start tomorrow."

"You're so lucky," Bethany says; "you don't know how lucky you are, having a mother like Imogene, and a daughter too . . ."

She lingers at the door. I'm afraid my resolution will buckle and she'll stay and drink and talk and cry but I manage to hold firm and give her a tight hard hug around the shoulders. "Good night, Bethany, I'll never forget what you tried to do and please forgive me."

I listen to her lonely footsteps plodding down the stairs, hear a small sniff, then the street door opening and closing behind her and I know if I look out the dining room window I'll see her bulky, lone figure, head down, diminishing round the Crescent.

Poor Bethany. But I'm not sorry enough to ask her to stay.

12.

I think about eating something, can't bear the thought, and pour myself another vodka, a large one. Then I run a hot bath, lie in the tub balancing my glass on my stomach, think how I'm drinking way too much and perhaps I'm genetically programmed to be an alcoholic like my father.

I start to drift into sleep and then, suddenly, I'm back in the night of Mother's party again, I know exactly what's going to happen next and I'm helpless to stop it.

I'm right here in the tub, having soaked for hours turning the hot tap back on with my toe each time the water cooled, and either I'm dozing or the water's running because I never hear him come in or the door close behind him until, sensing movement, my eyelids flicker open and there he is at my side, his brown bathrobe open and his erect cock inches from my face.

He's begging, "Touch me my darling, hold me, put me in your mouth, suck me, you know I'll do anything for you, anything in the world, so please won't you love me? Won't you do it for me? It isn't dirty, it's a beautiful thing and then I can do it for you, and it's so safe, please oh please!"

My body spasms in revulsion and my glass topples, spilling ice onto my warm stomach. I sit up and press my face against my-pulled up knees, my eyes clenched shut to banish the image as I've tried to do for so many years, but it's too late and the scene plays itself out yet again as I know it will forever, over and over.

I watch myself leap from the bathtub and snatch up my towel; hear myself cry, "You drunk piece of shit, get away from me!" and him grabbing for me, reaching for my breasts, his hands on me, his lower lip soft and wet and trembling *"My darling! my darling!"* while I yell "leave me alone! Don't touch me! Get away from me or I'll call Mother! Do you want her to see you like this? *Fuck* you!" when he rocks back on his heels, his face all bunched up as if I'd hit him.

Then I'm out of the tub, wet and trembling; out the door and slamming it behind me and Mother is right there outside in the passage, her eyes blazing: *"What were you doing in there with Daddy? I heard what you called him!"*

Oh jesus god. He's her husband. She loves him. What can I do? How can I tell her? What will she think? She'll hate me but I say it anyway, "He had his *thing* out. His penis. He was going to—he tried to—it was *disgusting*" while, from behind the closed door, I can hear him weeping.

"You're drunk." Mother's voice is icy cold.

"He's a pervert. He wanted me to suck his cock."

She takes a threatening step forward. "How *dare* you say such a vile thing about Daddy!"

I start to cry, my tears of rage mingled with hysterical laughter. "At least he said it would be *safe!* At least I wouldn't get *pregnant!*"

"You filthy little liar!" Mother smashes me across the face so hard that I'm flung backwards against the wall and my towel falls off. "Get out of my sight!" she cries, "Go to your room!"

I crouch on the floor, naked and shocked. Her rings have cut my mouth. I wipe my lips. There's blood on my fingers.

The bathroom door is open now. Mother is on her knees beside my father, holding him and rocking him, his bald head buried in her lap. His arms hang limply to the floor and he's making small, soft sounds.

"It's all right," she's crooning, "Oh my darling it's all right. Everything will be all right . . . ."

I throw some things into a suitcase and take a taxi to the train station where I spend the rest of the night on a bench, shivering with cold and shock.

Monday morning first thing I apply for a transfer to the Young and Rubicam head office in New York, there were fewer visa restrictions in those days and later, when a job opens up in the San Francisco office, I move again, as far away as I can get.

I run. I run. And I never came back.

I think of the way he secretly watched me through the years, waiting his moment.

I make damn sure Caitlin never goes near him.

PART THREE

1.

I'd forgotten Caitlin was planning to cut her hair and when she trundles her baggage cart down the ramp into Terminal 3 at Heathrow, wearing a snuff-colored suede jacket I don't recognize, she has to draw level with me where I stand behind the barrier separating arriving passengers from their meeters and greeters and shout "Mom!" not once but twice.

"Look at you!" I grab her and hug her, then hold her away from me so I can see her better.

She fluffs her short haircut. "What d'you think? Do you like it?'

"It's different. I guess so."

"Dad doesn't. He was grumpy. All he said was 'at least it'll grow again.'"

"Men don't like changes."

It's been less than two months, but Caitlin already seems older. Her face is losing its young fullness, her cheekbones are more pronounced, she looks more like Mother than ever. For the first time I see her growing up and away, becoming herself, leaving me.

Now she's pulling forward the blonde-ponytailed young man standing behind her. "This is Peter Mayer. We sat together on the plane."

He's tall and slender, wears jeans and a navy parka with lots of zippers. His handclasp is firm, his eyes blue and direct. "Hello, Mrs. Foley, it's nice to meet you, I'm sorry about your mother." We have a brief, disjointed chat among the surging crowds before he kisses Caitlin lightly on both cheeks European fashion, she tells him, "*auf wiedersehn!* Email me!" and he lopes away toward the tunnel for Terminal 2 and his flight to Frankfurt.

We head for the parking garage, Caitlin none the worse for her long journey, chatting all the way. Peter is a German fellowship student at the University of California medical school, he plans to be a thoracic surgeon, isn't his English perfect and he speaks French and Danish too, four languages, so *embarassing!*

"Good looking boy," I say.

"Just someone I met on a plane." She adds a touch reprovingly, "And he's not exactly a *boy,* Mom, he's twenty-four!"

Suddenly my young daughter is dating men.

And now it's ten a.m., we're hurtling west in our lavender Ford, I'm squinting over the steering wheel through sweeping curtains of rain and driving dangerously fast to keep up with traffic and not be forced into the far left lane among block-long EU trucks who will never notice us drowning in their wakes of muddy slush.

I had at least two more glasses of vodka last night, followed by a too-short night of turbulent dreams. The effects of the four aspirin I took earlier are wearing off and I feel horrible. My head pounds. Caitlin is fiddling with the radio, producing bursts of static or pulsing rock while to my right the cars hurl past at 100 mph. I'm still not comfortable driving on the left, hate the habitual high-speed tailgating, the constant lane changing, the belligerance. Americans regularly tell me how polite and kind they find English people, but that's because the Brits vent their frustrations on the motorway and when there's a wreck it's spectacular with a high body count.

I'm exhausted when we finally pull up outside No. 12, but at least the rain has stopped, the sky is lightening and the sun making a watery though uncertain appearance.

Mrs. Ship pops out the front door like a Jack-in-a-box. "There you are, Caitlin dear. Glad you made it over in one piece.

Nasty plane crash in the Middle East, sixty-three people killed, it's all in the paper, I took it up earlier with the post, not that there's much, mostly bills" and trudges indefatigably up the stairs with a bag gripped in each red-knuckled hand.

"She's *just* how you said," Caitlin cries happily once we're inside the apartment. "And this place is so *great!* It's like a palace! Such high ceilings! I can absolutely see why Granny didn't want to leave. I wouldn't either. Where am I sleeping? With you?"

I lead the way to my father's office. "I thought you'd rather be on your own."

"*His* room." Over the years, as a result of my silence and Mother's refulgent adoration, my father has grown in Caitlin's mind into a near-mythic blend of heroism and romantic self-destruction. Now she wanders around his private space touching everything. She runs her hand over the surface of his antique walnut desk, the empty book shelf upon which she can place her shoes and other possessions, the curves and gilt coils of Mother's wall mirror. She's curious about the darker rectangle behind the door where Rio de Janeiro used to hang: "What a weird place for a picture, like he didn't want anyone to see it." She sits on the bed and strokes Felicity's duvet. "This is nice. Did you buy it?"

"Granny's friend lent it to us. You'll meet her soon."

"When do we see Granny?"

"Later this afternoon."

"What's wrong with right now?"

"She had a bad night and will be tired. Why don't you unpack and wash up?"

"Okay." But Caitlin makes no move to rise. "Mom? Can you tell me yet why Grandpa never came to see us in San Francisco?"

"He was too old to travel."

"Not all *that* old. And if he had been, couldn't we have come here? I never knew him. Never even met him and he was my grandfather. I *should* have met him."

"I've told you why."

"So he had a drinking problem." She shrugs. "Lots of people drink."

"Trust me on this one."

"He must have been lonely."

"It was his own choice."

Caitlin's face instantly assumes its stubborn look and she draws a quick breath for a spirited rebuttal.

"Want some coffee?" I ask. "I'll fix coffee."

"You're not going to talk about him, are you."

"Not right now."

"Are you ever?"

"I don't know."

"Okay, I won't bug you." She sighs. "Can I have tea instead—I'm off caffeine."

"Tea has caffeine in it too."

"Not herbal tea—though you wouldn't have that, will you. You never do. I'll buy you some."

"You'd be surprised," I say.

We carry our cups into the dining room. Caitlin gazes at the clutter on the floor. "What's all this?"

"Stuff of Granny's I need to go through."

"Great! I'll help you!" She's ready to dive in then and there, kneeling on the floor, a Waterstone family album in her lap, turning pages. "These are *amazing!* Look at the clothes! The hair! And everybody's so serious, kind of grim looking—didn't they ever smile in those days?" She points. "Who's that?"

"I think she's my great grandmother."

"What did they call that bunched-up pile of stuff on her butt?"

"A bustle."

"How did they sit down?" She turns pages. Gasps. Chuckles. "Look at the poor babies! Just imagine wearing all those layers of petticoats and shawls and stuff, you'd think they'd suffocate. And all that laundry without washing machines!"

"There were maids for that."

"Terrific—unless you were a maid!" Now, Caitlin is gazing at a solemn-faced small boy in a sailor suit who sits cross-legged on a lawn. Immediately behind him a woman with a long chin and heavy eyebrows clasps a bundle of drapery from which can be glimpsed the sweetly chubby face of an infant.

I tell her, "The little sailorboy is Granny's uncle George. The baby is Alexander, her father."

"My great grandfather! He was killed in World War I, right?"

"In 1917. Granny wasn't even born when he died, and her brother Theo—your great uncle—was only two."

"What about George?"

"He died first, at the Battle of the Somme."

"Both of them. That's *so* sad." Caitlin turns another page. "Who's this girl? She looks familiar."

I look down at a heart-shaped face framed by a cloud of dark hair, at intense eyes and a wide, generous mouth. She wears a white blouse under a black sleeveless jumper which in those days was called a gym tunic. "That's Mother—your granny—when she was about twelve."

"And this is her again?" Mother is seventeen now, a teenage vamp, eyes narrowed against cigarette smoke. "She was so beautiful, wasn't she. Look at those eyes!" The pages turn. "Wow, who's *this* guy? He's *gorgeous!*"

"Granny's brother. Your great uncle Theodore."

"He could be Granny's twin." Caitlin clasps the album to her chest. "Oh, I want this! I must have it! Can I, Mom? Please?"

"Of course."

She gestures widely, "What about all the rest of it?" and when I hesitate, "Don't even *think* of tossing them out! They're our family. They're who we come from! They're *precious!*"

During lunch of soup and salad, we move onto comfortable routine matters. Caitlin thinks she did well in midterms; she's boycotting eggs to protest the raising of battery chickens; she's thinking of getting a job driving a pizza delivery van; and they've thrown Alan out of the apartment. "Not because he's a boring miserable geek or anything, but because he's so mean," complains Caitlin. "Like, we bought a used washing machine for $50, but he wouldn't kick in his share, not even a lousy ten bucks! We have this guy Cliff now. He's Okay."

The sun disappears and the rain returns but Caitlin is still full of energy. She asks for directions to the Internet cafe and the health food store, makes a hurried trip to her room, returns wearing an orange slicker and bright chestnut boots, a bulky package in her hand. "Here's your mail! I forgot. There's a card from Dad in there too."

I find various neighborhood notices, an invitation to a friend's daughter's baby shower, and a bundle of magazines. Liam's card is the iconic image of a line of steel workers eating lunch on a swinging I-beam a thousand feet above New York City. "I miss you," he says. "I'm sick of hanging out with the guys."

Caitlin leaves. I crash gratefully onto my bed and fall into a dizzy cycle of overlapping images: of hurtling trucks;

tidal waves of muddy water; beribboned and bonneted babies; my father's beseeching mouth—eventually waking to the slam of a door and Caitlin at my bedside, her jacket dripping onto the rug. "Mom? I've put the tea kettle on. It's so fun here! You go into all these neat little places for different things and the store clerks call you 'Dearie!'" She's bought carrots, onions and beets because one should eat seasonal root vegetables, and a package of chocolate cookies as a treat. She has e-mailed Peter Mayer, wonders whether Germany is colder to live in than England, and how sad to think that his and her great-grandfathers might once have fired at each other across no-man's land from their respective trenches.

2.

Mother is smiling and holding out her arms, yesterday's melt-down might never have happened and I think how much better she's looking until Caitlin's involuntary intake of breath when I realize how catastrophic the change will seem for anyone who has not seen Mother on a daily basis. Caitlin will have been imagining her languishing in ravaged glamor like La Traviata, not as a sick old woman with sparse hair and jaundiced eyes. However, after that first flinch she controls her face perfectly. "You're looking great, Granny! *Much* better than I expected."

"That's what they all say," Mother agrees. "Isn't it *absurd,* at my age! But look at you, darling! You've gone and cut your beautiful hair, how *could* you, it's so pretty when it's long!" She reaches up arms like sticks and pulls Caitlin down onto her chest. "Give Granny a big kiss! Where have you been, you naughty thing? You never come down to see us anymore. I don't know what you girls get up to these days—probably just as well! Sit down here and tell me *everything!* "

"There isn't much to tell," Caitlin says. "I have a full class load. The apartment's working out Okay and we have a new roommate called Cliff."

"Is he very special?"

"Just somebody to share the rent."

"Never mind, darling, it'll happen soon, you'll see. Somebody wonderful will come into your life. And what else are you doing? Are you in the school play? I'm sure you are! I bet you're the leading lady!" Mother breaks off at the arrival of her supper tray—bouillon and lemon jello—complaining as usual how it's far too early and how on earth do they think one has an appetite so soon after tea, then asks whether Caitlin remembers that night before the talent show when they sat up till ten o'clock rehearsing her poem. "Not like that, darling, I'd say; you don't just rattle off the lines any old way, think about the meaning! And give them some life: 'In *Xan*adu did Kubla *Khan* a stately *pleasure* dome decree!"

Caitlin asks, "What talent show?"

"When you were in the Upper Fourth! How could you have forgotten? I remember it so well. And you said it simply beautifully; you got an Honorable Mention! I was so proud of you!"

Caitlin says, "That must have been my mom," and Mother says "Of course it was, Penelope, and I remember it as if it was yesterday!"

On the way home Caitlin says, "There's this chart on the door."

"I know."

"They shouldn't have that hanging up there so she can see."

"I don't think she can read anymore, even with her glasses on, and if she could it wouldn't mean much to her in kilos."

"Oh." Then, "Mom?"—in a small, guilty voice, "Granny smells. Have you noticed? I mean, she's clean and all, but there was this bad odor underneath like it was coming through her skin."

"I suppose she does. I don't notice anymore."

"What is it?"

"I'm afraid it's the cancer."

Caitlin flinches again, and crosses her arms over her chest as if to hold her own body together. "I never thought you could *smell* it!"

"At least she's not in any pain," and I touch her lightly on the shoulder when what I want to do is take her in my arms, hold her tight and protect her from all sad and fearful things like loneliness and death.

I don't expect to fall asleep easily, I'm afraid of my dreams, but this time I need not have worried.

We're at the beach, Caitlin, Mother and I, in California. Caitlin is two years old, round and scrumptious and naked except for a frilly pink bikini bottom. Mother must be in her mid-sixties but from the back looks half her age, slim and youthful with great legs, wearing the red sundress with the blue flowers which is old and faded now.

It's very calm, very warm, the waves are gentle and rythmic as if the ocean is quietly breathing.

I lie drowsily on my stomach watching them build a sandcastle. Mother is digging the moat while Caitlin decorates the castle walls with shells and pokes feathers into the turrets to be pretend flags.

Now they're going down to the water, hand in hand, to fill Caitlin's pail. I watch my daughter bend over, see those fat dimpled backs-of-knees, that pink frilly bottom up in the air and my throat constricts with love.

Mother holds tightly to Caitlin's hand, she's having just as much fun, she could build castles and collect shells and jump over waves all day, she's a wonderful mother, a fantastic granny. How often in the past she's sighed how much she'd longed for ten children, and how I'd glow with pride when she hugged me, saying, "But if I had to have only one, Penelope, thank goodness I got you!"

The peace is abruptly broken as a helicopter thumps overhead, its shadow casting an instant of coldness on my bare back.

Caitlin calls, "Mom! Mommy!"

I lie on my rug and wave. I'm lazy. "In a minute."

"No, Mom! Now!"

"Here's a big one coming!" Mother cries, "Look, Granny's going to get all wet!" She swings Caitlin into the air as the wave soaks her to the waist.

Caitlin screams with glee and kicks her legs. *"Mom!"*

The helicopter thuds overhead again, there should be some ordinance against flying so low on a public beach.

"Mom *wake up!*"

And I'm awake in darkness, it's cold, and Caitlin is shaking me by the shoulder. "It's somebody from that place," she cries. "Beech Grove. It's Granny! She's gone crazy, maybe she's dying! You have to come *now!*"

3.

Mother is crouched on the floor, naked save for a sagging diaper. Her skin stretches drum-tight over a spine like a row of doorknobs, there's an angry-looking swelling on her right flank and her abdomen is a yellowish mass of pitted bloat. She's weeping and beating her hands against something or someone invisible. "Get her away from me! *Make her leave me alone!*"

Tonight's duty nurse, the older woman with the cast in the eye, is no match for Mother on a rampage. Poor devil, she's lost her cap and her grey hair hangs in her eyes. "She started up about half an hour ago," she gasps. "Banging on the walls and screaming."

"Where's Mrs. McQuarry?"

"Went home."

"*Home?*" I think, how could she? How *dare* she—but of course McQuarry goes home at night to her family like anybody else.

The nurse quavers, "I've rung her, and Doctor too. If Mrs. Sayle's upset she's supposed to have a syringe but I can't get anywhere near her. She says I'm trying to kill her."

Mother's eyes have narrowed to frenzied green slits. "I know who you are, I know why you've come!" She screams and wrenches at her flaccid breasts. "I won't go with you! *You can't take me!*"

Without thinking, I snatch up my father's old bathrobe and drape it over her shoulders, then sit on the floor beside her, pin her flailing arms tight against her sides and rock her back and forth. I whisper, as if to a small child, "Hush now, it's all right, this is Frank's dressing-gown wrapped round you. He loves you.

He won't let her get you and nor will I. You're safe now. It's me, Mummy; it's Penny."

"Penny!" Mother clutches at my hands. "It's *her* again, bending over me and staring at me with no eyes. She's come to get me and as soon as you go she'll take me away."

"She can't do that. Frank and I are here now."

"Don't leave me! *Please don't leave me!*"

And I tell her we're not going anywhere.

4.

Mother drops into a sleep like a coma following her shot but I sit beside her for the rest of the night knowing that, if she should wake for any reason, she must find me there. Caitlin refuses to go home alone and sleeps fitfully on the couch in McQuarry's office. We return to No. 12 when the morning shift has come on duty, and return at ten o'clock to supervise Mother's move into larger and better quarters on the ground floor right beside the office for which McQuarry, feeling responsible for last night although she should not, refuses to accept any extra payment.

Although still strongly sedated Mother is in constant, frantic motion, jangling the silverware on her meal tray, ringing her bell and plucking at her quilt. "She's had enough valium to knock out a horse," McQuarry sighs uneasily, "But it doesn't help. She's far too restless, it's wretched for her. And Pen, she's lost her wedding ring. We've searched all over her old room."

Mother yells, "They've stolen it of course, like my lovely topaz. I took it off when I washed my hands at the restaurant and left it behind on the basin. I rang them afterwards of course but it wasn't there, somebody took it—well of course they would, it was beautiful. Daddy gave it to me; I would have left it to you when I died. That Irish woman says it might have been sucked up into the vacuum cleaner bag but I don't believe her. She's lying. They're all the same. I don't like this place, Penelope, I don't know what I'm doing here. Why did you make me come here? When am I going home?"

Caitlin spends the rest of the morning on hands and knees searching every inch of Mother's old room with no luck. "Could somebody have actually stolen it? Could they be so mean?" Her voice trembles on the brink until, in sudden hope, "might it have fallen down the toilet? It could have, it would have been loose, her fingers have gotten so thin."

I don't remind her that Mother can't manage the toilet anymore and agree that's what most likely happened. In the meantime Mother, shrill and hostile, has accused each Beech Grove staff member in turn of theft and, when cocktail time rolls around and Simon, impervious to my warning phone call, shows up for his visit, she accuses him as well.

He states firmly, "Nonsense, Imogene! It'll turn up tomorrow, you'll see."

Mother's eye is steely. "You're lying, it'll be in your own pocket. Or Penelope took it, she's always hated me," then the nurse comes in to give Mother another shot and I lead Caitlin away. She's white and shocked, she has barely had any sleep since she arrived and is beyond exhaustion, she needs hot soup, she needs the chicken I was planning to roast for tonight which, forgotten, lies cold and raw in the refrigerator.

Simon says to hell with the chicken, we're coming home with him.

By the time we're back at his house in his lovely warm kitchen Caitlin has the dry heaves and her face is the color of putty except for the skin beneath her eyes which looks as if she's been punched. Simon gives her a measuring glance, fixes her a mug of hot tea with brandy in it (he's growing used to restoring the Foley women), then sits her on a stool, hands her a garlic bulb and an onion and tells her to chop them both up fine while he tosses various ingredients into a cuisinart, adds herbs and dumps the result into sizzling olive oil. We don't talk about Mother. Next he produces various bottles of unlabelled wine he brought back from a recent trip to Tuscany and stages an impromptu tasting. "Bit of a risk, local wines don't like to travel out of their valleys, but I tried this one last night and it seems to be holding up rather well. What do you think?" He sniffs and swirls. "Shall I go back to Lucca and get some more?"

After the third or fourth taste I protest we're drinking too much; he says who cares, nobody's driving.

Caitlin's color is improving. She's no longer in shock but still anguished for Mother. "What'll we do about her ring?"

Simon is pragmatic. "Buy another one in the morning and pretend they found it somewhere. She'll never know the difference."

"Of course she will, she's worn it for most of her life."

He looks at her and his face softens. "You poor little girl." He lays his hand tenderly across the back of her neck. "And you just got here. It's too bad."

Her eyes are huge and dark. "I didn't know it would be like this."

"Of course not. How could you?"

Caitlin stabs viciously at her onion. "I hate it when people die."

"But they always do. It's part of being alive."

"It's *ugly*."

"It's truth. Death isn't romantic and graceful the way they show it in films, and you see and hear things you'd much rather not. Believe me, I've lost some dear friends over the last few years, way too many, and I know."

"I'm sorry," Caitlin says.

"I've come to think that death is harder for the people who have to live through it and watch, like you and your mother right now, than for the person who's actually dying."

Caitlin has finished with the onion. He hands her a knob of Parmesan cheese and a grater, she sets to work, the tears leak from her eyes and trickle down each side of her nose and she knuckles them away. "I thought there'd be more time and we could sit together and talk. There was so much I wanted to tell her." She turns away, grabs a paper towel and mops at her eyes. "Half the time she doesn't even know who I am. She thinks I'm my mom."

Simon wonders, "Do you suppose that really matters?"

"It matters to me."

He dips a spoon into his sauce, tastes, considers, and adds more basil. "Do you remember what they say? How your whole life is supposed to pass in front of you when you're getting ready to die? Right now, Imogene could be re-living every experience she's ever had while, for all you know, you've blended with all the other girls in her life. You're not just Caitlin; you're also your mother when she was young, you're Imogene herself, *her* mother, and on and on. Push that thought a bit further and imagine yourself, Caitlin Foley, and all those other girls who are also you, are living all your different ages at the same time. Can you get your mind around that?"

"I'm trying. You mean that in Granny's head I'm young like I am now—but I'm also Mom's age, and old like Granny? And they're me? Her whole life going on at once? It's like science fiction." Caitlin's hand slows on the grater and eventually stops. "I think *maybe* I get it—if that's what you're saying."

"Einstein said it a lot better."

"And what about the other people in Granny's life she loved, like her husband, her brother and her friends—are they all in there too? "

"We'll find out when it's our turn, won't we."

"And right now it's Granny's turn. I feel so sad for her."

"But perhaps it's exciting too. Perhaps it's unbelievable. I like to think there are times when it's unbelievable." Simon samples his sauce one more time and declares it ready. He hands me a mixture of garlic and olive oil to spread on the bread slices I've cut, sprinkles them with cheese, slides them under the grill and tells Caitlin to set the table. "You'll find everything you need, silverware, mats, napkins, all in the drawer behind you."

"I wanted to tell her I love her," Caitlin says.

"Do you seriously think she doesn't know that?" Simon drains the noodles and slides them into a brightly patterned bowl.

"If only there was something we could *do!*"

"There's nothing. We must let Imogene do her dying in her own time and in her own way. In the meantime," he says briskly, "To comfort the living, there's nothing quite like Italian food!"

Caitlin stares up at me from her bed, where she's wrapped like a mummy in Felicity's duvet. "He's nice, isn't he? Simon?"

"Very nice."

"What he said about dying, all that, it kind of makes sense, that we're all in her head at once. And Mom? Last night? You did just the right thing with Granny. How did you know to wrap her in Grandpa's bathrobe?"

"I didn't. It just seemed the right thing to do."

"That's even better. You acted by instinct. I felt so dumb; and I was scared." Caitlin shivers under the duvet. "Who's the old woman with no eyes?"

"It's just the drugs."

I kiss her goodnight like the child she used to be and, for me, always will be and she wonders, "Was Grandpa on drugs when he died?"

'Of course. He was in a lot of pain."

"Was it horrible?"

"Not at all, he went very gently."

And I remember I said and did the right things then too, only for the wrong reasons.

My father looks small and fragile lying there in his white bed, and so pale he's almost transparent. His hands lie quietly on the coverlet, not recognizably human anymore but fan-shaped paws because the pads of muscle at the base of his thumbs have wasted away. He's blue around the mouth and his speech is labored. "They say I'm dying. Is that true, Penny?"

"Don't tell him!" Mother has begged me; "He dreads dying, he's terrified!"

She has been keeping up a fierce fiction that he will soon get better and go home and has enlisted the support of the doctor, who is young and merciful.

Personally I'm not at all surprised my father's terrified considering the harm he's done and I have no mercy. "Yes, it's quite true."

He anxiously searches my face. "Are you sure? You're not just saying that to be kind?"

Kind? Coolly, "I promise."

He moves his head on the pillow in a sideways nod of acquiescence. "That's such a relief. You can't believe how much. Thank you, Penny. You see, nobody will give me a straight answer, they treat me as if I'm a child, or an imbecile."

"You're welcome."

"I know Mummy means well but she shouldn't try and protect me all the time."

I ask curiously, "Aren't you frightened?"

He looks at me as if I'm mad. "Of course not, I'm bloody relieved. I'm so tired, you see, Penny. I can't hang on much longer."

I tell Mother she need not keep up the charade because he knows. She's furious with both of us—with me for telling him, and him for his obvious relief which she finds not only insulting but a personal betrayal—while he's impatient with her for crying when she should be glad for him. He begs me, "Do tell her to go away, Penny; there's no time for that kind of rubbish now" and Mother rages how he's a selfish brute, it's she who'll be left all alone because her daughter hates her and has moved half way across the world, and he closes his eyes and wanders off somewhere inside his head.

Clearly, Mother and I are fast becoming irrelevant to him and he recalls our living presences with effort.

He watches entranced while convoys of warships sail past his window on wide grey seas. I know this because when he remembers he points them out to me: "There's the old *Renown*; the *Newcastle*; and the *King George V*! There they go! See, Penny?" His crystalline gaze wanders the walls of his little room and up to the ceiling and he smiles as he greets old friends and comrades at arms. "I say, there's old Bunkie! What a long time it's been! How are you, old chum? Keeping fit?"

Now he's sitting in an armchair, "Somewhere on the rocks by the sea." He can't move his arms and legs, they seem to be tied down, he doesn't understand why. "Hellish weather too," he complains, describing the black waves snatching at his feet, the lightning which sizzles around him into the smoking water, the rolling thunder. "I suppose I should be scared but I'm not, you know. Odd, isn't it. It's all rather grand. Can't you hear the thunder? Are you sure? It's so loud, Penny."

Mother says it's just the drugs; my father insists it's all real; the doctor, who no longer treats him like a child, suggests it's the random electrical charges of a system shutting down and my father is entranced. "You mean I'm watching myself die? How jolly interesting!"

Once he opens his eyes and says, "I wish we'd got to know each other better, Penny, I think we'd have got on rather well, but it couldn't be helped, things being as they were. None of it your fault, of course. Bloody shame, really."

I wonder what he means but he never tells me because he dies the next day, quietly and gently.

And although I can't cry for him, his death leaves a barren space inside me and an ache which never heals.

5.

Caitlin and I go to the jewelry store right after breakfast where we stare at trays of wedding rings and argue whether Mother's ring was rose or yellow gold.

I think it was rose gold; rose was more fashionable when she was married but Caitlin is certain it was yellow so that's what we choose and Caitlin, whose fingers are slender and tapering like Mother's, tries it on the fourth finger of her right hand instead of the left, "Because Granny says you should never put a wedding ring on your left hand before you're married or you'll be an old maid!"

On the way home, sadly, "She's always talked about my wedding. What my dress would be like, and wearing the Waterstone family veil and how she was going to Harrods to buy her dress, olive-green to match her eyes. And how many children I'd have. She thought three would be nice. 'We're all only daughters,' she'd say, 'me, Mummy and you, you *must* have more than just one!' She couldn't wait to have great-grandchildren. She won't see any of that now."

I tell her Granny has had a lot of fun over the years imagining it all, and imagining's probably better anyway because she can make it exactly the way she wants.

In addition to the ring Caitlin has the excellent notion of bringing Mother's portrait over to Beech Grove now there's sufficient wall space in her big new room. "She can see it from her bed, and think she's at home after all!"

John, the nurse, finds a picture-hook and he and Caitlin hang it from a convenient piece of molding but Mother, torpid with tranquilizers, is quite indifferent.

Nor does she register much interest when I say proudly, "Look what we found," put the ring into the palm of her hand and close her fingers around it. "It's your wedding ring! You dropped it down the loo and the plumber found it in the bend in the drain. Wasn't that lucky!"

"Are you sure it's really mine?" Mother languidly tries it on, complains it's too loose and gives a tight, croupy cough. Despite the warmth of the room she caught a cold while out of bed in the night nearly naked.

I tell her, "Of course it's loose, you've lost weight and your finger's thinner. That's why it fell off in the first place."

"If you say so."

A practical girl, Caitlin has brought a length of black velvet ribbon and threads the ring onto it. "You can wear it round your neck instead. It'll be much safer."

"What a good idea," Mother says, and coughs again.

McQuarry is concerned about Mother's cold. It's gone to her chest, she has a slight fever, she could develop pneumonia, and Dr. Cameron prescribes antibiotics.

I think of the cocktail of drugs already coursing through Mother's frail body with antibiotics now added for good measure and wonder how long she'd last if it all just stopped—then remember the pain, how it would burst through the failing morphine barrier and how that's not an option.

6.

We have dinner with the McBrydes that night, all of us, including Simon, Bethany and Lord Storey who has come fifteen miles by taxi from his ancestral home, Deep Combe, because his driver's license has just been revoked.

Felicity has cooked my chicken and a second one too since there are seven of us. There's wild rice, baby peas and a salad, with caramel floating island for dessert—a feast for which no-one has much appetite.

Bethany mourns, "It's all happening so fast."

Of course it hasn't really been fast at all, but now that Mother's end is close we're not ready. I share Caitlin's regrets. Mother and I have never had the talk I'd hoped for, there's so much I'll never understand, and Simon's theory that it really doesn't matter is only a theory and no comfort.

The Colonel is talking about a living monument to Mother. "What would you think, Penelope, if we plant a little grove of birch trees in the Victoria park as a memorial to Imogene? She loved—loves that park. I'd be happy to find out about it; ring the committee chaps, do the donkey work. All the time in the world, after all." And unexpectedly lyrical, "It's a birch that comes to mind, thinking of Imogene. White and slender and dancing in the wind."

Lord Storey, bitter, sighs how it's too bad he has to lose his license just when Imogene needs him most. "That police chappie said I was driving too slowly and was dangerous. What bloody rubbish—how can it be dangerous to drive slowly? Haven't had an accident in years! How'm I going to see her now? Can't afford a taxi every day."

I offer to pick him up tomorrow afternoon so he can visit Mother; he accepts with alacrity and invites Caitlin and me to lunch provided we stop at the supermarket on the way over and buy it.

The Colonel, still musing on his birch grove, is sure we'll find a spot she'd like, "Maybe down on the south lawn? Jolly nice view of the river from there!"

I agree how that sounds ideal and I too would imagine Mother as a birch, if she was a tree.

Simon asks whether I've thought of holding a wake for Mother, which prompts an intense argument over who should be the host.

Felicity says, "Poor Penelope can't possibly have it in that cold flat, and with all those stairs. Not that Imogene wouldn't have *wanted* to have it there but—"

"I've known Imogene for sixty-five years," Lord Storey says. "The wake will be at Deep Combe."

"That's too far for a lot of people," Bethany says. "Especially if they're older and don't drive. Scottie and I can do it at our house!"

"You don't have the space," Felicity objects at once. "It's a shame we can't have it outside in our garden but if we open up the dining room onto the porch there'll be plenty of room and it *ought* to be warm enough."

Simon says with finality, "We'll do it at my place—if Penelope and Caitlin have no objection."

We don't and the matter is settled.

"He'll do a lovely job," I tell Caitlin on the way home, "Just the way Mother would have liked. He'll have a caterer, with lots of nice wine and food and all the trimmings."

"I've only just gotten here," Caitlin sighs. "I can't believe we're talking about her dying and her wake already."

She goes sadly to bed. I lie awake for a long time, gazing up into the shadowy ceiling, remembering the day Caitlin was born. I woke earlier than usual and lay quiet and still with my hands splayed across my huge, hard stomach which was moving with a life all its own, aware of a faint tingle touching the back of my neck, a feather-light shiver along my spine, and knew this was the beginning, that the baby would come soon and there was nothing I, nor anybody else, could do to stop it.

Just as Mother would have known forty seven years ago at her Aunt May's house as she stood at the window and gazed out at the birch trees.

Just as, now, nothing and nobody can stop her dying.

7.

Deep Combe is a rambling gothic pile located fifteen miles out of town at the end of an overgrown driveway. It is architecturally significant, owned and operated as a tourist site by the National Trust and Lord Storey occupies what were once the housekeeper's quarters. His small rooms are bachelor-shabby and very cold since the heating either doesn't work or has been switched off to save money, but it doesn't seem to bother him.

Caitlin and I huddle in our overcoats, our breath smoking, in the flagstoned kitchen which smells of soot and of the ancient springer spaniel which lies like a matted rug in front of the unlit stove. We eat the quiche, French bread and salad we've brought, and the earl supplies a potent blackcurrant cordial which burns its way down to our stomachs and spreads its way welcomingly to our extremities like an infusion of antifreeze.

Before we leave, he proposes a tour of the gardens which I understand are internationally famous.

It is not, at first blush, a tempting invitation. Although they must be gorgeous in the summer, the formal flowerbeds and rose gardens are bare, the water garden is a frigid bog and the ornamental lake clogged with dead leaves.

The maze, however, notorious for its diabolical layout (a pile of bones was once found in the north-west quadrant, rumored to be human) and which now has a lookout post in the center from which lost and panicked summer visitors can be directed to the exit via megaphone, is actually improved in winter when its towering evergreen walls are free of encroaching deciduous growth. The earl is clearly proud of it. "Follow me!" he cries as he plunges through a gap in the brush.

The old spaniel, deciding enough is enough, waddles back to the dubious comforts of the house like a laden barge returning to dock. We watch its retreating rear with envy before following Lord Storey into the outer loop of the maze before turning—and finding ourselves quite alone. Where did he go? We turn the first corner into a long curving alley with no apparent opening either to left or right, the dark walls tower over our heads and sound is deadened. "Lord Storey!" I call, "where are you?" and feel my voice smothered as if by a cold, damp blanket. "He'll be just around that corner," I reassure Caitlin, but he's not there and it's a dead end. We retrace our steps, or think we do, but now can't find the gap we came in by.

Caitlin says, "Imagine what this place would be like on Halloween! Where'd they find those bones, anyway?" Which is when, with a gleeful *'Boo!'* Lord Storey materializes right in front of us through an angled slot we'd never have noticed.

He roars with laughter. He probably pulls this trick on everybody and we've quite made his day. We don't let him out of our sight again and follow hard on his heels, twisting from passage to passage, right, left and right again. In places, low down, there are holes in the thick hedge through which despairing, lost souls must have clawed their way back to civilization. I sincerely hope the earl knows where he's going because nobody will be manning that central lookout station until May 1st and I've stupidly left my cell phone in the car, but at last he shoulders through an overgrown aperture we would never have found on our own and we're in the center at last, standing in a circle of unkempt lawn with a raised platform in the middle.

"It's even more fun at night," Lord Storey says.
"Did you ever bring Mother here?" I ask.
"Just once. At a dance before the war."
Caitlin wonders, "Did you tell her about the bones?"

"Everyone knows about the bones. But it's nonsense about them being human; they were just some animal, probably badger."

I try to imagine the young lord dragging my mother, giggling nervously and protesting in evening dress and high heels, ever deeper between the high bushy ramparts while the lights and the music fade behind them. "Was she scared?"

"You bet she was. That was the whole point," the earl confides rather grimly, "And I wouldn't let her out till she'd given me a kiss."

Caitlin demands, "And did she?"

"She'd have done anything by then."

I imagine this circle of grass more than half a century ago, moonlit and sinister. "Poor Mother!"

"That was mean," Caitlin says.

"It was," the earl agrees, "Very mean, but I wanted to punish her a bit."

We climb to the top of the platform, lean against the rail and gaze over lunging coils of hedge to the roof of the great house, its myriad gables and chimneys hovering in the mist like a mirage. Caitlin asks, "Why? What did she do?"

"Turned me down," the little earl says ruefully. "I begged her to marry me; even went down on my knees." He repeats, "my *knees!* Poor Imogene, she was so embarassed, told me not to be a silly ass, she couldn't possibly marry me, I was far too old. Then she laughed. That little trilling laugh she has. Such a pretty laugh but it can cut to the bone."

Caitlin is fascinated. "When did you see her again?"

"Not for years. The war started, she stayed in London and I was posted to North Africa. Her brother was a junior officer in my regiment so I was able to get news of her. Heard she'd got engaged to Sayle which made me bloody angry because he was even older than me."

"Did you see much of them after the war?"

"Ran into them a few times but not if I could avoid it. Too painful."

"You were still in love with Granny! That's so romantic!"

"There was never anybody else," Lord Storey says with dignity. His antique check cap is dark with moisture and the water drips from its peak onto the rosy tip of his nose as he ruminates on long ago disappointments and bad choices. "Mind you, she could have had anybody—*anybody!* She danced across the top of the world; everything came to her with the snap of her fingers; she had a marquis and a duke chasing after her, even some Hollywood chappie, but to give her her due Imogene never much cared about rank or money. She was a romantic. God only knows why she picked Frank. Tiresome sort of chap, no sense of humor and always had to have his own way but maybe she found him a challenge. He didn't give in to her all the time like the others, and he was a handsome enough bugger when he had his hair." The little lord absently passes his hand across his own still luxuriant white thatch.

"She loved him," I say.

"I suppose so. I'm sure she thought she did—she was his driver you know, in the war; glamorous sort of life for a girl, heady stuff, you should have seen her in her WRNS uniform, with that little hat. She wasn't supposed to wear it tilted over one eye like that. *God!*" The earl falters to silence and vigorously blows his nose. "Shouldn't be gossiping like this, it's not right, you're his daughter and poor old Frank's been dead ten years, should let bygones be bygones—" though between the upwelling memories, his adored Imogene's imminent death and the powerful cordial kicking in, the temptation is clearly too much. With sudden bitterness, "Nothing was the same after the war. Everything grey, sad and broken, and all of us suddenly so poor.

Her family had already lost everything—well of course you know that: father dead when she was a tiny little thing; mother hanging on to the old life come hell or high water; that brother of hers—damn nice chap but quite useless—and her with no more idea of managing money than a baby. Not her fault, mind, wasn't raised to it. Marriage wasn't the way she expected either. Frank started hitting the bottle, and then there was the problem in the plumbing department—not that she knew anything about *that*. Frank should have told her. I begged him almost to the day he married her: 'You've *got* to tell her, old man! It's only right.'"

Caitlin wonders, "Plumbing department?"

"A man's—you know. Internals." Lord Storey has said too much but realizes he's gone too far to stop. The three of us are quite alone but he throws a furtive glance over his shoulder and lowers his voice so we have to lean toward him. "Frank spent two months in hospital, you know; six operations; shell fragments in the lower regions." When Caitlin and I both look puzzled, "You know—" the earl flushes to his ears—"*Below the belt!*" and gestures toward the front of his dungarees. "They x-rayed him over and over. Didn't know much about radiation then, long term effects, all that, and gave him far too much. Poor old Frank. Never the same."

I have a hard think about too many x-rays below the belt. Is Lord Storey implying my father was sterile?

Caitlin the biologist is way ahead of me. "He couldn't have been sterile or he couldn't have had Mom."

"No, well, obviously not," agrees the earl, now crimson with embarassment. I'm sure he has no problem discussing the breeding of dogs or horses, but human sexual function is clearly out of his league. He confides, "The real worry was in case he *wasn't*, and the result was below par. If you follow."

There's a pause while we work that one out, then Caitlin gives a wise nod. "Birth defects!"

"Hit the nail on the head!" Lord Storey is clearly relieved not to have to say it himself. "Frank was terrified, absolutely *bloody* terrified that his child, if he managed by some miracle to sire one, would be a monster. It obsessed him. Even wanted Imogene to sign a paper saying she agreed never to have a baby. Told me about it, asked my advice, needed to be told he was doing the right thing. 'No other choice,' he said, 'don't you agree?' and I said 'don't even think about it, old man, it's not right, not legal, you've got to talk to her. She's young. She'll have her heart set on a couple of kiddies, for Christ's sake *tell* her!'—but he didn't dare in case she left him, so she married him not knowing and then it was too late. Criminal, really. *Bloody* man. And it's been on my conscience ever since. Maybe I made a dreadful mistake; maybe I should have told her myself and to hell with Frank. Not that she ever complained, mind; always pretended she was happy as a lark. Pretty noble girl, really. Though all's well that ends well; she had her child after all—" he pats my hand, so cold where it rests on the rickety rail—"and there's jolly well nothing below par about you, is there, my dear!"

Caitlin has drunk a lot less of Ada's wine and drives us all back to Beech Gove. She has no trouble driving on the left and declares the country lanes to be a fun challenge.

Afterwards, having left Lord Storey at Simon's house where he's spending the night, "Poor dear old boy," she says as we labor up the stairs of No. 12, "Fancy worrying so much for all these years! How he must have adored Granny!" As we re-enter the apartment and close the door behind us, "Of course you do realize that if Grandpa *was* sterile then he isn't Grandpa!"

What I had to do to get you . . . I don't tell her that the thought has already crossed my mind after reading those letters. Then, of course, I'd dismissed it out of hand—but so much could be explained if Francis Sayle was not my father—his remoteness, his coldness and even, in some twisted way, his pathetic, drunken advances.

"He obviously *is* Grandpa, though," Caitlin says comfortably as she hauls off her wet boots, "Granny's always telling people how you and he are alike as peas in a pod! Although," in afterthought, "I suppose she'd have to say that, wouldn't she."

8.

Caitlin and I spend the next morning sorting out Mother's closet. At least, Caitlin sorts; I sit on the bed and watch, thankful Caitlin is here because I can't bear to touch Mother's things: Her sad little rolls of stockings, her blouses, skirts, jackets, sweaters and dresses all smelling faintly of *her*.

Here again is her little black wedding suit; the navy check she wore on her first trip to San Francisco; the floral sundress, faded and worn beyond repair and here (I shudder) are Mother's fox fur neck pieces, the height of elegance in the 'thirties and 'forties, stored in a pillowcase with mothballs for nearly fifty years. They're pathetic with their limp, boneless legs and glass eyes, I've never seen anything look more dead.

Caitlin wonders, "Should we take those things over to her?"

"You've got to be kidding.'

"I'm serious. It's the sort of thing she'd like. Happy memories she can touch."

And she's right, of course.

Mother's face lights up as Caitlin knots their horrid little paws across her chest. "Dear Ferdie! And dear old Freddie too! Fancy seeing you again! Their names are Ferdinand and Frederick Fox!" Mother strokes their balding heads with a trembling hand and gives a phlegmy cough while, with each breath, a film of yellow mucus billows in and out from her left nostril. "Dear Theo gave them to me as a wedding present. He was always giving me presents though he couldn't afford it. He used to spoil me so! It wasn't a big wedding, there was just Mummy, and Theo who gave me away, and a Navy friend of Daddy's who was best man, Bunkie Montgomery—no relation to the general—poor darling, he was so nervous he dropped the ring! And of course Dorothy took charge back at the flat, she passed cheese biscuits and poured the drinks even though she was supposed to be a guest."

Caitlin asks the right question straight away. "Dorothy worked for you?"

"Of course she did, darling. She was Mummy's maid, wasn't she. Such a sweet little person, the only one who stuck with us all through the war. She said she'd taken care of Mummy all her life and wasn't going to leave her. And after Mummy died, and I got married, the dear thing came to me. I couldn't possibly have managed without her! I cooked sausages for our very first dinner at home after the honeymoon—how on *earth* was I supposed to know you put fat in the frying pan?—and they caught fire and Daddy threw the whole lot out of the window. He was so angry and said 'you mean you can't cook at *all?*' I was always a bit scared of him when he was angry but Dorothy said, 'don't you worry, Mrs. Frank, you've got me to help and I'm going to take you in hand.' She'd come over every afternoon to make our dinner and I'd pretend I'd done it myself so he'd be pleased with me. She saved me over and over again! 'It's our secret,' she'd say, and she never did let on! She took care of me when I was expecting you, too. That was another secret. Of course I never thought he was serious, I was sure he'd change his mind, it was only when the years went by and I found I wouldn't ever be allowed one that I started wanting it so desperately. After I turned thirty it was all I thought about, day in, day out. A baby of my own. I begged and begged him! And when it finally happened Dorothy would make me take my iron tonic, and rub lanolin into my tummy so I wouldn't get stretch marks. I thought Frank would have done that but he said it made him feel sick, seeing my tummy all big and bare." Mother takes my wrist in a grip like dead leaves. "Personally, though, I think she's getting a bit above herself. She's terribly bossy, always giving me more pills, says I have to take them for my cold but they're much too big and I only pretend to swallow them. Aren't I naughty! Look!" She pats feebly at the pocket of her yellow velvet jacket. I thrust my hand inside and find six blue and white capsules. Mother's antibiotics. "Go on," she giggles, "Flush them down the loo!"

So I do because what difference can it possibly make now?

9.

Caitlin has taken a long hot bath and gone to bed in her little room from which all traces of sad old man have been banished by the hairbrushes and cosmetics on the desk; the new suede jacket slung from a doorknob; the tall chestnut boots leaning companionably toward each other beside the chair.

As I return to the dining room I can see her light is out. Good. I'm carrying my grandmother's hand mirror and the photograph of my father I have unearthed from my bottom drawer and for the first time in my life I study his face in minute detail, that squared-off jaw and the brooding eyes under thick dark brows. Then I study my own. Decide, although the coloring is the same, that feature for feature we're actually not alike at all—which still proves nothing because, as Miss Bannerman has pointed out, I'm my mother's daughter through and through.

But if I'm not my father's daughter, then who could he have been, and how? Was Lord Storey telling the truth about the radiation—though why should he lie?

I try to put myself in my father's shoes when Mother first blushingly broke the news of her pregnancy. What particular moment would she have chosen? Would they have been in bed? At breakfast? Taking a walk together? Drinking a cocktail on their tiny London patio?

"You can't be," he'd have said, "It's impossible!"

And Mother's voice, surging with happiness, "Well it's not, it's happened at last and I'm going to have a baby!"

How did he survive those endless months of female congratulations and excitement, and the ribald male banter: Well done, old boy! What took you so long? Shot in the locker after all, hey?—all the while wondering what horror might be growing inside Mother's womb.

Then the day arrives, the baby is punctual, but Frank Sayle is not there, he doesn't have to see it, he can escape the worst for at least a few hours because Mother's in the country and he's safely in his Admiralty office in London alone with his dread, praying to every god he's ever heard of.

And his prayers are answered because it's no monster who appears but a robust baby girl, 8 lbs. 3 oz., 21 inches long, the right number of fingers and toes, everything perfect.

A miracle!

What shattering relief my father must have felt, before deciding, because he wasn't a fool, that he didn't believe in miracles.

What would he have done then? Would he have let the matter rest, or been compelled to know for sure?

Even though he suspected he'd regret it for the rest of his life, I think he'd have found it more unbearable not to know—supposing Mother insisted on having another child who turned out *not* to be perfect—and would have had his semen tested in a modern, peace-time clinic.

And upon learning that his sperm was thoroughly dead? What then?

By now I've arranged my father's letters in more or less chronological order, according to the dates on the envelopes, and find what I'm looking for almost at once.

On July 15, 1950, while Mother is still recuperating in the country:

'How you could have done this will forever be a mystery to me and I can neither understand nor forgive you,' he writes in corrosive hurt and bitterness. *'However, as agreed, we shall continue together and I shall house, clothe and educate your child. I'm sure you will agree this is an exceptionally generous*

offer. *With regard to your paramour, whose identity (fortunately for him) remains a mystery, I understand that he is out of your life and has undertaken never to try to see the child.* (He can't even bring himself to say my name). *You have given me your word on this, not that I can now regard your word as holding much currency. In fact I doubt I can trust you ever again.*'

Mother's paramour; the archaic word somehow lends final credence to the story.

Oh, poor Mother. Never having been told of my father's radiation treatments, she would have written off his adamant refusal to have a child as stubbornness and a determination to keep her all to himself and, once I was born, been sure he would accept me and grow to love me. How could a man not love his own child?

But when the child wasn't his? When that child was a cuckoo in his jealously guarded nest, a living embodiment of betrayal paraded before his eyes every single day?

How could she? He would have wondered in despairing rage and, *Who was it?*

I sink my chin in my hands and strive to recall whether Mother ever mentioned a name in such a way as to suggest a deeper involvement than mere friendship, but can think of none. Nor do I remember any man who, when I was a child, ever betrayed more than casual interest in me.

I leaf slowly through the Waterstone albums, carefully studying the faces of Mother's young male friends and relations. Some photos are missing, leaving four little glued-on corners to mark the ghostly rectangles where they had once been attached. Had they fallen out over the years and been lost, or deliberately removed lest Frank Sayle observe too close a resemblance with a man other than himself?

After a while the faces are blurring together, I lean my cheek in my hand, close my eyes, and once again Mother and I

are walking down that hot, dusty street, then crunching up the gravel path to a glossy black door. She pulls at the bell, and a stout woman in a dark dress with a white lace collar ushers us into into a room with a sofa, armchairs, and a table piled with papers and magazines. To the right of the door, a staircase curves upwards to the second floor. It has a wonderful, wide bannister. I'd love to climb that staircase and swoosh down again but instead I'm ordered into the back garden to play.
"I won't be a minute," Mother says.
"Can't I come up with you?"
"Not this time, Penny."
"Please. I want to."
"I said no."
She's unusually adamant and I flounce crossly outside where the garden is as dull as I expected, just a small square lawn with untended borders with nothing to explore and no trees to climb, though I find the remains of a dead animal in the grass: a small coil of intestines and a bony snout (a vole?) which is more promising. A lean cat with dirty grey fur slinks through a gap in the hedge. I throw a stick at it, dig a hole under a laurel bush and give its victim a decent burial, *Our father who art in Heaven hallowed be thy name and bless this poor vole*, while the cat lies on its belly and watches with sullen yellow eyes.
Soon, Mother appears and it's time to go. She's quiet and distracted all the way home.
Now, I wonder, was she seeing Him?
Did they make love?
But no, the visit was over so quickly and anyway, according to the bargain I'm sure they would have struck—the honorable bargain, Mother would have said—the sexual part of the relationship would have ended as soon as I was conceived.
Did she take me to that house because, against Frank Sayle's express decree, my real father had begged to see me? The

thoughts and images scald through my head. How did he feel, watching from an upstairs window while the daughter he'd never know scolded a cat and buried a dead rodent?
   Did Mother ever see him again after that?
   Do I want to know?
   I don't, not really.
   Instead, I feel a deep and unexpected sadness for Frank Sayle. I look for the photo of those three Navy boys mugging for the camera in Colombo under the equatorial sun and wish I'd known him then, when he was young and whole, before the tenderest parts of his body were laced with steel shrapnel. I think of his months of surgery and pain and Mother, whom he loved to obsession, begging for a baby. I think how he kept her secret through all those later years while involuntarily watching and waiting for some alien trait to emerge in me, some feature, expression or mannerism, some *clue* so that, to his infinite despair, at least he'd finally know.
   No wonder he drank, especially when I began to look so like Mother when she was young and he was doubly reminded of what he had lost—and in a flash of blinding clarity I suddenly understand everything.
   There he is that night in the bathroom, crying, his bathrobe open and his swollen cock thrust against my shocked face, begging, pleading, "Touch me, darling, you know I'd do anything for you so please won't you love me? It isn't dirty, it's a beautiful thing and then I can do it for you, and it's so safe, please oh please—" and of course he wasn't seeing me at all, he was seeing Imogene his young wife; he was desperate with love and longing; he was pleading with *her,* long ago, before I was born.
   Pleading with Imogene, to whom he'd never dared tell the truth for fear he'd lose her.

Oh that poor, sad man—and poor Mother, who had only longed for a child.

I lean my head into my hands and grind my knuckles into my eyes.

Now I understand it all, Mother's blind loyalty as well as her corrosive guilt.

I can understand how she'd both loved me and hated me because how could she not? She had given up everything only to have me walk away from her, flaunting my own independence, invalidating her sacrifice and her entire life.

No wonder she needed valium to help her sleep.

I think, what a fucking tragedy.

Caitlin demands, "What are you doing? What's all this?"

She's standing over me wearing her suede jacket over Pooh-bear pyjamas. Her short, dark hair stands up in spikes.

"I thought you'd gone to sleep."

"Couldn't. Guess I'm still jetlagged. Saw the light was still on and thought I'd make myself some tea."

"Help yourself. The kettle just boiled."

She returns with her mug; leans over my shoulder while I gather up my father's letters—the letters from the man who is not my father—into a pile which I bind again with their rotting white ribbon and slide back into the folder. "What are those?"

"Grandpa's letters to Granny."

"Love letters?"

"Some of them."

"Can I read them?"

I think, *no way, not now or ever.* I say, "It's midnight."

"Will you take them back to San Francisco?"

"I don't know."

"Take them to Granny. She should have them. She loved him."

10.

The days pass, two then three—and Mother hangs on, all eyes and febrile, exhausted chatter, a speaking skull fringed with fox fur, her throat ribbed like the hull of a boat leading up into the deep cavity under her jawbones, while her eighteen-year-old face beams down on us from the wall.

The package of letters sits beside her on the table, once or twice she asks to touch it and hold it, then forgets it's there.

I ask her whether she's seeing thunderstorms in her head and she looks at me as if I'm crazy.

Each time I leave she asks me to check her closet in case the old woman has come back; each time I assure her she's gone for good but I'm not sure she believes me.

Caitlin is endlessly, tirelessly helpful.

It's she who borrows Felicity's station wagon and hauls away a load of major garbage, including Mother's bedroom rug and its disintegrating pad, to the local dump.

Who acts as chauffeur, not just for me but for Lord Storey whom she collects each afternoon after she's dropped me off at Beech Grove.

Who walks me around the apartment, forces me to decide what furniture to keep and what to discard, and who contacts shippers and auctioneers.

Who deals with Mr. Durrage, the gnarly old painter sent up by Millicent the attorney, who will paint the whole apartment white (two coats of latex, semi-gloss enamel on the woodwork) for £2,000 which amply fulfills the redecoration clause in the lease, much to the ire of Mr. Pye who insists that the 'honorable thing' is to pay him his ten grand.

And now it's four o'clock in the afternoon, pretty Neela brings in Mother's tea tray, Mother says, "Thank you, Dorothy!" and invites me to pour.

I ask on impulse, "Do you remember Daddy's friend Bunkie?"

She smiles. "Bunkie Montgomery! He was such a dear!"

"What happened to him?"

"Poor Bunkie! Surely you remember, darling? It happened just six months after the wedding. Such a sad, stupid thing—going through the war without a scratch then run over by a bus on Piccadilly! Daddy was heartbroken."

I wipe her nose with a tissue. "Are you saying he was killed?"

"Of course he was killed. Thrown up into the air and dead before he hit the ground."

Caitlin leaves for Deep Combe to pick up Lord Storey. Mother tells her, "Hurry back, Penelope!" and picks at her quilt with little yellow claws.

I sit on the bed, hold her hands in mine and think how this could be my very last chance. I disrespect the word closure, it's become devalued currency, but in some cases it's essential. This is one of them.

"How cosy," I say. "Now it's just us."

Mother's glance flits anxiously around the room from corner to corner, shadow to shadow, bathroom door to closet. "Shouldn't you look inside?"

"I promise you she's gone."

"She'll be back." Mother lowers her voice to a whisper. "I know who she is now. I should have guessed all along."

"Who? Tell me!"

"Can't!" Her lips are a white seam.

"Sure you can."

She sighs; her head moves restlessly on the pillow. "All right. If you promise never to tell anyone else—"

"Of course I promise."

In a whisper, "Dorothy, of course."

I'm shocked. "It *can't* be Dorothy! She loves you!"

"I know, and that makes it even worse, what I made her do. Can't you understand? She's in hell because of me. She's never forgiven me. And now she's coming to take me there too."

"She'd never hurt you!"

Mother sighs with a sound like tearing cloth and her eyes fill with tears. "I hurt her so badly. I took criminal advantage of her and she wants revenge."

"Nonsense!"

"It's true! Poor Dorothy! 'You mustn't, Miss Imogene', she'd say, 'It's a wicked sin!' She was staunch Chapel but in the end I broke her down and she helped me. 'Don't you ever tell,' I said; '*Swear it!*' 'You can trust me to the grave and beyond,' she said, and she never did tell a soul. She'd say, 'I gave my life to the Waterstones'—and for her, love and loyalty came before God."

"Dorothy wouldn't want you to be upsetting yourself like this." I dry Mother's eyes with a tissue, then search among the bottles and jars on her night stand. I take her hand and gently massage her fingers one by one with lemon-scented moisturizer. "This smells lovely. Doesn't it feel nice?"

"Bliss!" Her breathing is hoarse and painful and the mucus billows in and out.

I say very softly, "It was because of the baby, wasn't it."

Mother snatches her hand away. *"What baby?"*

"It doesn't matter anymore. Penelope knows all about it."

Mother's eyes fasten fiercely on mine. "She *can't* know. She mustn't. Don't tell her. She'd never forgive me."

"How could she not forgive you? She wouldn't be here on Earth without you. You gave her life."

Mother gives a deep sigh and her eyelids droop.

I take her hand back and stroke round and round, soft and hypnotic. "You can tell me about it, you'll feel so much better, nobody else will ever know," and at last, so faintly I have to lean my head down to hers, "She'd bring me messages from him," Mother whispers. "When and where to meet him. And if Frank should come home unexpectedly—he'd do that sometimes, he never trusted me, he knew how men were attracted to me and how they watched me—she'd say I was out shopping, or having tea with a girlfriend. Oh, poor Dorothy. But she loved me! And so did *he,* the poor lamb. He'd do anything for me. He'd always told me that, so I asked him to prove it. Please! Do this for me, just this one thing, I'll never ask you for anything ever again! When he refused I begged him and begged him some more and he gave in in the end even though he hated it. I was wicked. *Wicked*!" Her eyes flick open again and gaze deeply into mine with bewilderment which shifts to relief and then to recognition. "Why yes, I thought it was you!" she says, and smiles.

Who does she see? Her husband? Her lover?

I slide my hands over her wrists and up the twig-like forearms, searching for the right words, the most important words in my entire life. I say, "Trust me, Imogene. There's no way Dorothy went to hell. She did it because she loved you. And you're not going to hell either because you love Frank and Penelope and there's no room for love in hell."

Mother frets, "If I was a Catholic I could just have confession and it would be all right again but I simply *can't* believe you can be forgiven by some silly boy with a white collar on who's no better than anybody else."

"There's nothing to forgive. You wanted a baby, which was your god-given right, and nothing could have stopped you." I suggest, "You were a force of nature."

"A force of nature!" Mother smiles. She likes that.

"If you hadn't had a baby, Penelope wouldn't be here, and nor would Caitlin. You gave them life, and it's God who creates life, not the Devil. The Devil only destroys."

"God wants to punish me."

"Why should he bother? You've been punishing yourself for years and years and you've done a very good job. But you can stop now. It's all over. Penelope knows, and she loves you anyway. Don't you understand? It doesn't *matter* any more."

Mother moves her head restlessly on the pillow. "I fought for Penelope tooth and nail, but she went to America and never came back. Married some frightful workman. Can't remember his name."

She closes her eyes. A moment later she coughs wetly, her eyes open and focus on my face, and she's back inside herself again. "Penny darling!" she exclaims. "There you are! What a nuisance, getting this cold. You'd better not kiss me, I don't want you to catch it too. Sit down over there. Don't go away yet."

"I'm not going anywhere, Mummy. I'm staying with you." And on impulse, "I didn't tell you my news! Johnathon and I are getting married!"

"Oh darling, that's wonderful!" Her smile is luminous. "You'll be so happy! I love that boy like a son, he's everything I could have wanted for you and he'll take such good care of you. You'll live in a beautiful house in the country and I'll visit every day! When's the wedding?"

"Very soon."

"You mustn't wait! Frank and I didn't wait once we'd made up our minds. We'll go up to London first thing tomorrow and go shopping. I haven't had a new dress in ages."

"Perfect timing; there's a sale at Harrods!"

Her little hands tremble across the quilt, "Please – Frank—" and I reach for his photograph in dress uniform with peaked cap and sword and hold it in front of her. I'm not sure how much she can see but she doesn't really need to.

"Darling Frank! He always said I was the most beautiful girl in London! I didn't have any jewelry, I sold it all because we needed the money, but there's this little florist on the corner who makes me bracelets of fresh flowers for practically nothing, lots of girls are wearing them now, I've started quite a fashion, you know!"

And now it's evening again and Caitlin returns with Lord Storey who looks cold and pinched and even smaller than usual.

Simon, the Colonel, Felicity and Bethany are here, and Johnathon too who came at once when I called.

"Dear Johnathon!" Mother cries, "Welcome to the family! Penelope, pour your dear man a whiskey!"

It's stifling and we're all sweating except for Mother who is draped in Freddie and Ferdie and complaining of the cold.

I pour a small measure of water into her tumbler and hold it to her parched lips. "Here you go, gin and tonic. Hope it's not too strong."

Mother puckers her mouth into a sipping shape. "Lovely! Thank you, Theo, but hadn't you better open the champagne?"

Bethany gives a sudden, stifled sob.

"Stop that,' Simon orders, "You can't cry now, this is a party."

Mother agrees, "Such a nice party too, but—" eyes darting—"Where's Dorothy? It's too bad of her to let me down;

she promised she'd come over this afternoon and make cheese puffs and polish my silver dishes" then accusingly, as McQuarry pokes her head around the door, "There you are! How could you be so late, they're all here already!"

Simon says, "She missed the bus."

Mother chides McQuarry, "How jolly silly of you! You should have phoned and I'd have sent Theo in the car. But never mind about that now, there're some olives and nuts in the kitchen; you can pass those round instead and George, darling, be an angel and build up the fire, it's terribly cold for May!" Then she beckons McQuarry up close. "It was terribly wrong of me, I've always known that. It wasn't fair. You will forgive me, won't you?"

"Of course I forgive you," McQuarry says.

"I couldn't help it, you see," Mother says grandly, "I was a force of Nature."

11.

The call comes at 2:00 a.m.

The window is wide open, the hot, stale odors dispersed into the frosty dark. Mother lies on her back, her arms neatly at her sides, her feet sheathed in white woolly socks.

Caitlin and I stare at the very old dead woman on the bed. We're silent because what is there to say? I think how this moment ought to be filled with drama and pathos. I'd imagined holding Mother in my arms when the time came and reassuring her once again that I loved her or, if I wasn't at her side, at least experiencing a pang of awareness at the instant of her passing—but I slept right through it all.

Caitlin says, "What a pity she died alone."

But there's no pity about it because I'm sure it's not true. "Don't worry about Granny," I say with certainty, "She was at a party, and then it was over and she went home."

The next few days pass in a blur while we go about the machineries of death.

The phone rings constantly. There are official condolences from the church women, the bridge club and the Conservative Committee, who must be dissuaded from sending elaborate wreaths and flower arrangements and the funds sent instead to the animal shelter as Mother would have wished.

Final details to be arranged with Hargreaves, and with Dr. Reed who is generously insisting on giving the funeral address.

There's the death certificate to be signed and Mother's pension to be terminated. I do this alone and it's the worst: dark and raining, the government building arid with its linoleum floor and brown walls, the clerk politely indifferent while Mother's life is officially signed off on by the Ministry of Pensions and the Inland Revenue.

Caitlin and I visit Mother in the viewing room at Hargreaves, downstairs where I have not yet been. It's a neutral space, beige curtained on three sides (I wonder what's behind those curtains but don't care to find out), furnished with a central dais to support the casket, half a dozen gilt armchairs for mourners, and a vase of plastic gladioli on a side table. I'm sure Mother would find this room tasteless in the extreme and her ghostly, derisive laugh permeates the air.

As promised, they have done a fine job.

Mother wears the new white cotton nightgown I bought her whose high lace collar covers her skeletal neck, and her skin is no longer yellow but ivory with the faintest blush on her cheekbones. Her patrician nose points arrogantly to the ceiling, her hair is combed back under a little lace cap and her pale lips closed over the sharp edges of her teeth. "She looks nice," Caitlin says; "Much nicer than Grandpa Foley." She adds, "He's the only other dead person I've seen."

"Me too." I think of Liam's father, wearing his best black Sunday suit with a green tinted carnation in his lapel, powdered and rouged, lying on white satin in his expensive mahogany coffin and looking far more dead than Mother. "Much nicer."

And then I send Caitlin upstairs while I tell Mother a final goodbye.

It's very quiet in that curtained space, heavy with a sense of absence.

I touch Mother's forehead, it's cold and hard, she could be one of those remote, marble angels they used to carve on tombs. I lean my face close to hers and sniff at her skin but there's no lingering odor, no human trace left at all.

I kiss my fingertips and press them to her cheek. You poor thing, I tell her silently. Oh you poor thing—but remember this: throughout your life, what*ever* you did, you were loved.

Poor, chapel-going Dorothy, a life-long burden on your uneasy conscience, loved you enough to risk the fires of hell, and one of your men loved you enough, despite bitter misgivings, to give you me.

I think how I'll never know for sure.

I've considered Lord Storey, who seems to have been available more or less at the right time (how strange to think that I might be an earl's daughter and the heir to Deep Combe), but it's clear to me that the little earl, too honest and simple to be a convincing liar, is not the one and knows nothing.

The most likely is Theo, her brother, who loved her. *I asked him to prove it. . . . begged him and begged him . . . gave in in the end even though he hated it. . . .* Theo and Mother looked alike enough to be twins so there'd be no awkward questions asked later on. As her gay brother he'd be doubly immune from suspicion. Theo could then safely play his role of favored uncle, visit me, indulge me and give me presents right up until—when? Growing older, might I have displayed some traits or mannerisms Theo thought dangerously revealing? Was his move to Tangier driven in part by sadness that he could not only never acknowledge his own child but must watch her raised by a man who didn't love her?

Was it Theo in that upstairs room in the tall grey house on the road to Beech Grove, Theo, who perhaps knew he was ill and wanted to see me for one last time?

Perhaps.

However, although Mother and Theo might have been convinced I was their natural daughter, am *I* so sure?

Miracles do happen.

Biology is not an exact science. X-Ray procedures would have been a hit or miss affair during the chaotic aftermath of the war while in busy labs, at the best of times, mistakes are made, specimens mislabelled and wrong conclusions drawn.

What a tragic irony if Frank Sayle was my father after all. I'll never know.

Only one thing is certain: that he loved Mother till the day he died.

I tell her goodbye. Touch her hard cheek one last time.

Then I untie the satin ribbon around the neck of her nightgown, tuck her husband's letters inside on her cold chest where her heart used to beat, button her up again and climb the stairs to join Caitlin.

12.

And now it's the funeral, in the chapel at the crematorium.

They run a tight operation up here, a funeral every half hour on the dot, mourners to assemble in the front courtyard not more than fifteen minutes prior, a twenty minute ceremony and then out to the parking lot in back.

A lot of people have come; Mother would be pleased at the turn out.

Mr. Pye is here, he offers me a clammy hand and insists, "No hard feelings, Penelope." He has every intention of coming on afterwards to the wake. *He'd never pass up a free glass of wine,* Mother would have sniffed; *Wants to get his money's worth.*

Johnathon is here, Rosemary at his side, hearty in heather tweed. She says, "I can't believe we never managed to get you over for dinner, Pen; you should have phoned!"

Bethany, and the MacBrydes.

Lord Storey, in a threadbare suit of immaculate cut, his cracked, ancient shoes polished to a mirror gloss. He says anxiously, "I shouldn't have told you all those things the other day, Penelope, but I was upset and not myself. It was an indulgence on my part and I didn't mean to burden you."

When I tell him I don't feel burdened at all but, on the contrary, I'm grateful, he looks puzzled but relieved.

Simon escorts Mrs. Ship, regal in her church hat with a dangle of artificial cherries on the brim who declares, "Won't hardly be staying on to do for them in the Crescent now Madam's gone; have to find somebody else now, won't they!" but I don't believe her for a minute.

Even Miss Bannerman is here in her navy suit, perhaps she always wears navy-blue in honor of Commander Francis Sayle. Caitlin and I are ushered to our front pew by two of the Hargreaves pall bearers and it's eerily like a wedding except for Mother's casket on the raised stage, placed front and center.

There are honey-gold curtains to either side of it, the pews are blonde wood and the casket (closed now) fits right in with the decor. The sun shines through a series of huge plate glass windows and it's all so light, bright and modern with such an illusion of outside warmth that we might be at Sunday worship in suburban California.

Dr. Reed takes his place at the lectern, the sunlight gleaming upon his iron-filings hair and snowy surplice.

We don't kneel but follow him in prayer sitting down, 'Our Father who art in Heaven,' then stand again for the first hymn, *Morning has Broken,* one of Mother's favorites. I look around at all the people here to sing for Mother and send her on her way, and congratulate myself for choosing cheerful hymns with no emotional pitfalls.

Dr. Reed's address, too, is upbeat. He reminds us all how Imogene Sayle was a special person full of love who brought the most unlikely people together, explains how she hasn't really left us but merely waits for us in the next room and, professionally conscious of time restraints, wraps it all up in seven minutes flat.

I've chosen *All Things Bright and Beautiful* for the second hymn and everything is still Okay until the second verse which is suddenly treacherous, *He made their glowing colors, He made their tiny wings,* when I think of Mother at my birth, watching from her window as the little birds poked for worms on the wet lawn and with no warning whatever my throat swells shut and I can't breathe, hear a gasping noise and realize it's me choking on tears. I was doing so well too, *damn* those tiny wings! My knees buckle and I collapse onto my seat, bury my face in my hands and the tears pour between my fingers and splash into my lap. Caitlin puts her arm around my shoulders and squeezes while everybody tactfully looks anywhere but at me, at us. This is England, after all.

Then the hymn ends, thank goodness, and they all sit down too.

Dr. Reed turns to face Mother on the dais. He intones, "We therefore commit her body to the ground, ashes to ashes, dust to dust, in sure and certain hope of the Resurrection to eternal life"—and to my astonished horror, in authentic theatrical finale which Mother would have thought fitting, her coffin sinks slowly down through the floor and the blonde curtains close together with a swish.

Caitlin sucks in her breath with a hiss and mutters *holy shit*, we stare at the closed drapes thinking how Mother will be down there in the fire *right now*, the shock jolts me back into myself and my tears dry up at once. I can't believe it happened like this, why didn't they warn me, it's outrageous, this would never happen in California—oh *surely* not—but no-one else seems to find it unusual. Dr. Reed gives the blessing, makes the sign of the cross, it's all over and Mother has returned to Frank carrying his love letters on her heart.

Everybody waits politely for me to rise but I dread getting up and being the first to go out there, imagining what I'll see—a tall brick chimney belching concentration-camp smoke—until I collect myself and reason that, with cremations scheduled precisely half an hour apart there should be a constant pall hanging over the whole valley and there isn't, and now I don't even remember seeing a chimney.

"Mom, it's Okay," says Caitlin, taking my arm, "Granny's gone, she's left the room. It's time we went too."

13.

Simon's white and gold living room, in which he serves Chardonnay and smoked salmon sandwiches at 2.30 in the afternoon, is bright and festive and I'm sure Mother would approve.

Everyone has come on from the crematorium except Mrs. Ship who has been picked up by William's father and driven back to the pub. At Caitlin's inspired suggestion I have given her Freddie and Ferdie as a keepsake of Mother and in my last view of Mrs. Ship she's sitting proudly upright in the front seat of the van, the limp pelts in her lap, stroking them as she would a favored pet.

Mother's friends approach Caitlin and me, one by one, to kiss us or shake our hands and say how they wish we weren't going back to America so soon, how much they'll miss us and how we must stay in touch, and I know I'll miss them too and that we'll exchange Christmas cards for a while—but inevitably the cards will grow fewer and the memories fade because, without Mother, there's no glue to hold us together.

Simon will continue his successful career and have his work photographed in prestigious architectural magazines.

The MacBrydes will happily nurture their organic garden.

Miss Bannerman can spend endless happy evenings relishing my father's sketch book while Lord Storey, who for the first time since I've known him looks dazed, fuddled and impossibly ancient, will probably follow his beloved Imogene before next spring.

For just a moment I consider giving Bethany the portrait of Mother; then decide not to. Even Bethany will soldier on and anyway it's mine, it will hang in my own living room in San Francisco and eventually will belong to Caitlin.

"Keep in touch, Pen," Johnathon says; "I'm sure we'll be seeing you again one of these days."

"Of course you will," I say with a brilliant smile, but I know they will not.

Just as everybody is leaving a messenger shows up from the crematorium to deliver two packages. One, the token to be sprinkled on the rose bed in the Victoria Park, is tiny; the other is larger, sealed, neatly tied with string. It's warm to the touch and comes complete with Customs' declaration. The process has taken three hours from start to finish, including driving time.

14.

We land in San Francisco in mid-afternoon and Liam is waiting, looking huge and solidly American in his bulky leather bomber jacket. Caitlin launches herself into his arms, he holds her tight, ruffles her short hair and looks a question at me over the top of her head. I nod that all is fine, that I'm fine.

It's cool and breezy, the sky a hard, flawless blue and there are whitecaps on San Francisco Bay. The first rain has fallen, the tawny hills are shot with winter green, and the traffic on the 101 North is terrible as usual.

It's good to be home.

Liam lays his right hand on my thigh and I feel his warmth through the fabric of my jeans.

Caitlin suddenly speaks from the back seat. "I met Johnathon, Dad."

"You did, huh."

"No worries there!"

I ask, "Why should there be worries?"

"Come on," Caitlin says, "the cool looking old boyfriend? The one you nearly married? And you telling Dad not to fly over?"

"Let's leave it right there," I say.

"Okay, Dad, here's the report," Caitlin says. "Johnathon's real nice and not bad looking for an older guy, but he's too smooth and too much Mr. Perfect. *Way* too perfect for Mom."

Liam's hand moves to my kneecap and squeezes. He makes a queer sound half way between a choke and a hoot. Can he be laughing?

I place my hand over his and press.

We spend Christmas day with the Foleys and I enjoy myself with Liam's family for the first time.

Mother cast a long shadow and there'd be restraint on both sides; now she's gone there's relaxation and acceptance, I'm hugged with sympathy as a fellow traveller on the road of life, "One goes and another comes," Granny Foley says with irrefutable logic, and attention reverts to Maureen's expected baby girl with a spirited argument about names.

Liam has shopped for his brothers-in-law respectively at Home Depot and Grand Auto, while the rest of the family benefit from the duty-free gift shop at Heathrow airport: a silk scarf for Deirdre, a Princess Diana memory book for Maureen, touristic T-shirts for the kids, a fluffy toy penguin for the new baby and, for Granny Foley, a flagon of Chanel #5. She's startled and a little flustered, can't hide a sudden pink flush on both cheekbones, I suddenly wonder whether anyone has ever bought her perfume before and am so glad I thought of it.

We're home around 6.00 o'clock, and Peter Mayer arrives at 6.15.

Within that time frame, astonishingly, Caitlin has changed both her clothes and her persona. She wears slim black slacks, a crimson silk turtleneck, and glossy black boots with high heels. The girl in jeans playing on the floor with Deirdre's and Maureen's children has suddenly become a beautiful grown up woman.

"Stop that," Liam tells me when the door closes upon them.

I demand, "Stop what?"

"Wondering how she'd like being a doctor's wife in Frankfurt."

"How did you know what I was thinking?"

"Because you're a mother."
I guess you can't fight it. It's scary.

15.

The year turns and it's 1998. Sirvas and Segal are expanding, I'm promoted to Senior Copywriter, and flirt with a move to the client side of the business. Either way I'll be making more money, but I find I'm less excited than I thought I'd be. I stop coloring my hair, my badger stripes are reappearing, people seem neither to care nor notice and I wonder who I thought I was kidding.

Then I ask myself whether I want to spend fifty hours a week with people I don't particularly like when I don't need the extra money.

I tell Liam, "But that doesn't mean I want to have another baby."

He says, "So write your book, that novel you said you never had time to finish. What was it about anyway? I always wondered."

"It was kind of autobiographical, I guess like most novels; it was about a girl on her own in the big city and how she got there. But it wouldn't work now, I'll have to start over."

Liam shrugs big shoulders. "So what do you have to lose?"

The shipment of furniture arrives in mid-January, all my favorite pieces: the cedar chest, the drop-leaf dining room table, Mother's little desk, and the paintings. When I unpack Rio de Janeiro from its crate the brittle, brown-paper backing is torn and scrawled on the back side of the canvas, visible for the first time, is the artist's signature: *Francis Sayle, 1922*. Miss Bannerman was right, he did have talent.

16.

Caitlin returns for spring break in late February.
Her first night home, in my dreams, I find myself struggling through the maze at Deep Coombe, Mother at my side wearing my father's bathrobe. She's edgy and cross: "That old fool's gone and lost us! I knew this would happen!"
I drop to my hands and knees and struggle to part the hedge but it closes up again quicker than I can rip it out. When at last, sweating and swearing, I manage to tear a small hole I'm stopped by a layer of chicken wire.
"Penelope," cries Mother, wringing her hands in agitation, *"Do something!"*
When I tell Caitlin about it in the morning, she says Mother's sending a clear message that she's been in the box too long and wants to move on. "I would too if I was her. Wouldn't you?"
So we cross the Golden Gate Bridge, turn up onto the Marin headlands, and drive until we find the perfect spot.
It's a sunny, breezy day, the grass is springy underfoot and stippled with clover, yellow daisies and early lupine.
Liam waits on the road beside the car while Caitlin and I hike down the hill picking flowers as we go until we're standing on the edge of the cliff. Immediately below us the waves are breaking onto the black shingle beach and, further out, the barking sea otters are lolling on their backs at the surf line.
Off a cliff into the sea, Mother said; *Somewhere lovely.*
We've brought a silver spoon, a rare survivor of her wedding silverware, with which I toss the first of the ash. It's amazingly fine, I'd no idea. The wind catches it and it hangs suspended for a long moment in an elongated S.

Caitlin and I recite a prayer and take turns tossing Mother's ashes into the wind along with the flowers.

By the end of the prayer we're only a quarter of the way through the box and Caitlin wonders, "Do you think Granny would mind if we went a bit faster?"

I say I don't think she'd mind at all, the faster the better, so we fling Mother's ashes over the cliff and can't tell where she lands, or whether she lands at all. We know she'll be content though, whether she floats on the wind or alights gently upon the ocean and the strip of beach with its wet black pebbles, and I think of her as I always will, young and barelegged, wearing the red and blue flower-patterned dress in which she'd always been so happy.

THE END

About the Author:

British-born Mary-Rose Hayes is the author of eight previous novels, including the TIME/LIFE bestseller *Amethyst* and two political thrillers co-authored with Senator Barbara Boxer. Her books have been translated into sixteen languages. She is a teacher, lecturer, and co-director of an annual writers' conference in Tuscany, Italy. Previous occupations include medical research, fashion modelling and the international delivery of sailboats. She lives with her husband in Northern California.

Contact
Facebook: Mary-Rose Hayes
Website: www.mary-rosehayes.com